# REDEYE

SYNTELL SMITH

ISBN: 1-952506-93-X

ISBN-13: 978-1-952506-93-2

Copyright © 2024 Syntell Smith Publishing Published by Syntell Smith



To obtain permission to excerpt portions of the text, please contact the author at syntellsmith@gmail.com

Scene Divider graphic courtesy of iStock by Getty Images

Library of Congress Cataloging-in-Publication Number: 2023919894

Cover design by Markee Books

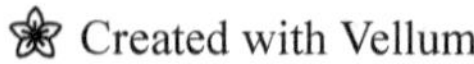 Created with Vellum

*This novel is dedicated to Kid Cudi and Haim. Thank you for the kick-ass song that inspired this work.*

# FOREWORD

*"Adam gave Eve his rib… But it was not enough."* - Anonymous

# PROLOGUE



SOUTH BEACH, MIAMI

Saturday, June 2001

"I brought you something," Nate said.

The hotel room was barely lit. Noise from the hallway was coming in faint as he focused on the task at hand. She was standing next to the bed as he opened his suitcase and started fishing through the carefully packed articles of clothing.

*She was still standing.*

"Here," he said as he pulled out a gift-wrapped box and brought it over. "Sit, sit!" he said, as he took a seat himself on the edge of the bed. She accepted the gift, looking down at him. He regarded her as a goddess. It felt so fitting for him to look up to her, he truly and deeply worshiped her.

*Why is she STILL standing?*

"You didn't have to," she said, as she opened the gift.

"It's your favorite, remember? First edition. You said it made such an impact on you when you read it."

She held the fresh new copy of *Cane River* by Lalita Tademy and sighed. "You remembered."

"Of course, how could I forget? I would never forget and

"

never *could* forget even the slightest detail when it comes to… why don't you sit down so we can talk?" Nate asked.

"Because I can't stay."

"Yes, you can…"

"But I'm not going to. I'm sorry," she said flatly.

He reached out as she took his hand and he looked into her eyes.

"I know you want this to happen but—"

"No," he interrupted, shaking his head. "You don't have to explain… I understand."

He fought back the tears and caressed her arm, then lifted his head to put on his best smile. "You should go. They're getting kinda wild out there… someone's gonna wonder where you are…"

"You coming?" she asked.

"I'll be in the lobby to meet everyone for the farewell party."

She nodded, and as if time accelerated somehow, she turned and took two steps, then the sound of the door closing behind her echoed in the room.

It's Sunday now. The company farewell party was over, and everyone was checking out. For the last two years, the firm had worked on the court case for Deutsche Bank. Scanning records, printing emails, providing OCR cleanup, and creating a document database for the attorneys to reference.

The two-year document scanning contract was completed, and it was time to move on. Group pictures were being taken, as goodbyes and hugs were being exchanged. Nate left his hotel room dragging his wheeled suitcase down the hall. He was on the third floor as he walked into the empty elevator and watched the doors close in front of him.

In this moment of solitude, his emotions finally got the best of him like an overflowing pond breaking down a weakening dam. He exhaled a stifled cry and let the tears streak down his cheeks in a moment of utter defeat. He almost wanted to howl a loud and anguished cry, as if his leg were broken from falling off a bike. But, unfortunately, it wasn't his leg that was shattered to pieces.

The elevator car shifted to a halt as he gathered his composure for a second. The floor indication light was on '2' and suddenly the doors split open in front of him. He quickly stepped back and wiped his face of any tears as an elderly couple stepped inside to join him. Just before the doors closed again, two women walked to another elevator car that was opening on the opposite side.

One of them turned towards him, and they locked eyes for what felt like an eternity. She saw him in his frail, defeated state. Eyes still red, face caught off guard, revealing a crestfallen broken shell of a man. He dared not let her see him like this. He needed to let her know that he was going to be alright.

It was too late to smile, but he saw her acknowledge him and he, in turn, nodded while simply raising his hand in an attempted half-hearted wave. And like that, the door was closed again.

That final awkward exchange would be the last memory he would have of her. He would probably never see her in person again. He would move on. He had to. He couldn't let her break him. He had to carry on and never dwell on what could have been. To do so would drive him mad, to the point of no return, and he simply refused to let that happen.

**1**

———

# THE HUSTLE

New York City

August 2013

"Ben Affleck can't be Batman! Are you out of your fucking mind?!"

The news broke the internet last night, sending message boards, blogs, and Twitter ablaze in an outcry of protest. It was a few minutes after nine in the morning and podcasters Calvin Reid and Kate Fitzsimmons were recording their weekly show in a broadcast studio in downtown Manhattan.

Calvin was wearing a blue short-sleeve T-shirt, with the legendary comic book artist Jack Kirby's name on it, inside a circle. Wearing dark horn-rimmed glasses and sporting a baseball cap turned backward on his low-cropped gray hair, he sat next to his co-host shaking his head.

"C'mooon Calvin, give Beanboy Ben a fair chance. I think he can pull it off!"

"Kate, no offense, but you're a woman, you don't know jack about comics…"

The two started a few minutes of guffaws and mock arguments until Calvin said, "I wanna hear from today's guest commentator… blogger, photographer, and overall jack of all trades, Nate Durant… what say you, Nate?"

"All I can say is the jury is still out… Ben can probably play the smooth, yet aloof billionaire type that is Bruce Wayne, but The Dark Knight will be the challenge of a lifetime. Affleck's dabbled in action with *Paycheck* and *The Town*, and don't forget, he played Daredevil. Say what you will about his performance, he did that role justice. Pun intended. Christopher Nolan is producing the film, right? It was his call, and I trust Nolan."

After the podcast finished, everyone took off their headphones as the producer worked the soundboard and signaled that the recording light was off. "We're clear!"

"Thanks for stepping in, Nate!" Calvin said, with a handshake.

"No problem."

Nate fanned a hand through his sandy blond hair as he stood up from his chair at an even six-foot-one. His boyhood smile beamed from ear to ear. He was wearing a long-sleeved blue button-down dress shirt draped over a pair of loose-fitting denim jeans.

"Hey, lemme get your headshot again. I got some new scouts looking for extras for *Law & Order*, as well as other local New York productions. Movies too!"

Nate rifled through his knapsack and inside was an eight by ten photo of him with his contact info typed neatly at the bottom.

"Here ya go," he said to Calvin.

He noticed Kate was stealing a few glances at him, while pretending to check her smartphone.

"Good, you better answer when they call. What else you got planned today? From what I hear, you're a regular renaissance man."

"Well, I'll be heading to Bryant Park near the library until 11:30 am for some writing, another podcast at noon, a tech expo

I need to cover and do an article for, a listening party around 5 pm…"

"Damn boy! Don't you ever sleep?"

"I am unfamiliar with that concept, what is this 'sleep' you speak of?" he asked, with a chuckle.

"Why you burning the candle at both ends? You got some terminal disease and don't plan to live past 45?"

Nate pulled out his phone, did an unlock swipe, and showed him his home screen. "You see that?"

Calvin looked at a picture of an obese young man who looked like he was over four-hundred pounds.

"Okay?" he said, not getting the message.

"That was me… seven years ago."

Calvin did a double take, going back and forth between the screen and the man standing in front of him, "Bullshit. What the hell happened?"

"Bariatric surgery. Got three-fourths of my stomach cut out and my intestines got rerouted, affectionately known as the Gastric Bypass."

Calvin did a nod of approval. "I've heard of that. Well, I must say, can't argue with those results. It's like you were an entirely different person."

Nate put away the phone. "The procedure is only the start. Since your stomach is the size of a small pouch, your enzymes can't break down your food like you used to. It's a dramatic life-style change. You need to take supplements to get the nutrients you'd normally get from food. And don't get me started on issues with extra skin once you start losing the weight."

"That still doesn't explain why you're doing over seven jobs a day like you West Indian."

Nate smiled at the comparison. "When I looked like that, I was a prisoner in my own body. I couldn't walk up steps, I was ashamed to ride the bus, and I *hated* going anywhere during the summer. Despite all that, I was lucky enough to find someone who would love me, and we got married."

As soon as Nate said that, he noticed Kate stopped looking at him and immediately walked out of the recording booth.

Nate turned his head, and then looked back at Calvin. "Suddenly I'm unattractive, huh?"

"There's nothing out there that'll repel a woman more than a married man," Calvin said.

"The good ones, anyway. The bad girls still make their passes at me. Once I decided I was going through with the surgery, I made a promise. When I lost the weight, I wouldn't just settle for a regular nine-to-five job. I'd find a way to work damn near 'round the clock. Weekends are dedicated to my wife, Cynthia, but everything else… is the hustle."

"Alright man, I'll let you get going," Calvin and Nate shook hands again. "Anybody tell you that you look like Brendan Fraser?"

He headed towards the exit. "Yea, around 14 years ago when *The Mummy* first came out and I was over 300 pounds," Nate said sarcastically. "See you around, Cal."

"A seven-letter word meaning, "To settle down or be calm"?"

"Compose," Nate replied.

The Great Lawn in Bryant Park was located behind the main branch of the New York Public Library in Midtown Manhattan. Nestled between Fifth and Sixth Avenue, as well as 40th through 42nd Street. The area was a well-known place to go "People Watching." Offering free Wi-Fi since 2008, it also became a networking hub for screenwriters, app developers, and online gamers conducting various campaigns in the virtual world.

"Six-letter word for Portuguese dollar?" someone else called out.

"Escudo!" Nate answered again. He couldn't remember the last time he did a crossword puzzle… they were too easy for him.

"Hmmm, fits. Thank you!" the stranger replied.

"No problem."

Nate was sitting on a green metallic tablet chair, browsing Tumblr on his MacBook Pro. He knew nearly every person around him and the projects they were working on. Freelancers were even known to swap assignments amongst themselves in the secluded group. Another writer approached the area and greeted everyone with, "Happy Friday! Anyone sell that Great American Novel yet?"

There were grunts and moans for replies as Nate smiled to himself. You couldn't find a surlier group of people, even in a bar, and the group kept to themselves, not sharing any depressing news.

Like the average emasculated married man, Nate had a guilty pleasure of occasionally looking at images of porn. He had no particular preference, but being previously overweight himself, he favored Big Beautiful Women, aka, BBW's.

He was scrolling through countless pictures on his dashboard when one made his fingertip freeze in mid-air. Nate's eyes bulged as he took in a shallow gasp of air. The woman was spread-eagled, revealing a bush with a huge stomach and a massive bosom. Any other time, those would make his body react a certain way, but it was the face he was concentrating on the most. He *knew* this woman.

After a double take, he squinted to study and try to identify her since the face was the furthest from the camera. Without a doubt, it was her.

"Stephanie?" Nate whispered.

People look at naked people online all the time, but when it's someone you know… he shook his head and then examined the background. She was sitting on a green leather chair in what appeared to be an ordinary room. There were no windows or any other furniture. Her blond hair was down nearly to her shoulders, she was wearing eyeshadow and there was a silver chain around her neck with a heart charm laying on the cleavage.

*She never wore makeup or jewelry… this can't be her, a twin possibly?* He mused to himself.

A wolf whistle from behind startled him. "Damn, she is hot!"

Nate slammed the MacBook closed and looked up to see Hiram Weyler standing behind him. The Jewish film school playwright was wearing slacks and a buttoned-down white dress shirt. A copy of the current week's The Village Voice newspaper was tucked underneath his armpit.

"Hiram, what the fuck? You mind not snooping on me?"

"Hey sorry, man… you looked like you saw a ghost or something, then started mumbling to yourself. Just seeing what was wrong?"

"Nothing's wrong… keep what you saw to yourself, you hear me?"

Hiram put his hands up, and the newspaper fell to the ground. "Hey… I didn't see anything." He picked up his paper and walked past him.

Nate looked around and noticed others were watching him. He nearly jumped out of his skin when his ringtone exploded from his pocket. He fished out his iPhone and answered while the onlookers went back to what they were doing.

"Hello?" he said to the receiver.

"Nate, it's Clancy… got a film screening that I need a 250-word review article on, if it's good I can shop it around to the usual mags, give you $65.00 if you have it in by Monday."

Clancy was a freelance headhunter, always looking for writers of articles to be placed in all forms of media.

"What movie?"

"Can't tell ya, you want it?"

"Hmmm, can you do $100.00? I'll double the word count."

"Alright, sending you the email, print it and be at the theater by 8 pm." Clancy hung up the phone. A second later, the email notification went off and Nate opened it.

"*Prisoners*? Never heard of it." He skimmed the email for details of the film and the location. His phone flashed with another incoming call.

"Hello?"

"What are you wearing?" a female voice asked.

"Nicky! How's it going, you freak?"

"I'm just sitting here in the tub, thinking about you and masturbating."

"Uh-huh, fascinating," he replied nonchalantly. The stand-up comedienne would flirt with mannequins if they were anatomically correct.

"Got a slot on my amateur hour show tonight at 8 pm, guarantee you a pair of c-notes and a blowjob, you in?"

He thought about it, boring film screening or stand-up set? *You should have paid more, Clancy...*

"Yes, to the gig, but I must decline the offer for oral sex. It might be frowned upon by my wife."

She let out a disappointed moan. "I swear, I'll wear you down someday… okay, be at the Times Square Comedy Club by 9 pm. I'll slip you in the middle of the lineup, then hopefully between my thighs…" she hung up.

Nate rolled his eyes and stood up. "Hey anyone want a film screening review? $65.00 for 250 words, 8 pm tonight on the lower east side?"

"I'll take it!" someone called out.

Nate pointed. "Give me your email and I'll forward you the details. Print the email and be there. Don't leave me hanging, man…"

Clancy would be furious he subcontracted, but he didn't care.

After packing up, he started walking towards Sixth Avenue. The picture was still stuck in his head.

*It couldn't be her… what are you doing out here, Stephanie?*

The Century 21 department store was at 22 Cortlandt Street, several blocks from the Freedom Tower as it neared completion. Cynthia Durant maneuvered up and down the aisles in the women's section. She couldn't help but smile as she found every item fitted her athletically fit body perfectly, because it hadn't always been so.

While her husband, Nate, had weight loss surgery several years ago, Cynthia went from a size twenty-four to a size nine on her own, while supporting him. She remembered a time when she had to buy clothes from secondhand thrift stores and remote full-figured boutiques outside the five boroughs. She walked up to the cashier and paid for three outfits with her credit card.

After leaving the store, she took a stroll down Fulton Street heading west. It was a few minutes after four-thirty, as she window-shopped various stores while turning the heads of businessmen (and a few women) as she passed. She loved to walk long distances. By the time she arrived at the South Street Seaport, it was five o'clock.

Cynthia walked into the Watermark Bar, a fairly new place that was part of the resurgence of the seaport after being hit hard by Hurricane Sandy last year. Taking a seat in the back facing the entrance, she ordered a mojito and waited. A tall Hispanic gentleman in a charcoal-striped suit took the seat next to her. His skin was olive-colored and his black hair was slicked back. He cleared his throat several times in a feeble attempt to get her attention.

"Don't I know you from somewhere?" he asked her, after being ignored.

She turned to look at him and smiled politely. "I don't think so."

He nodded. "My apologies." He let a few minutes tick by, while he tried to think of another line. "I uh, loved you in *Femme Fatale*. It was very erotic…"

The compliment tickled her, she turned once again and looked at him, "You saying I look like Rebecca Romijn? Would that make you Antonio Banderas?"

"I've been told I favor him several times," he said, flashing his best smile.

"Well, Anton, I hate to break it to you, but I'm married." Cynthia raised her left hand, revealing her wedding band. "Ten years this coming October." She leaned in and whispered, "Now, I'm going to let you down gently, because you're a nice guy. I'm waiting for my friends, who will be here any minute, and I don't want you sitting here when they arrive, okay? Get up, walk away, or I'm throwing this drink in your face."

She waited for him to leave. When he didn't, she gripped the glass in front of her.

"Okay, wait… before I walk away, I just need to know one thing. You said you've been married for ten years, right? After all that time, what makes him still worth getting up in the morning compared to a guy like me?"

She sighed and looked at him, with her icy blue eyes, moving a blond curl of her hair to the side. "Because he loved me when I weighed 350 pounds."

He flinched at the revelation.

"Something tells me you wouldn't have given me the time of day back then… which is why you're not giving it to me now. Bye-bye!"

The man nodded at the insightful message. "Have a nice evening," he said with a wave, and slid off the barstool.

The bartender came back to Cynthia. "He hits on every woman in here… was that true what you said? I didn't mean to eavesdrop, but uh, I just can't see you… that way."

"Yeah, it's true, and just proves how shallow men can be. I'll have another, please."

"Coming up." He left to prepare her another mojito.

Several mojitos later, Cynthia smiled when she saw her friends, Jennifer and Gloria, walk in. They saw her and waved, then approached, greeting each other with air kisses on each side of their faces.

"I've started without you. It's been a day…" Cynthia said.

"Who you telling? Let's get a booth, have I got some dirt from the office to dish!" Gloria announced.

Cynthia ordered a chicken salad while her two friends ordered appetizers. Jennifer worked for one of the best stock-market firms on Wall Street. She was the shortest of the trio, but you couldn't tell from the high heels she wore all the time. Ebony dark hair, with brown eyes, and a shapely body, she was always mistaken for Cynthia's younger sister. Well-reserved, she also served as the voice of reason among the close group of friends.

Gloria was the wildcard. While working very hard not to be the stereotypical "Loud, Obnoxious, Black Diva," she couldn't help who she was. At six-foot-six and an even two-hundred pounds, she could play for the WNBA. Instead, she worked as a legal assistant for the district attorney's office. Gloria had just finished a long-winded story about the hostile work environment among all the prosecutors in the office, fighting over being first-chair of an upcoming case.

"…I'm telling you, it's so cutthroat it should be on prime-time television!"

"Oooh, speaking of… did you see *Devious Maids* this week?" Jennifer asked. "That show is really growing on me."

"I'm feeling it, too," Cynthia agreed.

"I hate Lifetime shows, they never last long enough, I'm still pissed they canceled *Army Wives*." Gloria dismissed.

"I saw the bag, Cyn… you swung by 21 on your way here? Wha'cha get?"

"Something for the weekend picnic at mom and dad's… such a bore."

Jennifer and Gloria looked at each other, "Riiiiight," they said in unison, sharing a laugh.

"It's true! All they're going to do is grill me and Nate like… *'How's the job search, Cynthia? When are you having a baby, Cynthia? Why don't you call so-and-so for a reference, Cynthia?'* It's going to be pure hell."

"Girl, if you're looking for sympathy, you're barking up the wrong tree," Gloria said.

"Right? Poor, little rich girl who used to be fat and now looks drop-dead gorgeous while married to the perfect guy for ten years?" Jennifer asked.

"First of all, I'm not rich, my parents are. I worked hard for everything I own, teaching kids for over seven years, and my *husband* worked his ass off, too. Second of all, I lost the weight, yeah, but it wasn't easy! I worked hard to support my husband after his surgery and we did it together."

"But admit it, you're 36, the two of you have been married ten years, what *are* you waiting for?"

"We're putting it in God's hands, Gloria… I believe there's a reason why Nate hasn't hit the bullseye yet. We've both been checked, and nothing's wrong with either of us, but I'm still a type-one diabetic. Getting pregnant means gestational diabetes… that can kill me."

"So, basically, you're scared of having children because you think you won't survive the labor? That's so selfish," Jennifer said.

"Fuck you, Jennifer! You squeeze a beach ball out your hoo-ha and see if you can whistle Dixie!"

"Calm down, girl! You're so defensive! Listen, I heard through the grapevine that HSA Charter School Two is looking for subs. Think you can handle some privileged black kids in East Harlem?"

Cynthia's eyes went wide. "For real, Gloria?"

"They started the school year already, but the deadline's September 10th to apply. They're doing interviews on the spot."

"Send me the details tonight. I'll call you when I get home if you don't…" she stood and took a fifty-dollar bill out of her purse. "I'm going to the bathroom before we go." She placed the payment on the table.

Two minutes after she left the table, Gloria and Jennifer made a grab for the fifty. Gloria won the tug-of-war and cheered triumphantly. She then replaced the payment for the tab with three tens and a five-dollar bill.

At seven-twenty, Cynthia entered their three-story condo in Williamsburg, Brooklyn, with the bags of newly purchased clothes and a doggie bag under her arm. She sighed, as she was greeted with a moist, steaming pile of dog poo, in the middle of the divide between the breakfast nook and the living room, a few feet from the front door.

After hanging up her jacket and Century 21 bag on the coat hooks behind the door, she took the doggie bag with her salad to the kitchen and put it in the refrigerator. She then took out some rubber gloves from the pantry drawer and a bottle of disinfectant and cleaned the mess. Ten minutes later, she rewarded herself with a glass of Louis Roederer Brut Rose.

As if on cue, Brutus emerged from the dark hallway leading to the first-floor bedroom. A Staffordshire Bull Terrier, the couple's prize pet, had a beautiful, healthy black coat, with a white patch down his chest. He walked up to Cynthia, as she sat behind the island in their kitchen, and looked at her with a pleading look.

"I'm not walking you, and you still got food in your bowl…" she scolded.

She stood up and walked to the living room, still sipping on her glass. Heading to their sectional in front of the television, she pressed the flashing button on their answering machine. The first message was from Duane-Reade Pharmacy, informing Nate to pick up his medication that was called in on his behalf. Next, was Gloria giving the information about the job she mentioned. The third and final message was from her mother, Barbara…

*"Hey Nate, Cynthia, it's just me reminding you about Sunday. Everyone's arriving at 2 pm. Please don't be late, and Nate, bring your camera. Don't pretend that you forgot it like you always do. Your father says 'Hi,' bye-bye!"*

Cynthia shook her head as Brutus jumped on the couch, taking a seat next to her and staring. She looked back at him. "You're lucky you have no idea who your parents are."

The dog tilted his head, as if he understood what she said to him. She turned to the coffee table in front of her for the remote when a knock on the door startled them both.

"What th…" she stood up and cautiously approached the door. "Who is it?" she called out.

"It's Isaiah, from across the street," A high, feminine voice called out.

Cynthia relaxed a little and opened the door to see Isaiah Deakins standing in front of her. He was holding a leash to his female American Staffordshire Terrier, Alexis. At five-foot-four, Isaiah craned his head up to address her. He was wearing tight beige cargo shorts with an orange polo shirt. His complexion indicated he was possibly mixed between African American and Asian parents. In the four years of living across the street from them, Nate and Cynthia had never asked about his ethnicity.

Six months ago, Isaiah started breeding unique types of pit bulls for money and had been fascinated with Brutus since.

"I know it's late, Cynthia, but I was wondering if you could bring Brutus over for a doggy date with Miss Alexis so they can get to know each other, sniff around and say howdy? Jorge took the rest of the pups out to Jones Beach to play with his cousins all weekend. It'll be nice and quiet."

Jorge was Isaiah's partner, domestic and business, for whatever schemes the couple hatched to make money. Cynthia suspected Jorge was bisexual because he'd flirted with her several times in the past, claiming to be flamboyant. Isaiah himself was gayer than David Hyde Pierce and twice as conservative.

Cynthia was planning to zone out in front of the television until Nate came home around half-past midnight, but Isaiah was always great for a drunken conversation and a sympathetic ear.

"Alright, you've been asking for a while now… let me get his toys and we'll be right behind you."

She got a leash and some chew toys, then put some dog treats in a Ziploc bag. The two owners and their dogs left the building and walked up the street.

## 2

## A DATELINE SPECIAL

Cynthia and Isaiah took the dogs around the block a few times while participating in idle conversation. Williamsburg had been gentrified lately, with their neighborhood being one of the most sought out locations in the real estate market. Cynthia's parents bought the condo for her and Nate after they had been together four years. It was considered a late wedding gift since her parents didn't contribute to any of their wedding expenses, since Nate was her second husband.

They made it to Isaiah's place, and he let her in. The couple was renting the house, and you would never know they kept more than six dogs there because the place was spotless. There was just something about gay people and cleanliness that she respected. Ten years with Nate and it was a miracle when he kept their closets organized.

"Isaiah, you have to let me in or your secret. Do you have a cleaning service come through every day or what?" she asked.

"Please, this is all me, girl… grime doesn't stand a chance in my queendom."

The living room had no couch, just a few love seats placed in a semi-circle. A flatscreen television was mounted on the wall.

Nate and Cynthia were still watching their 52-inch standard definition television he'd owned since 1998. Isaiah sat in the middle chair while Cynthia walked to his left and threw a rawhide bone to the middle of the floor, where Brutus and Alexis started chewing on both ends.

Isaiah grabbed the remote and turned the television to ION where an episode of *Cold Case* was on, then stood up. "I got mimosas in a pitcher from this afternoon. That sound good?"

"Pour it on," she replied.

He walked to the kitchen while the dogs gave up on the bone and started playfully chasing each other. After a couple of minutes, Isaiah came back holding a plastic pitcher and two glass flutes. "Awww, they're so cute. I can tell she likes him. She loves to play hard to get. When she's with a dog she doesn't like she just lays there and takes it like the bitch she is."

She laughed and accepted a flute, holding it up for a pour, then took a sip. It was cold and strong, so she took a longer pull.

"How old is he? Think he can still stud?" he asked.

"I don't know. Nate had him before we met, so probably twelve or thirteen years. How old issszat that in dog years?" her speech started to slur.

"Wow… he's a senior citizen. Collecting social security this one!"

There was a pause in the conversation as the dogs left the living room. Isaiah sensed something was bothering Cynthia.

"So, what's going on, girl? Rap with me…"

"Ugh, life sucks, that's all. Nate's working all the time and I'm not. My parents are driving me up the wall. My so-called friends are bitches, plus half the men in this city eye-bang me everywhere I go. But all I see in the mirror is that ugly, fat woman my first husband left for someone I look like now."

"I don't get that. From what you told me, back in the day the two of you were like "Mike and Molly" before there actually was a *Mike and Molly*. But you're both skinny now, so why can't you let your former selves go?"

"Because my head's fucked up… that's why I can't teach anymore. Those kids broke me down. My ex broke me down, my parents are breaking me down. The one person that should be in my corner is out there… coming home Saturday morning and leaving for work Sunday night. I'm a weekend wife, *that's* what's wrong with my life!" she giggled. "That rhymes."

Isaiah felt a vibration in his back pocket and pulled out his cell phone. He read a text and then tucked it back in his shorts. "Honey look, I don't know shit about straight men, but Nate appears to be a great guy. He works hard, but he's not your ex-husband. He loves you, girl…" he took a sip and continued. "If his jobs are keeping him from spending time with you, let him know that. Communication is the key."

"Yeah, you're right."

"I know I am! And I feel you on the job situation… I was an art teacher for P.S. 132 in Washington Heights for twelve gaddamn years! Once I came out, they called me a pedophile, said I was being too close to the male students, and they canned me. Being gay is the scarlet letter among educators. The mark never goes away."

"I'm so sorry Isaiah…"

"It's okay, I'll be alright." He sighed, then lifted his glass. "Hey, to the dedicated teachers of yesteryear…"

Cynthia held up her glass as well. "Hear, hear!"

"May those chalkboards stay clean, and those erasers stay dirty!"

The pair finished their drinks, and Cynthia was feeling tipsy. "Hey, let Brutus stay here for the night. Nate won't mind. I'm gonna crash over at our place. He'll wake me up when he gets in… and we'll pick up Brutus in the morning…"

"Okay, that's cool… Jorge texted me from Long Island. He won't be back until Sunday. I'm serious about making some pups with Brutus and Alexis. We gotta hammer out the details, okay girl?"

Cynthia got up and walked to the door. "I'll talk to Nate about it. It's up to him. I'm just the stepmom."

"You got my flute in your hand!" he called out.

She stopped at the door and looked at the glass like it appeared out of thin air. She started a snorting, laughing fit and walked back to hand it to him. "Here ya go…"

"Uhh, thanks," Isaiah said, with a chuckle. "You take care crossing the street, okay?"

She nodded repeatedly and then turned to the door again. After a few attempts, she got the door open and sauntered out into the street. The dogs emerged from their hiding places, and walked back into the living room. Brutus sniffed the chair Cynthia was sitting on and then walked over to Isaiah. The dog put his front paws on his lap, as to ask *Where did my mother go?*

He looked down at his face and whispered, "Brutus, ya momma crazy, boy…"

Nate arrived at the Times Square Comedy Club on Eighth Avenue at eight-thirty. He greeted everyone backstage and waited for Nicky to introduce the second performer in the lineup. She was a contributor and panelist on the MTV show *Girl Code* and had several other projects in development for the network. After cracking a few jokes, she brought out the next act and ran over to greet Nate with an aggressive hug.

"Thanks for coming, sweetie! You're on after the next guy in around 25 to 30 minutes… wanna quick handy to loosen you up?" she made a move for his crotch, which he quickly deflected.

"That's alright, Nic. I'm loose enough, thank you."

She had been over aggressively infatuated with Nate for as long as he'd known her. The playful banter didn't faze him, whereas anyone else would have considered her behavior sexual harassment a long time ago.

"How's the crowd? Can I go blue, or is it family-friendly out there?" Nate asked.

She gave him a look. "This is my show, and I'm as filthy as they come. Go nuts. I don't care, just be funny!"

He chuckled. "Alright, just checking."

"Everyone's got at least twelve minutes. If you get them hysterical, we can give you five more minutes. If you go twenty, I'll let you palm my tits," she instructed.

"You'd let me palm 'em if I bomb, you horny toad."

"Yeah, you right, but I wouldn't respect myself in the morning." She laughed and playfully slapped him on the ass.

"We're going to Latitude after the show. Got the rooftop to ourselves! You better sit next to me, so break a leg!" she went back out to the stage to warm up the crowd. After another fifteen-minute set, Nate was ready to perform next as Nicky made a formal introduction.

"This next comedian is the number one reason why I like white guys. No offense brothers! Ladies and gentlemen, welcome to the stage, my future baby-daddy, Nate from New York!"

There was a round of applause as he came out and she walked past him offstage. Nate waved, greeting the crowd, and adjusted the microphone on the mic stand.

"Thank you, thank you very much, everyone. I *am* Nate from New York, that IS my stage name," he opened. "How 'bout another round for Nicky?" that brought another round of applause. "She's such a kidder. She's just jealous because I actually prefer her friend Carly over her… I have a thing for redheads."

There were a few laughs from the audience, and Nicky yelled from backstage, "I can do red hair! All I have to do is change my wig!" that got a few more laughs.

"Yeah, but will the carpet match the drapes?" he barked back at her. "So yeah, Nate from New York is my name. I picked that name with the intent of traveling all around the world, comparing everywhere I go to New York. So far, it's not working."

The audience laughed. His comedic timing in his delivery was on point.

"I'm actually from Chicago, though. Born and raised, and every time I tell people that they always ask me the same question… *"You left Chicago to come HERE?"* guess that was a step in the wrong direction! Like Chicago is any better? I consider it a lateral move. You damned if you go, you damned if you stay!"

He stole a glance offstage and saw Nicky rubbing her nipples, a sign by her to keep going. Ten minutes later, he wrapped up his set with one last joke…

"I wanna finish my time by announcing, this October… I'll be celebrating ten wonderful years of marriage!"

There were "Awwws" and claps from everyone.

"And I would like to share with you all the secret to a happy marriage… don't get married in the first place! I'm Nate from New York, ladies and gentlemen. You've been great, good night!"

He walked off the stage as the audience gave him a standing ovation. Nicky came out and kept the show moving for the next set of performers. An hour later, all the comedians came out for the curtain call and took a bow. After the show, everyone exchanged pleasantries, took pictures, and signed autographs for a few lingering fans. Nicky handed out envelopes to everyone for payment and then made it out the back door, heading into the street.

It was eleven-fifteen at Latitude Bar and Lounge. Nate made his way up to the fourth floor, which led out to the rooftop deck. There were couches everywhere, with tables in the middle. People with drinks were standing around talking, enjoying the night air. Nate walked around and mingled for twenty minutes. He was about to leave when Nicky grabbed him from behind.

"Ah, ah, ah… I told you to sit with me, you little sneak… thought you could pop in and leave like you're doing the walk of shame out of my apartment? Guess again."

She pulled him to her group table, and they sat among her friends.

"Nate from New York, huh? You sure you ain't a pro? Nicky promised us amateurs! You killed tonight, like you were born for stand-up! Shit, made us all look bad!" one of the other performers said, while lifting his glass for a toast.

"Yeah, this was like my third time in front of a crowd. I do other things as well."

"That's right, this man does so many things, he hardly sleeps!" Nicky laughed.

"Well, keep doing what you're doing. And, Nicky, put him on first next time!" a comedienne joked.

Everyone shared a hearty laugh.

"Wha'cha drinking, baby? First one's on me," Nicky asked Nate.

"You know I'm a lightweight. You trying to slip me a mickey?"

"Hell no! Too easy! I like a challenge. I'll wear you down sooner or later, THEN wear you out!"

The laughs started up again. Nate said, "Just water, thank

you. I'm driving home tonight, and I need to be home by 1 am… or the wife will file a missing persons report."

"Hey man, how old are you?" a white comedian Nate only knew as "Scrappy Gee" asked.

He cringed. "What kind of question is that? How old do I look?"

"I only ask because you said you were married for ten years, unless that was bullshit…"

"Nah, it's true," Nate confirmed.

"Well, were y'all college sweethearts or something? You look like you barely 30!"

Nate turned to Nicky, who just kept quiet with a big, shit-eating grin. "I'm 42 years old, this past June…"

The table erupted with jeers of doubt. "Bullshit!" someone said.

Nate held up his left hand. "Hand to God. You wanna be dazzled some more?"

Nicky was laughing, with a cup of Jagermeister in her hand, as Nate pulled out his phone and showed everyone his home screen again.

"Damn, that's you?! You look like Yokozuna!"

Everyone laughed again.

"Yeah, check his gallery…" Nicky added. "…His wife used to be big, too!"

"Hey, props for turning your life around, man… you certainly are blessed," A gentleman said, as Nate put his phone back in his pocket.

"Thanks, and if I want to continue to be blessed, I'll need to hit the streets soon." He stood up and said his goodbyes, sliding out from the table. Before he started walking, Nate bent down and hugged Nicky. "Take care, Nic… stay sexy."

She whispered in his ear, "I sent you a nude selfie I took in the bathroom stall. Erase it from your phone after you rub one out when you get home."

"Nicky, if my wife divorces me, I'll kill you."

"Just break me off with that huge white dick of yours before you do, so I can walk through those pearly gates smiling."

He sighed and walked back to the staircase that led downstairs.

Nate parked at a lot on 49th Street between Eighth Avenue and Broadway. He climbed into his Chevy Tahoe and buckled his seatbelt. After checking his senses to make sure he was alert to drive, he checked his phone. There were twelve new messages, each with a photo attachment.

"Nicky…" He sighed and shook his head. He selected all the messages at once and deleted them. After turning the key in the ignition, the engine came to life, and he pulled out into the night. The hustle was over. It was time to go home.

Nate was crossing the Brooklyn Bridge a few minutes after midnight when his phone rang in the car mount. While keeping his eye on the road, he pressed the phone's speaker mode and quickly said, "I'm driving, call you later!" then hung up. A minute later the phone rang again, and he answered again. "I said I'm driving, call you back!" and clicked the phone off a second time.

The phone once again rang for a third time as he got off the bridge, so Nate pulled into a gas station and ripped the phone out of the mount. "What?!" he yelled.

"What the fuck, Nate? I just got a shitty 300-word review from a Paul Acevedo, who the fuck is this guy? Why didn't *you* go to the screening?"

"You should have paid more, Clancy. I subbed it out for another commitment, sorry."

"I give you the plum gigs, the money may not be good, but I make it up with the quality of the film! I don't deserve this disrespectful shit!"

"Some Hugh Jackman channeling "Special Victims Unit"-snore-fest is your idea of a plum gig? If he's not slashing someone with claws sticking out of his hands, it ain't worth watching! The last good movie you got me screening tickets to was *The Avengers*!"

"You know what? I take a lot of shit from you. These mags *ask* for you personally because you write pretty well, but don't think I won't cut you off in a heartbeat, buddy! You're nothing but a two-bit hack washout that wasn't even good enough for SNL!"

"Oh, hell no, you didn't…" Nate hung up the phone and slammed it on the dashboard.

The phone rang and he let it go to voicemail. It rang once again, and he continued to ignore it. Nate stepped out of the car and went to the convenience store to buy a Red Bull. He climbed back inside and when the phone rang again, he answered it.

"Say sorry, motherfucker!"

"Sorry, I was out of line," Clancy mumbled.

"You *ever* say some shit like that again, I will END you. You will be a fucking *Dateline* special. You hear me?"

There was a long pause. Then Clancy said, "Yeah, I got it."

"Don't call me with anything… for the next four weeks." He ended the call and threw his phone on the passenger seat. His left eye twitched as he grinded his teeth. He resisted the urge to break his phone and buy a new one. The engine came to life again, and he exited the gas station.

The Tahoe pulled up in front of Nate's place and he braced himself for whatever Cynthia was going to complain about when he walked in. He remembered her parents were doing something Sunday that they were going to, but there was something else he couldn't put his finger on that he was supposed to do.

After unlocking the door, he found Cynthia lying face down on the sectional with the television on.

"Hey baby, I'm home. Where's Brutus?" he started whistling and calling for him.

"The garbage has to go out, hon," Cynthia said, from underneath her tattered blond hair.

And that's what Nate couldn't put his finger on. He shook his head and continued scanning the room.

"Alright, I'll take it out. Where's Brutus, baby?"

She sat up and rubbed her head, looking like the room was spinning around her. "Don't get mad or anything…"

Nate spun and glared at his hungover wife. *Don't yell, whatever you do, don't yell…* "I come home after a long day, the first thing you say to me is, 'The garbage has to go out.' Now I can't find my dog and you tell me not to get mad? That's kind of hard to do. We're past mad… despite my calm voice."

He congratulated himself for his calm demeanor.

Cynthia was fueled by liquid courage and was thinking about what Isaiah said. *Communication is key… let him know.* "Um, Brutus is across the street… on a doggy date at Isaiah's place."

Nate rolled his eyes. "Really Cyn? You know they're breeding pit bulls for dog fights. What on earth were you thinking?" he turned around and opened the door.

She called out, extending her arm. "Wait, there was something else I wanted to tell… ahh, fuck!" her arm dropped in frustration as the door slammed.

Nate marched across the street and looked in a window into Isaiah's living room. He appeared to be injecting Brutus with a needle. Nate vaulted up the three steps to the front door and pounded on the door.

"Open the door, Isaiah!" he yelled. He would never raise his voice to Cynthia, but his neighbor was another story.

The door cracked over and Nate pushed his way inside, confronting the timid man. "What the hell are you doing? What was that you just injected in my dog?!"

Isaiah backed up, putting his hands in front of him. "Just some hormones! Calm down, man!"

"I am two seconds from calling Animal Control on your ass. You're making these dogs more aggressive so you can sic them on each other!?"

"No! I would never do that! I'm just breeding them for money! I swear!"

"Bullshit!" Nate spat.

"Look, look, look… I'll make you an offer right now… $350.00 and pick of the litter. Alexis is ready and ovulating, man… their puppies I could probably sell for $1,000.00 apiece. I'll even give you 15% of the total sale. We're talking another $600.00 Nate… aaaaakk!"

Nate grabbed Isaiah by the collar of his shirt. "Stay. Away. From my wife. And my dog. Got it?"

"Yeah, yeah, I got it, man. It's cool, it's cool…" Isaiah relented.

Nate let him go and gathered Brutus's toys and leash. With a whistle, the dog ran over and circled his legs a few times, then sat still for Nate to put his leash on. Without another word, they left the house and walked home.

After collecting the garbage from the kitchen and taking it out to the collection of bins in the side alley of the condo, Nate came back inside to find Cynthia sobering up with some coffee at the dining room table. It was ten minutes to one o'clock in the morning.

She looked up and saw the look on his face. "Sorry, hon I…"

"Forget it. Just please keep Brutus away from that kook, okay?"

She nodded, as he came over and kissed her on the forehead, then took a seat at the table.

"So, uh, how was your day?" Cynthia asked.

Nate took out the envelope Nicky gave him and a few hundred-dollar bills. "Did two podcasts, covered a Samsung pre-event about smartwatches… and I killed it at an amateur comedy show for $200.00! I'm getting more comfortable on stage now."

"That's great!" she praised. "Good for you! You had a better day than me today…"

"Why? What happened?" Nate asked.

"Ah, the agency was a bust… took the skills test, clerical test and they told me they had no assignments right now, and they'll give me a call."

"Yeah, I've heard that line before," he said, patting her hand. "Don't get frustrated. You'll find something sooner or later."

"Well, Gloria did mention a charter school was looking for substitute teachers."

"There you go! Right up your alley. I'd give them a call first thing Monday."

"Yeah, um, listen, Mom called to confirm us for their outdoor picnic thing they're doing out at um… Floyd Bennett… something."

"Floyd Bennett Field? That's all the way out at Jamaica Bay. Why the hell would they have something out there?"

"I don't know. It starts at 3 pm officially, but they want everyone arriving at 2 pm."

Nate sighed, "Fine… but I'm not…"

"Please bring your camera," she pleaded. "C'mon Nate."

"Babe, I spend at least four days a week taking pictures. I'd like to give myself a break on the weekend. If they want me there taking pictures, they should freaking *hire* me."

Cynthia sighed and decided to let him have the last word. "Fine, don't bring your camera… but you mentioning work brings me to another matter I've been meaning to discuss…"

He knew what was coming and made an effort to hide his annoyance. "Go ahead."

"Nate, you're working too hard…" she began.

"Cyn—"

"Please, hear me out, hon… please. I know my severance is gone, and it's going on three years since I worked…"

"Which is why I'm doing what I do," Nate interrupted. "I have to be the provider, baby. I do all this to keep a roof over our heads, to pay the insurance on the car, to keep the lights on and the internet running…"

"I know, I know, and you're knocking it out of the park, honey, but I never see you anymore. These last few years have been a blur… we've gone from *Nate and Cynthia* to *Cynthia and Him.*"

Nate stood up from the table. "Okay, would you prefer that I go back to being 'Overweight Nate', huh? 'Four-hundred-pound Nate'? 'Never going out Nate'? Or how about 'Can't climb a flight of stairs Nate'? Hmmm?"

She remembered those days and remained silent, looking up at him.

He leaned in. "I do this so I don't go back to being tha… that guy. He would be dealing with heart problems by now, and bad circulation in his legs. I'm not going back to that, okay? Not going to happen."

He whistled for Brutus and put the money from the table back in his pocket, then walked past her. "So if you insist that I slow down, give me a reason to… you know what you have to do."

Brutus met Nate at the door, and he put the leash on. "Going for a walk around the block."

The door slammed behind him, and Cynthia hung her head in frustration. *I'm trying, goddamn it, I'm fucking trying!* Her eyes watered up, and she quickly wiped her face, then stood up, washed her mug in the sink, and stomped upstairs to the master bedroom.

**3**

---

# OF COURSE, THEY DID

Nate felt terrible ending the conversation like he did but being non-confrontational is what has kept them both sane all these years. In the beginning, there were a few arguments during the so-called "honeymoon" period, around 18 months in. After six years of marriage, he learned that if there's a serious conflict between the two of them, it's best to air out your grievances, state your case, and in the event of a stalemate, walk away and let cooler heads prevail.

Now approaching ten years of "marital bliss," he was doing what he could to keep them afloat, so they don't go crawling to Cynthia's parents for help. Nate was definitely a night owl, and Williamsburg was peaceful in the early hours of the morning. He returned to the house at one-thirty and noticed most of the lights were off, as well as the television. He unhooked Brutus and threw his ball down the hallway. The dog chased after it.

There was a small lamp on the computer desk on the left side of the living room. Nate took a seat and wiggled the mouse on his Mac Pro desktop computer. The machine snapped out of sleep mode, and he once again thought of Stephanie's picture on Tumblr.

"Where are you, Stephanie?" he whispered.

He logged onto Facebook and searched for "Stephanie Grace." There were over 100 profiles that he scrolled through, and none of the faces matched the woman he remembered. He narrowed the list with applied filters. Looking for those living in or from Chicago, Illinois… that attended Triton College in River Grove… or worked for Image Processing Systems.

As he searched, Nate started thumbing his wedding band. It was a nervous tic he did when deep in thought. The band danced loosely on his ring finger because of all the weight he lost from the surgery. After searching through all possible filters, he still came up with no results.

*Maybe she got married and is under a different name… yeah, and her husband just lets her take provocative pictures to put on the internet!*

A half-hour later, searching through other social media platforms, he was starting to get tired. He had no idea why he was obsessing over this picture of her. Stephanie worked with him on various document scanning projects for IPS back before the September 11th terrorist attacks. For four years, on and off they were close friends, then they drifted apart. Now, a decade later, he stumbled upon her online. He didn't know what to think.

Nate erased his browsing history and shut down the computer, then checked his phone for any messages. After securing all the locks and windows, then making sure Brutus didn't go to the bathroom anywhere in the house, he made his way upstairs to the second floor. Cynthia was sleeping in their king-size bed. She was wearing a sleep mask, with her iPod playing some gentle whisper white noise in her earbuds.

He stripped down to his underwear, then climbed into bed, and noticed he had a serious erection. Not exactly earning the husband-of-the-year award after their argument, so cuddling with Cynthia was out of the question. He sighed and closed his eyes, and within a few minutes, he was sound asleep.

The scent of sauteed turkey floated upstairs where Nate was still sleeping Sunday morning. Cynthia had let him sleep in and started breakfast late after doing yoga from a paid program infomercial. It was almost ten o'clock when Brutus made his way into the bedroom and jumped up on the bed. He approached Nate, tongue hanging out of his mouth, and started a barrage of playful licks on his face.

"Ughhh! What are you doing, boy? I know what you do at night! Stop!" he protested.

He came downstairs after washing up, wearing sweatpants and a white tee-shirt. Brutus was a step behind him. Cynthia was over the range in the kitchen, finishing a crustless smoked turkey and spinach quiche in a skillet. Nate snuck a quick peck and took a seat at the kitchen table. The Daily News Sunday newspaper was waiting for him. He pulled out the comics section and started reading.

"Who ordered the doggy wake-up call?" Nate joked.

"He's been a bundle of energy all morning," she replied. "It's like he got a B-12 shot."

Nate thought about Isaiah and that injection he saw him give Brutus Friday night.

"Something on your mind, hon?" Cynthia asked.

"No, um, nothing…" he shook his head.

After their tense Friday night, they had spent all day Saturday walking on eggshells. They eventually made up and watched *Identity Thief* on Netflix. The comedy stylings of Melissa McCarthy made the couple forget about their fight, bringing them to the status quo.

"I almost made two, but I figured we'd split one… eat it

carefully. I'll bring you some water in 30 minutes."

"Thank you, baby…" he said.

Both of them were used to the routine of portion control, and Nate drinking liquids *after* eating instead of during.

They ate quietly for several minutes, then Nate said, "Cyn, I was thinking…"

She looked up from her plate.

"Do we really need to go to this picnic thing with your parents? Let's stay in… and I can make things up for Friday to you…" he added with a sly smile.

She smiled back. "Nate… we skipped out on them Memorial Day and the Fourth of July… those 'fireworks' were remarkable by the way…" she added with a wink. "We owe it to them today… then they'll be out of our hair until Thanksgiving and Christmas."

Nate rolled his eyes. "Fine. But remember… we're going to Chicago to see dad and my cousins one of those holidays. We also owe them. Haven't been out there since 2009."

"Fair enough, but you know mom and dad are going to want us hosting this year. We should do Thanksgiving in Chicago and deal with everyone coming here for Christmas."

"We hosted the Fourth of July here last year… your sister got drunk and threw a Wii controller at our 42-inch flatscreen in my man cave, while I'm positive your uncle stole our iPod dock and subwoofer."

"He did not! Stop saying that he did, it's here somewhere. We just misplaced it."

"Whatever, we are not hosting Christmas here, end of story." Nate resumed eating while Cynthia took a long swallow of her bottled water.

At noon, they started looking for clothes in their separate closets. Cynthia held up two of the three outfits she purchased on Friday.

"Which one?" she asked Nate.

One was a lavender strapless gown with a bow at the waist, the other was a knitted red dress with a rose-shaped bow in the middle of the waist. *What is it with her and bows?*

"Um, the red one."

She looked at his choice and then walked back into the closet and held up the third outfit and the lavender gown again.

"Which one, now?" she asked again.

He looked to see her holding up the lavender from the first two and an identical strapless gown only in black.

"The black one," he picked.

"That settles it." She put the black gown back in the closet and took the lavender selection to the bathroom.

"Why do you always ask for my opinion and go with the opposite of what I say?" he called out in a higher-than-usual voice so she could hear him.

"Because you have no sense of style, hon!" she replied with a grin.

He let out a mock chuckle, then got serious. "Um, all three of those look new. You didn't perhaps go shopping Friday after-noon after the temp agency?"

Cynthia didn't answer.

"Cyn…?" he asked.

"You should wear a tie. Don't wear a sports jacket and a banded collar like you always do."

Nate sighed. Cynthia always changed the subject when he confronted her about money or shopping.

She stepped out of the bathroom. The gown flowed as she walked… to find Nate scowling back at her wearing a pair of white slacks. She sucked her teeth and looked up at the ceiling.

"Can we discuss this later?"

"No, we can discuss this *now*," he insisted.

They looked at each other in silence.

"I'm not going to get mad. Just tell me how much and what did you use?" he asked.

They had three bank accounts. A joint checking account, a savings account with a credit union, and a prepaid debit account that is occasionally funded by Cynthia's parents when she asks them to.

"Three… from the prepaid," Cynthia admitted.

He nodded. "Fine." He reached over to the bed, picked up a navy blue collarless shirt, and put his arm in the sleeve. After tucking the bottom into his slacks, he buttoned it up to his Adam's apple. A few moments later, he was dressed in a matching white jacket in front of her and stepping into his loafers.

"I hope that's the most expensive of the three," he said calmly.

"The red one was only six, the other two were $1,200.00 each."

"Hmm, I still like the black for contrast purposes. We'd be polar opposites."

"Ten minutes after we step outside, you're going to regret wearing white, I promise you." She walked out of the room and headed downstairs.

He shrugged. "At least it's before Labor Day," he said to himself, then followed her out.

It was a quarter to one, and they were going over what they were taking with them. Nate put his phone on vibrate. He was not taking any work-related calls. Cynthia found a purse that matched her lavender dress and checked the contents, making sure she had plenty of sugarless gum to chew.

Nate examined the Tahoe thoroughly, knowing that Cynthia would sneak his camera inside so he could take pictures at the event. The previous night, before going to bed, he put his equipment in a gym bag and locked it in his personal safe. Cynthia was waiting in the passenger seat, adjusting the air conditioning. The sun was beaming with a high temperature of 82 degrees.

"Let's go! Quit stalling, I didn't hide the camera, silly!" she called out.

He climbed into the car and gave her a skeptical look. She fluttered her eyelids innocently, and he grinned, turning the key to the engine. Nate took the I-278 to the Belt Parkway. Traffic flowed steadily for a Sunday afternoon. The trip took them a few minutes over an hour as they arrived at Floyd Bennett Field at 2 pm.

There were several signs posted as they pulled up to the checkpoint. A guy in a security uniform holding a clipboard approached as Nate rolled down the window.

"Uh, Nate and Cynthia Durant?" he announced.

The guard checked the clipboard and waved him through. "Parking area is on the left, just follow the path."

"Uh, am I missing something? What's with all this security?" he asked.

"The Goss's rented the entire area for the next six hours. It's closed to the public."

Nate looked and noticed that the signs indeed said "Closed for Private Event" on them. He nodded. "Of course they did," he said, as he drove inside the entrance.

Nate parked at the designated area where over 30 other cars were parked.

"Quite the turnout," he said, stepping out and slamming the door behind him.

Cynthia was on the other side bent over, she reached underneath the passenger seat and pulled out Nate's gym bag with his photography equipment.

"Oooh, well looky what I found underneath the seat!" she said, in a sing-song voice.

*Don't yell, whatever you do, don't yell...* Nate gasped in shock. "Cynthiaaaaaa…" he growled.

A female's voice called out from across the lot, "Is that my big sister and her attractive husband I hear over there?!"

"Oh great," Nate whispered, with a sigh.

Vanessa Goss, in full stride, jumped on Cynthia with a spirited embrace. The two giggled and screamed, greeting each other. Cynthia's younger sister was a bundle of spontaneous combustion. Her fiery red hair was tied in a ponytail, she was wearing a tea dress with a floral print. At five-foot-eleven (with heels), she was neck-in-neck with her older sister.

She took a moment to wave to Nate. "Hi, Nate! Daddy's looking for you. Apparently, there's a few local assemblymen attending that he wants to get a few pictures with."

"Hey, Vanessa." He waved back unenthusiastically.

Cynthia held the gym back up and waved it for emphasis. He walked around to her side and took the bag.

"We're going to have a discussion about how you learned the combination to my safe," he grunted.

"Took me three tries. I figured it'd be our pin, your birthday, or your mother's birthday."

Nate took out his camera, placed the strap around his neck, then the gym bag over his shoulder. With a quick peck on her cheek, he whispered to Cynthia, "I love you, but you drive me crazy."

"I know." She smiled back at him.

He walked away from the sisters and slipped into *Professional Photographer* mode.

Vanessa gave her sister the once-over. "I love this dress! Where did you get it?"

"I'm not telling, you'll turn around and buy it for yourself..."

The two giggled again. Vanessa had idolized her sister since puberty. They were eight years apart but acted like twins, always confiding in each other and never competing for their parent's affection. Both always felt equally loved by their parents and they couldn't be prouder.

They started walking from the parking lot. "I'm warning you now, sis. Mom's on a serious kick about grandchildren. One of her friends just bragged about grandbaby number five and she is jealous to the point of stealing one!"

"Oh, great!" Cynthia hissed.

"Dad's all about investors, of course. Kissing ass everywhere. He's going to be hounding Nate for pictures..."

"I know, I know... who else is here?"

"Mostly cousins, grandma Goss, uncle Dwight, and Aunt Krystin, the gang from the old neighborhood, a few of my friends from the network..."

"They still keep in touch? After two years?" Cynthia asked.

Vanessa was a former daytime television morning show meteorologist. From mid-2009 to 2011, she delivered weather reports to millions of viewers across the country. Then, after a rough night of drinking, she had a meltdown live on the air and was let go. After a quick stint in rehab, she was finally starting to get her life back together, weighing several options for a comeback.

"I've been hearing about a few slots opening up for weekend personalities. I'm hoping to find someone to put in a good word."

Cynthia was proud of her sister. "Alright, sis, you're doing better than me. Let's go meet mom and dad and get this over with."

They disappeared into the crowd of partygoers.

Nate moved through the number of guests, identifying himself and taking pictures. A majority of Cynthia's distant relatives recognized him and posed. Others were caught off guard for candid shots, reacting once he moved on.

He took a moment to rest his camera and walked over to a silver-haired gentleman in a gray pinstriped suit, who was speaking to an African American woman wearing a blue pants-suit.

"Ma'am, if this guy tells you about a bridge in Brooklyn he wants to sell you, trust me, he'll make you one." Nate joked.

Christopher Goss turned around and smiled. "Nate! Glad you could make it!" He hugged his son-in-law and turned to introduce his guest. "I'd like you to meet Annette Hollingsworth, Assemblywoman from Albany County."

"Nate Durant, how do you do?" He shook her hand politely.

"I was just telling Mrs. Hollingsworth about the projects that Goss Brothers Construction has been involved with all around the world…"

Goss Brothers Construction was Christopher's pride and joy. He started with small building contracts originating in Pittsburgh, Pennsylvania back in 1948. With only a handful of dedicated men and his G.I. Bill, Christopher managed to build his company into a multi-million-dollar firm that serviced four continents.

"…Nate, please tell us your amazing story of courage after the events of September 11th."

He was prepared for the subject. Christopher loved using Nate as a patriotic selling point with potential people of influence. "I was born and raised in Chicago and did a lot of contract work in data entry and document scanning from the time I was 22. After seven or eight years, work started to dry up, so I got my IT Certification. Then the towers went down, and I was on the first Amtrak to New York. I had no friends, no family here, but I walked straight down from Penn Station to Ground Zero and picked up a bucket."

"What a remarkable story, young man," Annette replied.

"I was worried when my Cynthia told me she was ready to re-marry so quickly after meeting Nate," Christopher started. "But he assured me that he was an honorable man, and after ten years, he's been true to his word." He hugged Nate's shoulder for emphasis.

The assemblywoman tilted her head with a familiar nod. "Durant… from Chicago, you wouldn't happen to be related to *Jeremy* Durant, would you?"

There was a moment of silence as Nate and Christopher exchanged glances, then Nate cleared his throat. "He's my father."

She then pointed at him. "Yes… I saw the CNN special about him!" She cocked an eyebrow. "Didn't you used to be fat?"

Nate blushed, as Christopher attempted to deflect the conversation. "Madam Assemblywoman…"

"Um, if you'll excuse me, I believe I see my wife calling me." Nate gave an uneasy smile and walked past the two, disappearing into the crowd.

"All I'm asking for is to come in and record an audition tape, Josh," Vanessa pleaded.

She was making a case to fill in for one of the network's weekend anchors, who was going on maternity leave in a month. Josh was one of the producers looking for a replacement.

"Your meltdown has over a million views on YouTube. You're synonymous with an image we don't want, Vanessa."

"I've been clean and sober for 18 weeks and the camera still loves me." She leaned in and whispered, "I just got my tits done. I'm up to a 40-Triple-D," and raised her eyebrows.

The new producer took a quick glance at her cleavage and swallowed hard. "Wear something short and *tight*. 10 am Wednesday, studio J."

She clasped her hands together. "You won't regret this! Treat yourself to some paté." She nodded to the table of appetizers. After watching Josh walk to the spread, she giggled and thought about outfits to wear.

Nate was drinking a bottle of water when Cynthia walked over to him. "Thank you for being a good sport about this."

"Yeah, yeah," he scoffed. "I'm pretty much ready to go, you?"

She nodded. "We've made our appearance, and you've suffered enough. Let's say our goodbyes and head to the car."

They threw away their utensils and froze as they saw Christopher Goss talking to someone.

"Is that?" Nate asked, "Oh no."

Cynthia was stunned and dumbfounded.

Nate tried to pull her away, but she didn't move. Her eyes were fixated on her father. And Sylverton Withrow III conversing with him.

"Cyn, c'mon, while they don't see us. Please, he's not worth…"

Cynthia pulled out of Nate's grasp and made a beeline across the field to confront her ex-husband.

Nate followed quickly behind, whispering some sense to her. "Baby, don't make a scene, at least don't hit him first. If he hits you, I'll deck 'im for you."

"Cynthia! Isn't this a pleasant surprise?" Sylverton began.

He was five-foot-seven, with red hair and freckles. Nate alternated between calling him *Howdy Doody* or *Archie Andrews*, especially with his overbite. Wearing a dark sweater vest over a white spotted dress shirt and brown slacks, all he would need is the capital 'R' on his chest.

"Hello, Sylverton," Cynthia greeted coldly, then turned to her father. "Daddy, can I speak to you for a second?"

"Oh, don't steal him away on my account. We were just about done, right Chris?"

"Uh, yes, that's correct. Um, whatever you wish to discuss, my dear, can wait until I wrap things up here." Christopher reached over to shake Nate's hand. "And thank you for all the pictures you took here, son. You'll send me copies, right?"

"Along with the bill, sir…" Nate said, with a wink.

The elder winked back and quickly stepped away, leaving the three awkwardly looking at each other.

"I must say, you two look great. I'm extremely jealous," Sylverton remarked.

Nate put on a fake smile and attempted to pull on Cynthia's wrist.

"What are you doing here?" she demanded.

"Uh, your father invited me at the last minute. What's with the attitude? Hey, I know things ended badly between us, but there's no need to hold a grudge…"

Nate stepped between them. "Right, we were just…"

"I don't care if my father invited you. Next time, I'd appreciate it if you just politely decline."

Sylverton glared at Cynthia. "Wow, you haven't changed a bit, have you?"

Nate sighed. He was baiting her, and she bit… hook, line, and sinker. "Cyn, please," he whispered. "He's not worth…"

"It means that despite being happily married to someone I'll admit *is* better than me, you're so petty… WHOA-WHOA!"

He didn't get to finish his sentence, because Cynthia was removing her shoe, with the intention of stabbing him with the heel. Nate was able to restrain her, cup her mouth closed to prevent her from screaming, and drag her to the parking lot.

Sylverton shook his head. "Same 'ol Cyn…"

**4**

---

# I WOULDN'T USE A FORKLIFT TO KICK HER OUT OF BED

THE RIDE BACK HOME WAS TENSE. NEITHER ONE OF THEM SAID A word as they both got out of the car. Cynthia opened the front door and slowly walked up the steps to the bedroom. Nate took off his jacket, pulled out his phone, and lowered his gym bag next to the computer desk. He started his way up the steps when he saw Brutus run out of the bedroom and down the steps, followed by a pillow that hit him square in the face. He nearly fell backward, as a bedspread followed the pillow down the steps when he looked up.

"Hon, I didn't do anything…" he started.

"That's right! You didn't!" she barked back, slamming the bedroom door behind her.

He sighed, as Brutus looked up at him.

"I hope you have a spare bedroom in the doghouse we'll be sharing tonight."

Cynthia woke up in bed alone at ten in the morning. After a shower, she opened the door and came downstairs in her robe to find a note from Nate.

*Photoshoot… only job today. I'll be home early. Mid-afternoon early. I'm sorry - Nate*

No more than twelve words. That was Nate, brief and emotionless. She crumbled the note and threw it in the trash. The coffeemaker finished her mug, and she took it over to the phone. She dialed a number and held up the headset as it rang.

"Hello?"

"Yes, is this Alice Simmons?" Cynthia asked.

"Yes."

"Good morning, my name is Cynthia Durant. I was formerly a substitute teacher for Amsterdam Elementary under my maiden name Goss. I heard you are holding open interviews from now until September 10th?"

"Yes, yes, we are. Do you have time for a brief phone interview?"

The call went back and forth with a series of questions, then Cynthia hung up the phone with a ten-thirty appointment for Thursday morning. She prayed that this would be the opportunity she's been waiting for. After going upstairs for a change of clothes, she decided to take Brutus outside for a walk.

The Hampton Inn was down the street from Madison Square Garden on 31st Street between Seventh Avenue and Sixth. Nate got off the elevator on the third floor and walked down the hallway to room 301. He knocked on the door three times.

"Yeah!?" a voice behind the door called out.

"Backup photographer," he replied.

"Have your ID out."

Nate took out his wallet as the door opened. He flashed his driver's license and a kid no older than twenty said, "Take it outta the wallet."

He rolled his eyes, pulled the ID from his wallet, and handed it to the kid. He was wearing jeans and a generic Nike football jersey, with a black baseball cap turned backward which read, 'Plumperpass.com'.

"Alright, looks good." He handed it back to him.

Nate put the ID back in his wallet and walked inside. "It's a fake."

"Fuck, really?" he asked.

"No, dumbass."

"Fuck you, man," the kid replied, and closed the door.

Nate ignored him and looked around the hotel room. A queen-size bed was surrounded by lights. There were guys with camcorders, a main photographer, and two interns. A tall, white bald gentleman, wearing slacks and a plaid shirt was addressing everyone in the room.

"Okay people! We got six hours until the room goes to the next group and four scenes to shoot. Two minutes! We're shooting in two minutes! Places, people!"

One intern grabbed a boom and adjusted the microphone at the end. The second intern knocked on the bathroom door, then left the room. The man in the plaid shirt walked over to Nate and handed him an Android smartphone.

"You, go into Instagram and Snapchat… post pictures every ten minutes."

Nate accepted the phone, but he had some difficulty maneuvering the home screen and pulling up the app drawer. The man saw him fumbling and took the phone back. "Whatsthematter with you?" he asked.

"Sorry, I… I use iPhones. I don't know anything about…"

"Geez, it's 2013, man. Team Android's taking over." He opened Instagram on the phone and handed it back. The main photographer emerged from the bathroom and closed the door behind him. He stepped forward and received a few instructions from the guy in the plaid shirt.

The bathroom opened again, and two women and two men stepped out. One woman was a full-figured African American wearing a skinny two-piece green bikini. The other woman and two men were white. One of the men disrobed, revealing his nude body as the other woman dropped to her knees and proceeded to stroke his penis, building an erection.

Nate kept it all business. He approached the female performer and introduced himself. "Hi, I'm Nate, uh, you wanna do an intro promo?"

"Sure," she said, fixing her hair and adjusting her top.

"Okay… recording…"

"Hi, this is Cotton Candi. We're shooting my new scene for Plumperpass.com, and for $29.99 a month, you can have all access to the number one adult site for full-figured women and get a piece of the action. See you there!"

Nate completed the recording, checked it on the replay, and posted it on Instagram. "Got it. Okay, how about a few shots?"

She nodded and reached behind, removing her bikini top, revealing a pair of huge breasts, and covered her nipples. Instagram had certain guidelines that prevented users from showing certain body parts, and nipples were at the top of the list. Nate began to snap a few pictures with the phone.

"Alright, performers on the bed, we're rolling in five!" yelled the guy in the plaid shirt, who then took one of the video cameras and adjusted it for recording, then started monologuing.

"Okay, it's Monday, August 26th, 2013, 10:35 am. Director Destro with Cotton Candi, that's C-A-N-D-I and Terry Knox… hold up those IDs please… good. Alright, we're rolling…"

Nate took pictures only with the phone as the social media photographer, posting on behalf of Plumperpass to Twitter, Snapchat, Instagram, and other social media. The main photographer shot the scenes from all directions, but after an hour, he started to stare more than shoot, as the two performers engaged in intense sexual actions.

"Christ, Tim's hard again. Get him out of here! Can't take a picture without drooling on himself," plaid shirt pointed at Nate. "You! Hey you! Can you shoot better with an actual camera than you do with an Android phone?"

"This ain't a basketball in my backpack."

"Think you can shoot the rest of this scene without nutting in your pants?"

"A job's a job. I can compose myself. My fee goes up, though."

"What's your price?"

"$200.00."

He snorted. "$150.00. For $200.00 you better be in there actually fucking!"

Candi and Terry grinned at each other. "I'm all for that," she said, with a wink.

Nate blushed. "Fine, $150.00." He then tossed the phone to Tim as they escorted him out and opened his backpack, pulling out his camera.

"Excellent... shoot this right, you're my new go-to guy. Let's go! We're almost done, here! Candi, get that ass in the air. Places... action!" plaid shirt pointed to Nate. "You! Make her ass look so good you'll wanna eat it."

"No problem," Nate replied.

A half-hour later, the *Money Shot* was filmed, and the scene ended. Towels were given to Candi and Terry, who went back into the bathroom. The crew started stripping off the sheets and packing up their equipment.

Plaid shirt came over and introduced himself. "Name's

Destro, I'm the director. I can tell by your stance and angles that you're the real deal."

"Thanks."

"Tim was all over the place. Your pictures actually told a story. You used the lights real well, too. I'm taking $50.00 from his cut to get you that $200.00. He can go back to shooting department store catalogs."

"Appreciate that." Nate smiled.

"You got an eye… stick with me and your dick will thank you."

Nate chuckled. "What did you say your name was again?"

"Destro."

"Like the G.I. Joe villain with the metal face?"

"As in Destroyer of pussies. I used to perform myself before I found my real calling behind the camera."

Nate blinked hard. *A loss to the industry, I'm sure,* he said to himself.

"Anyway, I'm making you my main guy when I shoot in the city. How far you willing to travel? I'll take you along like my bitch."

"I'm local only… and I'm *nobody's* bitch."

Destro shrugged. "Fair enough. I got six scenes here in the next two months. Keep your phone on for the call, okay? You're gonna make so much buck and see so much crazy shit. You'll be sucking me off in no time."

He winced. "Hey, keep the euphemisms to a minimum, okay? Talk to me straight."

"Easy, easy, man… be cool." He nodded to the bathroom, "You wanna meet Candi? Usually, I don't have her talk to the help but you are in my cool book. C'mon, let's go say hi." He led him back to the door and knocked twice. "Candi! Got a minute?"

The door opened as Terry walked out, fully clothed. Inside, Candi was still naked and typing on her phone.

After years of taking pictures, Nate was comfortable in the company of nude people. He rarely got flushed or flustered. Candi was five-foot-four and two-hundred and eighty pounds. Her cup size was a massive 50-N and natural.

"Candi, this is, uh…" he balked, not remembering Nate's name. Nate grimaced and then stepped forward. "Nate Durant, we met before. How do you do?"

Destro's cell phone rang and pulled it out of his pocket. "I need to take this." He walked out of the room while answering the phone and leaving Nate alone with Candi.

They both smiled. "Uh, nice shoot," he said politely.

"You used to be fat," she replied flatly.

"Yes! how did you…?" Nate gasped, thrown by the comment.

"I can always spot someone who's had *the bypass*… your scars are faint, but visible, from the skin removal surgery."

He blushed as the talk became more friendly. "Um, have you thought about it? Surgery, I mean. *Those* must really wreak havoc on your back," he said, looking down.

She shimmied a little. "Yeah, but I don't plan on doing this too long. I'm almost 40. I probably have a good five or six years of shelf life in the business. That's why I have other endeavors."

Nate was impressed. Meeting an adult film star who was so well-spoken was virtually impossible. "Oh yeah? I do other things, too. Podcasts, movie reviews, music and television shows. I'm even an amateur stand-up comedian, I'm writing a book, and I DJ for clubs."

"Nice! I do promotions for my brother who DJs and produces music for local rappers. They like to use me for their flyers."

"I bet."

They shared a laugh, which made her breasts jiggle again. "Do you have a YouTube channel?"

"Huh?" he asked.

"Caught you staring…" she joked. "A lot of DJs put their sets on YouTube so others can listen and they can get discovered."

Nate tilted his head, struck with an idea suddenly. "Hmmm, I never thought of that… ahem, sorry for staring," he added apologetically.

"It's okay." She took a step closer and whispered, "between the two of us, let me ask you something. Your dick get bigger when you lost the weight?" she raised her eyebrows.

He chuckled politely, and cleared his throat. "Um, no comment."

The mention of his penis did suddenly give him a growing hard-on. He snapped out of it and put on his professional face again. "I, um, got to go… it was nice meeting you…"

Nate stepped back as she waved and let out a sultry chuckle. "See you around!"

Nate stepped out of the hotel and started walking out on the street. He opened YouTube on his phone and searched for Stephanie Grace. After scrolling down a few videos in the results, he stopped mid-stride.

"Found you!" he cheered.

Remembering that she loved to sing and was very good at it, he found a YouTube channel that featured her performances. Standing in the middle of the street, he played a video and watched as she sang Adele's "Rolling in the Deep." She was standing in the middle of a room wearing a Jay Cutler Chicago Bears football jersey.

After reading the comments, he noticed she indeed had a Facebook page under the name "StephanieSymphony." The page had pictures and videos from performances on stage, as well as pictures of her in a hair salon.

"Well, I'll be damned," he whispered. Remembering the picture from Tumblr, Nate clicked on the button to send her a friend request, then put his phone away and resumed walking towards Seventh Avenue. He had an appointment for lunch to keep.

Cynthia took the G-Train to Carroll Street and walked down Third Street to Third Avenue. Her mother, Barbara Goss, was waiting for her in front of Whole Foods Market. She walked up and they greeted each other with a hug, but there was still tension between them.

They each found shopping carts and went inside. As they walked along the aisles, her mother finally spoke. "Your actions this past weekend were unladylike, Cynthia. I raised you better than that."

"I was within my rights, considering the situation. What possessed you to invite Sylverton? What did you think would happen the minute I saw him?"

"We do NOT have to explain ourselves."

"He's off limits, Mom! After the stunt he pulled back in 2008…"

"The Withrows are still close friends and investors, despite the divorce. We have to be civil to one another."

"Did you know Nate almost talked me into not going? But I insisted, out of respect for Daddy, but that respect is a two-way street! For Sylverton to be there, despite the relationship with his family, was very disrespectful to me."

"Oh, grow up! You sound like a 12-year-old! Talking about respect. When you're independent, standing on your own feet, and not relying on us to take care of you occasionally, *then* we can talk about respect!"

Cynthia stopped in the middle of the aisle. Her mother kept walking for a minute, then stopped and looked back at her. Cynthia then turned around and resumed shopping alone. She was in the frozen food section when her mother walked in front of her.

"Okay, I'm sorry for being so harsh. You're right. Professional relations aside, it was wrong to invite Sylverton." Barbara raised her hand. "I'm not going to promise to never invite him again to anything, but we *will* take consideration of your feelings before extending an invitation to him… okay?"

Cynthia stared at her mother, then said with a snort, "It's a start."

They finished their shopping and got in line to checkout at the cashier area when Barbara said, "You know, Trudy Sadanowicz just celebrated the birth of her fifth grandchild."

*Oh, here we go…* "Is that right?" Cynthia asked, feigning enthusiasm.

"Yes, so I was wondering when I'll be welcoming a grandchild myself. I mean, you still have time, of course."

"Of course," Cynthia repeated sharply.

She was trying to keep calm, gripping tightly on the handle of the shopping cart.

"I personally believe you and Nate are ready now, and since you're in between jobs, this would be the perfect time to get pregnant," Barbara finished.

Cynthia's eye twitched, then felt something on her lip. The cashier was just starting with her items on the belt and looked up. She gasped. "Um, ma'am, your nose…"

Cynthia felt underneath her nose and pulled her hand back. There was blood on her fingertips. "Oh!" she turned to her mother and told her, "Here's my card, pay for me." She handed Barbara her debit card and rushed away, looking for the bathroom.

Barbara sighed, knowing that she had no idea what Cynthia's pin code was, so she took out her own credit card and gave it to the cashier.

"Nate, when you asked me to lunch, I expected to actually eat instead of sitting here waiting…"

The Tick Tock Diner was busy, even though the lunch hour was winding down. It was two o'clock and Nate was sitting impatiently with his friend, Sean Kelvin. Sean was African American, with a medium build, and sporting a bird's nest hair-style of twisted braids.

"I think you met me here intentionally so we could talk about your 'so-called' problems of late," he said, while sipping his water.

Nate pulled out his phone and opened Tumblr. "Maybe, but first I need a second opinion on this…" he handed the phone to Sean.

Sean looked at Stephanie's picture. "Hmmm, a little thick for my taste, but I wouldn't use a forklift to kick her out of bed," he said with a chuckle.

Nate didn't find the joke funny.

"Um, sorry." Sean slid the phone back.

"She's someone I knew from Chicago, during the old document scanning days…"

"Okay."

"You think someone posted it out of spite? I feel an obligation to tell her for some reason."

"You think your wife will be okay with that?" Sean asked, with a raised eyebrow.

"Well, that's why you're here. I just found her Facebook profile. We haven't talked in over ten years. How do you break the ice? *'Hey how's it going? Long time! Anyways, I found this naked picture of you, how do you feel about it?'.*"

"If I were you, I'd leave it be. You don't want Cynthia to find out you're talking to some old friend and the reason you found her. Unless she's cool with you looking at porn on the internet."

Nate nodded, agreeing with his friend. Cynthia had a jealous streak that he'd only seen once while shooting a wedding in Westchester. A bridesmaid got too personal and started calling him at all hours of the day. Cynthia found out where she lived and the confrontation that took place wasn't pretty.

"Alright, how about this thing over the weekend with Sylverton? You think I handled *that* correctly?"

Sean laughed. "Man, I would have let her swing on him! After she beat the hell outta Sylverton, she would have come home and *spiked* your football in celebration."

Nate grinned at the euphemism. Sean had a way with words. He probably had over a hundred terms for sex. Terms no one else would even think of using. "You might be right. I just didn't want to make a scene."

They both checked their watches, growing impatient.

"Man, they're taking too long, I can't wait anymore, let's go somewhere else," Sean said.

"You know what? You're right. I'm going to surprise Cynthia by bringing home something for dinner, so she doesn't have to cook. I promised to be home by four. That's just enough time to swing by Urban Rustic."

They both stood up from the table and headed toward the exit. A waitress finally arrived with their orders. "Hey!" she called out. "Your order's here!"

They both looked back. "Give it to someone else!" Nate yelled back.

"Yeah, and get faster cooks! I shouldn't have to wait 20 minutes for a *fucking* BLT!" Sean added.

"Hey, fuck you!" she yelled back, then turned and walked back to the kitchen.

**5**

---

# STEPHANIE HAS DIED OF DYSENTERY

Barbara and Cynthia shared an UberBLACK with Cynthia getting out at the first stop. She retrieved her bags of groceries from the trunk and stepped onto the curb next to the back passenger window.

"We're going to see Nate's family in Chicago for Thanksgiving."

"Okay, what about hosting Christmas?" Barbara asked.

"Immediate family only... just you, dad, and Vanessa," Cynthia replied.

"Alright, I'll let your father know. Remember what I said." She rolled up the window, and the SUV took off. Cynthia sighed and fished out her keys.

Nate heard Cynthia jiggle the keys in the door and quickly took his place in the kitchen with the spread laid out. The door opened and he yelled out, "Supriseeeeee!!!"

Cynthia carried the bags in and looked astonished. "What's all this?" she asked.

Nate had a salad with a sandwich for each of them from one of her favorite organic sandwich shops in the neighborhood.

"I got you Urban Rustic! Your usual Ashokan Reservoir

salad, and I made a wrap with a Tahawus Sandwich. I settled for grilled cheese for me, then threw in some almond slivers with Tuscan kale. Whaddya think?"

Cynthia was speechless. Nate's smile beamed from ear to ear. She couldn't remember the last time he brought home dinner. She shuffled her hands and pulled out a pizza box from one of the grocery bags.

"I… I brought pizza from Whole Foods…" she mumbled, with some disappointment.

"Oh," Nate replied, crestfallen.

"Why would you do all this?" she asked, as she walked in, heading to the kitchen.

"I wanted to surprise you… th… that's why I yelled supri—" Nate stammered.

"You should have called and checked with me. Even a simple text…" she said in a condescending tone.

"You didn't say anything about going to the store last night. How was I supposed to—"

"Mom called this morning. It was a spur-of-the-moment thing," Cynthia explained.

*Don't yell, whatever you do, don't yell…*

She sighed. "So, what do we do? All this organic food will go bad by tomorrow."

"We eat the pizza and I'll just throw away the salad and sandwiches. I'm keeping my wrap and the grilled cheese, though. We can also save the kale and slivers." He collected the plates and threw them in the trash, then put the rest in the refrigerator.

Cynthia knew he was disappointed. "Sorry baby… thank you, though. It was a nice gesture."

Nate helped himself to a slice of pizza. "Yeah, yeah," then walked to the living room.

She said nothing else and started putting away the groceries.

After another evening of minimal conversation and watching television, Cynthia went upstairs to bed. She left the door cracked as an invitation for Nate to join her, but he didn't get the hint. So, she decided to get a head start on her slumber. Nate couldn't find anything worth watching so he just turned the television off and got on the computer.

Remembering what Sean said, he decided that it wasn't worth it to think about Stephanie anymore. He had checked Facebook all day and noticed she didn't accept his friend request, so it was time to forget about it. After checking his news feed again and reading a few articles, he was just about to log off when a message notification lit up.

@StephanieSymphony: "Hello! Who is this?"

Nate tilted his head. "Uh oh," he whispered. His fingers hovered over the keyboard as he debated typing a reply. "Fuck it," he said, and started typing.

@NatefromNewYork: "Sorry, I think I got the wrong person, thought you were a friend from Chicago."

He figured that would be the end of it, just a simple misunderstanding.

@StephanieSymphony: "WHO IS THIS? I AM from Chicago, and I only know one Nate. You don't look nothing like him."

*Oh shit*, he thought, maybe this was her but naturally she doesn't recognize the skinny guy in his profile picture. He needed to say something only he would know… he started playing with his wedding band while thinking, then snapped his fingers with an idea and typed…

@NatefromNewYork: "Stephanie has died of Dysentery."

He hoped she would remember.

@StephanieSymphony: "Nate? Nate Durant from IPS? It IS you! Oh my God!"

Nate smiled. During down times on assignments the two played an online version of the classic children's computer game The Oregon Trail. The quote was from one of the dire outcomes she suffered when failing to reach a certain destination. A notification lit up, indicating she accepted his friend request.

@NatefromNewYork: "It's nice to have found you on here after all these years."

A few minutes went by with no response. Meanwhile, his notifications pinged with multiple alerts.

@NatefromNewYork: "Uh, Stephanie?"

@StephanieSymphony: "Hold on, I'm going through your albums…"

He chuckled as the pings continued, with Stephanie liking and commenting on as many pictures as she could get through.

@StephanieSymphony: "Wow, I can't believe how much weight you've lost! And your wife! She's beautiful. I'm so happy for you!"

@NatefromNewYork: "Thank you. I wasn't sure if this profile was you. I found it through your YouTube channel. It said you're in San Diego. I never thought you would ever leave The Chi. How'd you end up in California?"

@StephanieSymphony: "It's a long story, we HAVE to catch up sometime."

@NatefromNewYork: "Sure, but I was getting ready to log off before you caught me. It's kinda late."

@StephanieSymphony: "Oh yeah, I forget, we're three hours behind. It's only 8:25 pm here. Alright, I won't keep you."

@NatefromNewYork: "It's cool, catch you tomorrow? My schedule's kinda light."

@StephanieSymphony: "Get you… 'My schedule's kinda light,' LOL, sure. Catch ya later, 'night!"

Nate closed his browser. *Well, contact made… no turning back now*. He thought. All he had was his doctor's appointment, and a podcast to record. It was eleven-thirty. He went upstairs and took a hot shower, then climbed into bed with nothing on. He hoped Cynthia would be up for a late-night tryst, but she was out like a light.

He sighed, *Another missed opportunity…*

The lawnmower's engine roared to life at exactly six o'clock in the morning. Nate did his best to tune it out, but after five minutes he growled and sat up on the bed. He noticed Cynthia was already awake, and he had a serious case of morning wood. He wondered if the erection was fueled by rage somehow, because that was all he was feeling right now.

Cynthia heard Nate stomp down the steps as she started sipping her protein shake. She gasped, nearly dropping her glass when she noticed he was naked and heading towards the door.

"NATE! Put some clothes on!" she screamed.

He froze with his hand on the doorknob and looked down. "Oh… right." He ran back upstairs.

Ten minutes later, Nate emerged from the house and looked both ways, trying to find the source of the noise. The majority of their neighborhood was brownstones, apartment buildings, and condos. There was, however, a townhouse on the right side of their street with a fenced-in backyard.

"Fermin… I should have known," Nate hissed.

Fermin Hall was a 50-year-old Filipino executive, who was obsessed with maintaining a patch of grass the size of a single parking spot. His lawn was surrounded by a series of hedges and exotic plants. The sound of the mower echoed from the back of his townhouse. Nate followed the noise through the side alley, walking past the garbage bins. He approached the ten-foot wooden fence and knocked on the door.

"Hellooooo? Fermin? FERMIN!" he yelled.

The engine cut off and footsteps approached the door. A few locks snapped, and the gate flew open. The stout old man looked up at Nate. He was an even five feet and over three-hundred pounds. Fermin was wearing a straw hat with a hideous white Hawaiian shirt. Wearing crocs with white khakis, he adjusted his gold wiry eyeglasses.

"What?" he asked.

"Do you know what time it is, Fermin? People are trying to sleep!"

"That's *Mister* Hall to you! Keep your window closed and you'll sleep fine! I don't even mow that long!"

"Look, there are noise ordinances about this sort of thing, you know? Landscaping services do this type of work for you, and they start at a decent time."

"I know my rights! I can do what I want on my property! Keep your window closed and mind your own business!" He disappeared back inside and slammed the gate.

"Sonofabitch!" Nate cursed.

By the time he walked back inside the house, the lawnmower started up again. "It's that damn Fermin…" Nate began. "Every couple of months he does this shit, I've had it!"

"Calm down, hon… wash up and I'll make you some…"

He shook his head. "I got the doctor's appointment, baby. I got to fast, can't eat anything."

"Oh."

He started back upstairs. "After that, I have a podcast at the District Council building. Pending any offers, I should be home before 4 pm."

"Okay, um, I'm meeting the girls for lunch at 1 pm, but before that, I have my hair appointment for my interview… I may get a new outfit for it as well."

He stopped in the middle of the stairs and gave her a look.

She sighed. "I'll find something under $300.00, okay?"

Nate nodded and resumed up the stairs.

"Good morning! Vanessa Goss here for Good Day New York, weekend edition. Let's go ahead and take a look at today's current conditions, followed by the forecast for the rest of your upcoming work week."

After filming her audition tape, Vanessa stepped away from the green screen stage as the cameraman cued up the last thirty seconds to check if the recording went off without any problems.

"Looks good."

"Thanks." She turned to Josh as the producer approached her. "Well? I think I still got it. No one is even close to being as bubbly as I am." She put on her best smile. "I'm willing to work my way back…"

"Uh, yeah, we'll call you with our decision in the next couple of days, okay?" Josh interrupted. "If it was up to me, I'd put you in the top three potentials, but it's a group decision with the other senior producers of the show. Keep your fingers crossed."

"Okay, thanks for at least giving me a chance. Now, if you'll excuse me…" she left the studio and quickly found the woman's bathroom. Inside the biggest stall at the end, she dropped to her knees and threw up in the toilet. After grabbing some toilet paper and wiping her mouth, she lifted her head with an uneasy look on her face.

"Oh no," Vanessa whispered.

"Are you taking your supplements?" Doctor Yoshi Edo asked.

Nate was sitting up on an examiner's bed without a shirt on, as the Japanese doctor examined each of his ears with an otoscope. "Yes," he answered.

"Any incidents with your pouch? Dumping, frothing, regurgitation, dizziness, diarrhea…"

He shook his head. "No, the last time I had the foamies was in June, after eating a piece of steak that came back up."

The doctor nodded. "I must say, you've done pretty well since the surgery back in 2006. I have your bariatric diary here." Yoshi opened up the binder he was holding. "Remember him?" the doctor held up a picture of Nate that was dated *December 2006.*

Nate winced at the memory. "That was the beginning of the excess skin. My arms looked like I could take off and fly around the room like Rocky the flying squirrel."

"That was at three-hundred and twenty pounds, dropping eighty post-surgery." Yoshi turned the page. "It took a while, but then you came down to two-hundred pounds even by 2008 and stayed there for the skin removal surgery."

"Which took some serious adjusting to!" Nate added.

"But the best thing is, you've plateaued now at one-eighty for the last five years with no signs of gaining any weight back. You've beaten the odds, young man. Keep up the good work."

"Thanks, doc."

"Don't thank me, yet. There's still one thing you need to do."

"Huh?"

"You need a medical alert bracelet to let medical professionals know you've had the Gastric Bypass. If you become unresponsive and they have to put a feeding tube through your nose, they won't know you've had your intestines rerouted. That can lead to complications. You should have ordered one by now."

Nate made a face. "Sorry, I'll get one right away. It just slipped my mind."

"See to it, everything else is fine. I'll see you back here in six months."

The New York Bariatric Group building was between 25th and 26th Street on Seventh Avenue. Nate left the building and stayed on Seventh, heading south. He took out his phone and took a seat inside a bus shelter for the M20 and M7 buses. The

FaceTime call rang several times before an elderly white man answered.

"Did you forget we're an hour behind you? It's not even noon yet!"

"Nice to see you too, dad," Nate said to his father, Jeremy Durant.

Jeremy's hardened face was wrinkled, like a worn baseball mitt, with bags under his dull blue eyes and slicked back hair. Several curled strands were at the top of his forehead, with a salt-and-pepper mustache and a soul patch underneath his thin, pointy nose. The elder Durant was pushing 70 with a bitter and battled old soul, so occasionally exchanging pleasantries with his son proved difficult. The two were not on the best terms.

"…and why can't you use Skype to call me like a normal person? I don't know anyone else who uses FaceTime. You're the only one!"

"Apple is a stable brand, dad… free from viruses and malware."

"Yeah, yeah…" Jeremy dismissed. "How ya doing, son?"

Nate noticed the M7 bus pulling up. He waved it off and it continued down its route.

"I'm fine, just came from a doctor's appointment. Still running around doing things."

"Hmm, you're looking a bit lanky in the face, there. I betcha the wind off the Michigan Avenue Bridge could knock you flat on your ass."

"I'm *healthy* and I'm eating right. Why is that a bad thing to you?" Nate asked.

"Because Chicago don't raise no pussies! You were big, but it was muscle. You were the baddest motherfucker on the block."

"Oh yeah, and everyone feared me because I could scan 1500 papers in an hour. I struck fear in the hearts of gangbangers on the street, c'mon dad, get real."

"Whatever. How's the swan princess?" Jeremy asked.

*Him and these nicknames!* Nate thought. "Cynthia's fine. She's been a little pissed lately. She ran into her ex at a party her parents had and everything came rushing back."

"Heh, women. All spitfires, son. Volatile and unpredictable."

Nate looked up and saw the M20 bus had stopped for him. The bus driver called out, "Hey! You're at a bus stop, not a phone booth!"

"I'm waiting for seven!" he lied.

"The seven bus was just ahead of me!" the driver barked back.

"It was crowded, so I'm waiting for the next one. Fuck off!" Nate waved.

The driver closed the door and pulled away. Nate looked down to see Jeremy's face grinning.

"What?"

"I see The Big Apple hasn't changed," Jeremy joked.

"Funny. Anyway, just a head's up, we're coming out there for Thanksgiving. Let Uncle Eddie and the cousins know."

"You sure? We've heard that before, then you always cancel or something."

"I'm sure, this time," Nate said, with a nod.

"Okay, it'll be great to see you…"

Nate actually saw a smile on his face and decided to end the conversation on a high note. "Okay, I gotta go. Don't think I was cool with that remark of yours about women, either. You're not exactly the expert authority on that subject, dad."

The smile immediately disappeared. "What the fuck is that supposed to mean?!" he yelled.

Nate regretted the remark as soon as he said it and didn't answer. *Fuck.*

"Christ, after all these fucking years, after serving my time, you still blame me for what happened to your mother!"

"Don't start, dad. I'll hang up this phone in an instant," he said, pointing at the phone.

"Look, I'm sorry about what happened, but I was within my rights to defend myself… she was drunk and out of her mind… she came at me with a knife…"

"And *you shot her dad!*" Nate screamed. "Right between the fucking eyes! I still see the look on her face! Never in a million years did she think you would actually do it. That look of shock… frozen in time. Twelve years of talking to shrinks and it's a miracle I'm not more fucked up in the head than I already am!"

Nate's face was bright red, and he was attracting stares from people passing by.

"Everything alright, sir?" a voice from his left asked.

He turned to see a patrolman and his partner next to a police car parked near the curb before the bus stop. Nate looked down and noticed Jeremy disconnected the FaceTime call. He gathered himself and calmed down. "I'm fine, officer."

He slowly put away his phone as the patrolman said, "We received a call that someone was loitering in a bus shed. You either take the next bus coming or move along."

Nate scowled as an M20 bus approached. "It just so happens, my bus is right here," he said, with a look of contempt. The bus stopped, Nate climbed in and paid his fare as the police officers looked on.

Cutler Salon was on Grand Street, a few blocks from where Nate and Cynthia lived. She walked in at eleven-thirty for her appointment and was greeted by her favorite hairstylist, Leila.

"Right on time, Cyn… have a seat and give me a second to get ready." Leila motioned to the salon chair in front of her.

Cynthia sat down and Leila came with a cape to button around her neck.

She cleaned her instruments and checked her phone for messages, then two minutes went by, and she walked back up to the chair asking, "So what are we doing today, girl?"

"I got an interview tomorrow…" Cynthia replied.

"Okay. Short and stylish or long and sleek?"

She thought about it for a moment.

"Daaaaamn girl! I'm digging the cut! You look like Beyoncè!" Gloria yelled.

With her new ultra-short hairstyle, Cynthia walked up the street to meet Gloria and Jennifer at 10 Hogan Place, which was the district attorney's office where Gloria worked.

"I didn't even think about her, but she did just do the pixie cut thing recently!" Jennifer added.

"It's for the interview. I want to look professional for them tomorrow."

"Nice! I'm sure they'll swoop you up. They'd be crazy not to," Gloria said.

"Okay, where are we going for lunch? We only have around 45 minutes."

"Let's stay out of Chinatown. I've had enough of noodles and rice," Cynthia said.

"McDonald's on Broadway, then?" Jennifer suggested.

"Nah, how about one of those sandwich places up the street from there?" Gloria suggested.

"Ooh, I know! Atera on Worth Street, before Church, it's got a little of everything," Jennifer announced.

"Works for me. Let's go!" Cynthia agreed, and the trio started walking west.

They found a table outside on the sidewalk and were served their meals, with 30 minutes left before Gloria and Jennifer were due back to work.

"So, guess who had the nerve to show up at mom and dad's party last weekend? Sylverton the scumbag…"

"What?" both her friends gasped.

"Oooh, girl, tell me you busted his face," Gloria asked.

"I was *this* close, but Nate stopped me, and we just left. Mom actually tried to rationalize reaching out to him!"

"Nah, there's no reason to still include him in your social circle," Jennifer said.

"Exactly! I told her that no matter the money he still might have, he's off limits!"

"Now, even though you wanted to beat his ass yourself," Gloria began, "*Nate* should have been the one to do it for you! He's your husband now. You should have been pulling *him* back, instead of the other way around! He should have been sticking up for your honor."

Jennifer nodded in agreement.

Cynthia sighed. "Nate's not the confrontational type." *Unless it's about his dog.* She quietly thought. "One of us has to be the rational one. He's just more level-headed, but it *would* feel nice if he kicked someone's ass for me."

"Yes girl, then you reward him with something special that you've never done in the bedroom, you know what I'm saying?" Jennifer said, with a smile.

"Break out those *handcuffs*! Clink! Clink!" Gloria added, while gesturing with her wrists.

The trio broke out in a round of laughs, then Cynthia said, "Y'all are so nasty!"

**6**

———

# MEMORIES OF A PAST LIFE

NATE FINISHED DOING A GUEST SPOT ON TVOVERMIND.COM'S podcast about the upcoming 2013-2014 Fall lineup of television shows and stopped by Hot97's broadcast radio studio. New York's most popular radio station and source for Hip-Hop music. Wrapping up their interviews were Ibraham, Lauren, and Pete, the trio known for their morning show.

Their producer did a hand gesture, and the 'recording' light went out. Lauren ducked out of the booth through the back door while Pete stepped out and met with Nate.

"Hey man, how's the coolest white guy in Hip-Hop other than Eminem?"

"Haha, I'm alright Nate, you doing alright?" Pete asked.

"Sure, just learning from the best. I was in the neighborhood and decided to pop in, see if you got anything up my alley? I heard about the shake-up back in June. Is it true that Da Fox left the morning show?" Nate asked.

"Ibraham stepped in, wanting to be more hands-on, so he and Lauren stepped in, and they kept me. I don't make the rules."

"I hear that, um, you need anybody for entertainment spots? I could occasionally do a segment about what to watch on television and in the theaters…”

Pete held his hand up to stop him. “Talk to the station manager. If you’re getting into *this* business, you gotta start at the bottom, like an intern or something.”

“Aw, alright…” Nate said, with some disappointment.

Pete patted him on the shoulder and walked past, but then turned and called out, “Hey Nate!”

“Yeah?”

“Let me get your email address. We got a listening party coming up for some upcoming rapper, you ever hear of ‘.38 Special?’”

Nate did a hard blink. “Um, yeah, I know him!” he lied.

Pete laughed. “Work on that poker face, I’ll send you the details. Peace!” He took out a pen and wrote down Nate’s email address, then resumed walking to a door at the end of the hallway.

Vanessa was home, sitting in the bathroom on the toilet. Her legs were shaking as she pulled up the stick she was holding underneath her and waited. It was the longest two minutes she ever stared at a pregnancy test. When she saw the blue plus sign appear, confirming her suspicions, the test dropped from her hands and fell on the floor. Her whole body shook now as the tears streaked down her face.

“I can’t believe this shit,” she whispered. “Fuck.”

Nate walked in at four-thirty, proud of himself for coming home early twice in the same week. He helped himself to a bottle of water and Cynthia tiptoed down the stairs and crept behind him. She placed her hands over his eyes.

"Guess who?" she said playfully.

He smiled and slowly turned his head while grabbing her hands and pulling down, then opened his eyes and yelled, "Whoa! What happened to your hair?"

"You don't like it?" she asked, "I cut it short for the interview tomorrow. The girls said I looked like Beyoncé!"

"Tha… that's not really helping much."

She twisted her face into a spiteful glare.

"I… I… I mean, I… hold on…" he snapped his head to gather his thoughts. "Wh… what's going on here? It's like ever since we ran into Sylverton you've been angry and edgy. I've dealt with it, but seriously… talk to me… what's wrong, baby?"

She grabbed a chair from the kitchen table, sat down, and lowered her head. "I… I'm just so frustrated, and I feel bloated. I know I've probably gained five pounds in the last week…"

Nate rolled his eyes. "Will you stop? You're always obsessing about your weight, you're fine… you know what? It's been a while since we watched the tape. You need some reassurance."

Cynthia's eyes got wide with fright. "No! I was kidding, I'm fine, Nate! Please, I don't want to watch the tape…"

"Get the kale from the kitchen and be downstairs in the man cave in five minutes. I'll be right back…"

Two minutes went by, and Cynthia slowly came down the steps with kale and some crackers for a snack.

Nate was still searching the bins and then cheered triumphantly as he held up an ancient videotape.

She sighed. "You burned it on a DVD, so why are we watching the original tape on this old VCR?"

"I like how it looks. It's like watching some old television show from the 80s in 480p."

Cynthia rolled her eyes. "It's like you were a film student in a previous life, geez."

Nate put the tape in and turned on the television. They looked at their former selves back in 2003, celebrating their nuptials. The ceremony was small, but extravagant. They got married at Riverside Church. Nate was a fan of the venue since the musician Björk had performed there several years earlier.

The reception was on a yacht as it circled Manhattan, a small gesture from Cynthia's father since he went all-out for her first wedding. They made the best of it and then went to Niagara Falls for their honeymoon.

The video finished and Nate turned to Cynthia. "There, feel better?"

"We were so big!" she replied with a daunting tone, "Yeah, thank you for taking me down memory lane… we really have come a long way…"

"Especially you."

"Don't knock yourself for taking a shortcut. It took a lot of hard work for both of us to get here." She leaned in and kissed him.

"You know… I have another tape here…"

Cynthia gasped. "Is that…"

"Uh-huh…" he grunted with a smile.

"You told me you burned that!"

"I did, I burned a copy on a DVD… kept the original."

"Oh, my God!"

"C'mon, let's watch it…"

She shook her head, "No! It would be like watching two elephants doing it on National Geographic!"

Nate's face brightened. "That's a great idea! We can narrate it with fake British accents like, 'Notice the male, ever so slightly penetrating the female with several well-timed thrusts…'." he started laughing.

Cynthia laughed too. "Stop!"

"Okay, well if not that…" he checked the box. "I think I got a few adult videos in here… Oooh! *Viva Vanessa*! We gotta watch this, Vanessa Del Rio was the very first porn star I jacked off to!"

She grunted. "Why do you still have those dirty movies? Gross! I'm not watching those!"

"C'mon, just the movie audition scene, or the three-way in the bathroom. You know women always have those fantasies about having sex with two guys at once…"

"I've already *had* sex with two guys at once… on my honeymoon!" she joked.

He gasped. "Oh! You are *so* going to get it now!"

She got up and he started to chase her back upstairs. Cynthia came up from the basement and continued up to the second floor, followed by Nate. The couple ran into the bedroom, and he caught up with her. She let him tackle her and they both flopped onto the bed.

"Gotcha!" Nate yelled.

They started play fighting, then looked at each other and started making out. The kisses became more intense as they started tearing off their clothes. Her bra flew off, exposing her breasts and she peeled off his briefs. He turned her around and mounted her. She was already wet and anticipating him, moaning when he penetrated, taking every inch of him.

Neither of them could remember the last time a momentous occasion like this occurred. He pumped furiously, panting with every thrust as she rolled her head back screaming, "YES!" repeatedly. He turned her over again as they began doing missionary, her legs shook with serious convulsions as her body gave in to a powerful orgasm. He pulled her body close, burying his face in her bosom, humping as hard as he could. He was approaching his climax, snapping his head back as he threw her legs up in the air.

"Don't cum in me! Don't cum in me!" she screamed.

Nate felt his accelerated heartbeat pounding through his eardrums as he pulled out at the last possible minute and shot his load all over her stomach and chest. The release put his mind in a state of euphoria as his body's nervous system crackled to life from head to toe. He went limp and fell forward, landing beside her face down. A second later, he pushed up and turned on his back, staring up at the ceiling.

Cynthia lowered her legs and started giggling as she traced her finger through the thick creamy gobs deposited on her body. "Whoooo... good thing I cut my hair short or you would have definitely messed it up," she said with a devilish grin.

Nate craned his head over to look at her and chuckled. "Damn, whatchu *do* to me!"

They looked at each other for a moment, then she said, "Thank you, honey... you're always there to make me feel special."

"That's because you *are* special, baby..." Nate said, caressing her face. "Don't let anyone else tell you different. Love you, Cyn." He leaned in and kissed her on the forehead.

"Love you, too, honey," she replied.

"You got that interview tomorrow, so get some rest."

"Do me a favor, hon? Can we cuddle? Just… hold me until I go to sleep."

"Sure…" Nate brought his arm across her back as she leaned into his chest. Within ten minutes she was sound asleep, with no mask or earbuds.

In the middle of the night, Cynthia got up and went to the bathroom. Nate opened his eyes and rolled out of bed. He crawled to the window overlooking Fermin's fenced backyard. He reached down and grabbed a hunting slingshot, along with a sack of landscape pebbles. Loading a handful at a time, he fired across into the small area of grass for several minutes.

The sound of the toilet flushing got his attention as he put everything away and returned to bed. Cynthia stepped out and climbed back into bed herself. Nate laughed to himself and closed his eyes.

At five-thirty the next morning, Nate woke up with a pep in his step. He came downstairs to find Cynthia in her bra and panties checking her resumé on the computer.

"Didn't expect you up this early," she said, as he poured himself a bowl of cereal.

"I wanted to be up early today for one particular reason…" he said, as he looked up at a wall clock.

At six o'clock on the dot, the lawn mower started up and a wide grin grew across Nate's face. Several minutes went by when suddenly there was the sound of the engine sputtering, and metal ricocheting. There were then screams of pain and cursing in a foreign language.

Nate continued to eat his cereal as the cycle repeated itself for ten minutes, then silence.

Cynthia jumped out of her skin when a sudden pounding began on the door. Fermin's voice was yelling from outside. "I know you're in there!" he screamed.

She turned to Nate who just waved his hand and shook his head, ignoring the angry shouts. "Just pretend we're not here, he'll go away."

Brutus started barking at the door for a minute.

Fermin knocked repeatedly for over five minutes before getting tired and leaving.

Cynthia gave her husband an unpleasant look as he celebrated his small victory… until the lawn mower started again and proceeded to mow the lawn.

"The bastard must have raked up all the rocks!" he snarled.

Cynthia shook her head and walked to the living room to turn on the television, while Nate furrowed his eyebrows. "This isn't over," he vowed.

"I want you to think about this decision, Miss Goss. Once you decide to terminate—"

"I'm sure, I'm positive." Vanessa interrupted.

She was in her OB/GYN office feeling very distraught. It was eight o'clock and her eyes were red from staying up all night crying and worrying.

"Have you… at least discussed your decision with… the father?"

She looked down at her feet with embarrassment. "I… uh, there are, um… several possibilities. I don't know exactly which one to talk to."

"It's okay, we don't judge here. If you're positive this is the way you want to go, I'll make the appointment."

"Tha… thank you."

It was the hardest choice of her life, but there was no turning back. Vanessa made her choice out of fear. And the reality was too harsh for her to imagine. She could look back and believe there were other options, but this choice… made the most sense now.

Nate was back at Bryant Park working on his novel. After leaving Saturday Night Live, he came up with an idea for a television series. When he pitched it to several networks and producers, no one was interested. A few years later, he transferred the concept into a potential first in a series of novels. He kept the project a close, protected secret, revealing the details of the story to no one.

He had a photoshoot soon, so he was wrapping up a scene he was typing when the phone rang, and he answered it.

"Hello, Nate from New York Photography, this is Nate… yes, it's $285.00 for a four-hour shoot. You get all the digital files, prints are .15 apiece for any size, 1 through 100, over that it's .10 for 101 through 250. Anything over 250 prints will have to be done with a third party of my choice and I'll give you those rates when we're ready to print."

He pulled out a notepad from his backpack and started to take down some details.

"Pictures will have a watermark on the bottom right corner, and I reserve the right to use six pictures of your choosing, for my portfolio and advertisements. I keep copies on a cloud server for six months and then they're deleted. You'll get a complimentary DVD and thumb drive with all pictures taken."

He listened as the caller asked a few questions.

"Um, no, I don't do video, only photography, but I know several videographers I can recommend. Okay, keep in mind I require an $85.00 non-refundable deposit once the contract's signed. Any cancellations 48 hours before the event requires a 25% payment of the remaining $200.00 for prep and time. 12 hours before that, it goes up to 50%."

The caller confirmed the stipulations.

"Also, I wear my own clothes, a traditional black tuxedo with a white shirt and *no* tie. I say this now because I've done non-traditional weddings, LGBT, Goth, Fantasy, among others and I look terrible in purple…"

There was a laugh on the other end, and another series of questions.

"Yes, I take PayPal. When? Okay, I'll pencil it in, let me have your email address and I'll send my standard contract for you to go over and sign. May I ask how you found me? Were you referred by somebody? Okay, thank you. I'll be in touch, have a nice day."

He ended the call, double-checked his notes, and packed up his MacBook. "Who the hell gets married on All Saint's Day?" he asked himself.

Cynthia approached the school at ten o'clock. The children were already inside their classrooms since the opening bell rang an hour earlier. Success Academy was a network of charter schools located across the interlocking four boroughs of New York City. Harlem Two was located on the far end of the east side on 128th Street between Lexington and Third Avenue.

Alice Simmons greeted Cynthia in the hallway leading to her office. The school administrator was wearing a navy-blue pants suit with a gold brooch in the shape of a book pinned to her lapel. She smiled and gave a hearty handshake.

"Thank you for being early. Step in my office and I'll be right with you."

Cynthia stepped into the office and took a seat in front of her desk. She fidgeted her fingers nervously and examined the desk to gauge the personality of her interviewer.

*No pictures of a spouse, child, or any family. No knick-knacks or personal items of any kind. This woman is cold as ice.*

Mrs. Simmons returned to her office and closed the door behind her. She walked past Cynthia and took a seat behind the desk.

"Would you like some water before we begin?" she offered.

"No, thank you," Cynthia declined.

Alice nodded. "Did you bring a copy of your resumé?"

"I did." She fished out a copy and presented it to her.

"Thank you." The educator accepted the document and looked it over. "So, tell me what happened at Amsterdam, I hear it's a revered institution."

Cynthia relaxed and started to explain. "I started there back in 2005 on a six-month probationary contract. I was then hired full-time as a homeroom teacher in the ninth grade. I preferred short-term curriculums like summer school and was on standby to sub in the event of emergencies like an illness, sabbatical, or even maternity leave."

"May I ask why you only commit to being a substitute and not just teaching one specific subject for as long as you like?"

Cynthia thought carefully before answering. "It's hard these days to find dedicated subs. I'd like to be the exception to the rule. Any teacher can sit there teaching ninth grade social studies over and over again. I like the challenge of moving around and teaching a little bit of everything. Keeps me on my toes." She smiled for emphasis on the last statement.

"That's an interesting way of looking at it," Alice said. She opened a drawer in her desk and pulled out a folder. Cynthia kept a straight face, but a twinge of fear crept up her spine.

"How exactly did you leave the school, then?" Alice asked, while resting her hands on the folder.

"Unfortunately, three years ago, they restructured, and all the teachers were reevaluated. Some made the cut, some didn't. I was given a nice severance package, and I took a year off after that to find myself."

"And did you? Find yourself?"

"Yes, I believe I did." Cynthia averted her eyes to the folder, wondering what was inside.

"Okay, I uh, took the liberty to contact Amsterdam for any references about you and I spoke to a…" she opened the folder and looked for the name, "…a Brigitte Swierczynski… wow, that's a mouthful. Do you know who she is?"

Cynthia's fingers tightened into a small fist on her lap. "Yes, she was in charge of all the faculty evaluations before I was let go." She didn't beat around the bush. "I take it she had some favorable observations about me," she said with a fake chuckle.

Alice looked down at the file and read, *'It is our determination that Mrs. Durant (formerly Goss) is a bucket of water applied to a burning building. She has the drive and determination to be a great teacher, but her greatest enemy is herself. By limiting to temporary curriculums and standing in for those who are unavailable, Cynthia performs well as a substitute teacher for a few weeks before suffering from the withdrawals of routine teaching."*

She looked up back at Cynthia. "Do you agree with that assessment?"

"Mrs. Simmons, I… I'm just looking for a fair shot to prove myself. I'm confident that these children…"

"Stop right there," Alice said sharply, "What do you mean *'these children'*?!"

Cynthia gave a surprised look. "Wha? Nothing! I meant no disrespect, I…"

"Mrs. Durant, I see this all the time. A disenfranchised teacher from an elite charter school downtown, forced up north of 125th Street, where they believe that teaching children of the ghetto is considered an act of charity. That we'll just welcome our *white savior* with open arms and let them show us poor, black people the way of the future."

Cynthia's jaw dropped from the accusation. "Oh my God! I… I would never think—"

"Well, I'm afraid we have no place for you here, Mrs. Durant."

"Th… this is prejudice! You can't just refuse to hire me because I'm white! How dare you?!"

"We're done here. The receptionist will show you the way out. Have a nice day." Alice closed the file as Cynthia stood up and stormed out of the office.

Outside the school, Cynthia checked her watch. The interview had only lasted twenty minutes. Her face was crimson from anger. She wanted to break something… and have a drink. There was only one person she could turn to this early in the morning.

## 7

# OH... OKAY

The loft was on Houston Street and Broadway, and
Sierra Smile adjusted her wig of big, curly red hair. Dressed up
as the famed X-Men and sometimes power-crazed villain, Jean
Gray, also known as Dark Phoenix, the 30-year-old cosplayer
stepped away from the mirror and struck a pose.

Nate was standing behind a tripod with his camera attached,
setting up in front of a painted background wall.

"We're all set, here." He looked at her as she approached and
let out a wolf whistle. "Wow, your costume is fantastic! You
made everything yourself?"

She nodded. "Yep, got all the material, stitched it, painted it
perfectly. Ready? We only have one shot at this."

"I'm ready." He looked at the two pyrotechnic artists who
stepped up and applied two special fire-retardant gloves on her
arms, then grabbed fire extinguishers and waited on their marks.

A third person held an ignited torch as Nate aimed his
camera. With a hand signal, the person with the torch lit the
gloves and Nate clicked away as Sierra posed. After ten seconds,
the two men with the extinguishers put out the fire, then helped
remove the gloves.

Sierra had no burns on her hands. "Whoo! I hope you got those pictures perfectly. We can't do that again!"

Nate checked and gave a thumbs-up. "I got you. They came out fine."

"Good. You should come with me to the New York Comic-Con in October. The turnout is massive! If you think *my* costume looks good, it's nothing compared to what you'll see there."

"Sounds great," Nate replied. "But I might be busy, my wedding anniversary is Columbus Day weekend, and I don't even know what my wife and I are doing yet."

"Awww, that's sweet. Oh well, I gotta change. Two more outfits and we're done."

"Alright." Nate watched her walk to the changing area.

Vanessa arrived at Cynthia and Nate's house at ten-thirty in the morning. She walked up to the door and knocked. It felt weird to her, arriving unannounced, but it's been an emotional 48 hours and she needed to talk to her big sister. Five minutes went by and there was no answer. She scratched her head.

"What the hell, Cyn?" she whispered.

Vanessa pulled out her phone and before she could dial, Cynthia called *her*. She answered the call. "Cynthia? I was just about to call you, girl. I'm outside… huh? You're where? Oh shit. Well, perfect. I'll be over there in a minute. Save me a bar stool."

She hung up and opened her Uber app.

Ten minutes later, Vanessa walked into the bar to see her sister and took a seat next to her. Cynthia was already nursing her third mojito.

"Shit Cyn, why didn't you call me twenty minutes sooner?"

Vanessa asked. "I would have come straight here. Would have saved me a trip!"

"Don't care, and the only reason I called you was because Gloria and Jessica are working this morning," Cynthia replied. She pulled a hundred-dollar bill out of her purse and slapped it down on the bar, "Get my sister any drinks she wants with this!"

The bartender came over to their corner with a judgmental look. "Alright ladies, it's barely 11 am and you're on a bender. For the sake of my conscience, I'm cutting you off unless you eat something."

Cynthia reached out and grabbed his collar, "I don't wanna eat something, Sam Malone. I wanna drink until I forget I was ever born! Now bring me some Absolute or I'll take my business elsewhere!"

Vanessa noticed the bartender's face and quickly stepped in. She placed her hand on Cynthia's shoulder. "Whoa there, sis… um, let's take this to a different bar so we can start at the same time, okay? I think I need to catch up to your level."

Cynthia turned to her and back to the bartender. She matched his fierce glare with one of her own… she wanted to test this guy but opted not to. Her hand released his collar and she stepped away from the bar, heading to the exit.

Vanessa pushed the bill that was still on the bar. "This oughta cover that little incident."

He slapped down and pocketed it. "Barely," he whispered.

She nodded and quickly followed her sister.

Nate pulled into his driveway back home at noon and noticed a stranger waiting in front of the door. He stepped out of the Tahoe and hit the alarm. "May I help you?" he asked.

Nate drew closer and noticed the clergy collar as the visitor introduced himself. "Mr. Durant I assume? I'm Father Gregory Harrison from the Community Worship Center."

Nate shook the extended hand of the priest, wondering what he was doing at their place.

Reading his mind the priest said, "I'm here on behalf of your neighbor, Mr. Fermin. He's contracted our services for a peaceful resolution to the dispute the two of you are having."

*What a chickenshit,* Nate thought. "Well, that's nice of you, Father."

"If you have the time, the three of us can meet at this location and talk things out." The priest handed him a card with an address printed on it. "He'll be available all day tomorrow."

Nate accepted the card and looked at it. "10 am tomorrow. Promptly. If he doesn't show, I'll shut down any other olive branches he sends over."

Father Gregory nodded. "Agreed. Have a nice day, young man." They shook hands again, and the priest walked past him up the street.

Nate unlocked the door and whistled for Brutus. The dog came down the hallway to greet him. He petted the dog, fished out a doggy treat from the kitchen, then walked to the computer.

There were no emails for new job leads, but Pete from Hot97 followed through with an 'e-vite' to the .38 Special listening party next week. He then checked Facebook and found a new unread message that was sent this morning.

> @StephanieSymphony: "The river is 629 feet wide and 5 feet deep… do you A) Attempt to ford the river, B) Caulk wagon and float it across, or C) Take a ferry across?"

Nate smiled and typed his reply.

> @NatefromNewYork: "Never ford the river!"

After a few minutes, Stephanie came online and resumed the conversation.

> @StephanieSymphony: "Right! How's it going?"

> @NatefromNewYork: "Doing fine. It's not too early over there is it?"

> @StephanieSymphony: "I got a half-hour, we just opened but my first appointment isn't due until 9:30 am."

Nate wondered how to bring up the picture from Tumblr, since Cynthia wouldn't be home anytime soon. This would be the ideal moment to discuss it… *Might as well go with the direct approach.*

> @NatefromNewYork: "Okay cool, because there was something I wanted to tell you, one of the reasons why I started looking for you in the first place."

Stephanie didn't reply at first.

> @NatefromNewYork: "Stephanie?"

> @StephanieSymphony: "Uh, Nate you're scaring me."

> @NatefromNewYork: "No, no, no… relax, no need to be alarmed. Just, do me a favor and check out this link… 'sexybbwsluts.tumblr.com Date Stamp: April 5th, 2012'."

He held his breath and counted the seconds as he imagined her waiting for the picture to load and her reaction.

@StephanieSymphony: "Oh... okay."

That wasn't the reaction he expected.

@NatefromNewYork: "Huh? Stephanie, that's you... naked."

@StephanieSymphony: "And? Nate, you knew I did magazine spreads back in the day, I told you. Big Butt, King, Legs & Tail. It's nothing I'm ashamed of."

@NatefromNewYork: "Oh."

@StephanieSymphony: "How did you find this picture?"

@NatefromNewYork: "I've been married for ten years. You don't think I look at porn? Anyways, I'm glad you're cool with it. When I first saw it, I thought it was... what do you call it? Revenge Porn."

@StephanieSymphony: "Well aren't you Mister Chivalry? Let me get this straight. You find a naked picture of me online, and do this valiant search... just to let me know? After all these years?"

@NatefromNewYork: "I was just looking out for you. Don't think too deep into it."

He realized how it looked, and he didn't want to give her the wrong message. It was time to clear things up now that the picture mystery was solved.

> @NatefromNewYork: "Stephanie, it's been a long time, and things between us ended… weird. I'm married now and I…"

He left the statement unfinished, not knowing what else to type.

> @StephanieSymphony: "Hey, hey, hey… that's all water under the bridge, Nate. Everything from Chicago I've put behind me. For a reason."

He tensed up remembering Miami and Chicago. *This was a mistake.*

Nate jumped when he heard the phone ring. He reached over and answered it. "Hello? Hey baby…"

"Hey honey, the interview was a bust so I'm hanging with sis, drowning my sorrows until I feel better… you better order something because I'll be in no mood to cook or do anything else when I get home."

"Awww, sorry about the interview…" Nate began.

"It's okay, I'm already over it. I just wanna get drunk and take an Uber home, don't wait up for me." She clicked off the phone before he could say goodbye.

He looked back at the screen and noticed Stephanie was offline. He thought about unfriending her, to avoid sending any mixed signals. *She didn't want you back then. She won't want you now.* Nate pulled up her profile and placed the cursor on the *Friends* button. One click, and it would all be over… Stephanie Grace will go back to being an obscure, distant memory, never to be bothered again.

He thumbed the ring on his left hand, while the finger on his right hand hovered over the mouse button for a moment, and then he pulled it away. Nate typed in a different website address and moved on to other matters.

Cynthia lowered her phone. "There, that's that… keep those shots coming!" she yelled. It was twelve-thirty, and the two sisters were at their second stop. Rudy's Bar and Grill was in the heart of Hell's Kitchen, between 44th and 45th Streets, on Ninth Avenue. The place was filled with surly construction workers, cabbies, and police officers during their lunch break.

*This is more Cynthia's crowd,* Vanessa thought to herself. Despite her recent medical procedure, she was hesitant to drink any alcohol, so she was nursing a glass of orange juice.

"I thought you were catching up," Cynthia said, noticing Vanessa's glass.

"This is a screwdriver," she lied, "I'm being stylish today."

Cynthia grunted in reply and then finished her martini. Vanessa waited a moment then asked, "So, you gonna tell me what happened, or do I have to guess?"

Cynthia let out a long sigh. "Bombed another interview," she began, and signaled the bartender for another martini. When it arrived, she took a slow sip and resumed her story. "This principal went off and made her decision the moment she reached out to that *bitch* Brigitte."

"Oh," Vanessa replied, shaking her head. "I knew she would burn you when you let slip that she was fucking that British guidance counselor. Brigitte's had it in for you ever since."

"That was over seven years and two boyfriends ago! How long is she goin' to hold a grudge? My God!"

She nearly shattered her glass as she pounded on the bar.

Vanessa tried to calm her sister down. "Hey, how 'bout we get some bottles and take this over to your place, huh, sis? Don't wanna get too ripped in public and make a fool of yourself when you can act crazy in the privacy of your own home."

Cynthia waved her hand down dismissively. "Forget it! That place is starting to feel like a prison, rather than a home, like the… the Taj Mahal! Did you know it was built to keep the emperor's wife in? A place so beautiful she'd never wanna leave! That's what the condo feels like now. See? I'm smart! I know things!"

Her voice was getting louder, and they were drawing questioning stares from everyone around them.

Vanessa pulled her arm. "Alright then, let's hit some stores. Spending a few thousand dollars always makes me feel better, huh? You can show me where you found that dress from the picnic."

That was the wrong thing to say because reminding Cynthia of the picnic also reminded her of Sylverton. Which made her even more infuriated.

Someone jostled Cynthia as they were passing by. She immediately turned around and yelled, "Alright! Who wants some?" and threw a haymaker at the innocent construction worker who was walking near her.

"Oh shit!" Vanessa yelled, jumping back.

As the construction worker fell to the floor, his four friends sitting at a nearby table stood up. As they approached her, Cynthia cracked her knuckles and swiped her thumb across her nose. "I haven't been in a bar fight since high school." A smile crept across her face as she asked the group, "Who's first?"

The first man was over six feet and three-hundred pounds, Cynthia socked him right in the jaw and he went down like a bag of potatoes. The next two grabbed each of her arms as Vanessa stood back several feet and looked on in shock. Cynthia tried to wiggle her arms free as a third slowly walked up to her.

"I don't usually hit dames," he said with a laugh.

"Too bad," she replied. "I like it rough!"

She kicked her right foot and caught him right between the legs, then brought her heel down on the top part of his boot.

With an agonizing howl, the man bowled over.

Vanessa took the opportunity to bash a glass over the head of each guy holding her sister's arms. Now free, she took Cynthia's hand and pulled her to the exit.

"C'mon! Before the cops show up!"

"My purse! Your purse!" Cynthia yelled.

"I got them both. Let's go!"

They made it outside and caught a cab. Vanessa opened the door and pushed Cynthia in.

"Hey!" she protested.

"Fifth Avenue and 50th Street, step on it!" Vanessa ordered, as she climbed inside and shut the door.

The taxi took off just as the police showed up. Vanessa let out a sigh of relief.

"So, you told her about the picture, and it was no big deal, huh?" Sean asked.

Nate was relaxing downstairs in his man cave, playing Call of Duty on his PlayStation 3. Sean was playing co-op online with him as they carried their conversation over their gaming headsets.

"Yeah, but then things got awkward… watch your six."

"Thanks… What do you mean *'awkward?'* Why do things get so complicated with you? You're a regular George Costanza, you know that?"

Nate laid out a round of suppression fire while Sean flanked the enemy.

"Watch the left, watch the left!" Nate barked.

"I got them!"

"So anyway, she started asking me how did I find the picture in the first place, and I'm all like *'I'm a married man, of course I browse internet porn…'* then she thinks I'm this knight in shining armor defending her honor, yadda, yadda, yadda, and then the bullshit from the past comes up."

Sean tossed a grenade and took out a jeep of insurgents. "Uh-huh, so what happened next?"

"She went offline and that was it. Okay now this time, don't shoot the dog! Let him bite the bad buy and bring him down, then walk up and cap him."

"Alright, alright, I can't help it if I get trigger-happy."

Nate waited while the German Shepherd attacked the guard from behind.

"Got him," Sean said. "So, if I were you, I'd cut all contact, unfriend her and keep it moving… but something tells me you're not gonna do that."

Nate made it to the checkpoint, ending the level, and a cutscene played. He sighed, saved the game, and logged off.

"Hey! Let's do the next level!" Sean yelled from his headset.

"I need a break. I'll hit you up when I'm ready to give it another go…"

"Aww c'mon man…" Sean yelled, before he disconnected.

Nate woke up alone in bed at eight o'clock the next morning. Either he was so tired from last night he didn't hear Fermin mowing the lawn, or the man hadn't bothered, as a peace offering for their meeting. After a quick shower, he got dressed and came downstairs to find Cynthia passed out on the couch.

She was sitting up, face to the ceiling… and Brutus was resting on her bosom.

"Now there's a Kodak moment if I ever saw one," he said to himself.

He didn't disturb either one of them. He just ate a bowl of oatmeal and left a note explaining where he was going. Before leaving, though, he snuck a quick picture on his phone. He figured it'd be a great laugh to share with Sean.

It was a forty-five-minute walk to the Worship Center, but Nate arrived at nine-thirty and was greeted again by Father Harrison.

"So glad you could make it. I applaud you two for attempting to settle this peacefully," the priest said.

"Right," Nate replied, deadpanned.

The two walked down the hallway to a private meeting room. There were no windows, and the only wall decoration was a cross with Jesus Christ being crucified on it. Sitting alone at a long table was Fermin. He was wearing a three-piece business suit with three buttons on the jacket. His glasses reflected the dim light coming from a lamp dangling from the ceiling.

"You're here early," Nate said.

"Yes, I like to get up with the sun, although you know that already."

"Hmph." Nate took a seat.

Father Gregory sat down as well and they got started. "Now then, from what I understand, Mr. Durant has a problem with you, Mr. Hall, mowing your lawn in the early hour of the morning and waking him up. Mr. Hall, do you think it's possible for you to…"

"I have been tending to my plants every morning at the same time for the last five months…" Fermin interrupted. "He didn't complain back then!"

"You just started with your lawn a *month* ago, and I've complained to the *police* since then!" Nate countered.

"Who are you to tell me what to do in my house?" Fermin asked. "I did my homework on you, Durant… I know about your father," the old man said, waving a wrinkled finger at him.

"Oh yeah? You know, then, what *he* would do in a situation like this, right?"

"Gentlemen please…" the priest pleaded for control.

"You'd be there mowing your lawn and my father would step out of the house, walk up behind you… and put two bullets in the back of your head!"

"Mr. Durant!" the priest cried out, as he did the sign of the cross in front of him.

"Your body would have fallen forward like a bag of bricks, and he'd go back inside to finish his breakfast," Nate finished.

"You're nothing but a Chicago thug! Your name may make boots shake out there in the windy city, but you're in Brooklyn now, so you can't do shit!"

"We do not swear in the presence of our Lord!" Father Gregory exclaimed.

"You know what? We're done here…" Nate stood up. "I can't deal with people like you. Take that any way you want." He turned to leave.

8

———

# A CALL IN THE MIDDLE OF THE NIGHT

THERE WAS A BUZZING THAT NATE BARELY HEARD. HE HAD TO convince himself he was dreaming because there was no way someone, *anyone* was calling for a job. Not this late on a Friday, or early Saturday, before the weekend. Without opening his eyes, he reached over, found his vibrating phone, and answered it.

He whispered, making sure not to wake up Cynthia. "Unless someone is dead, hang up this phone. Don't speak, don't say 'sorry,' just hang up and let me go back to sleep."

"Nate! It's an emergency!" a voice called out. Nate didn't even recognize the voice as family, so it was impossible that it *was* an actual emergency.

"Who's dead?" he asked. "Somebody better be dead."

"I'll be the one dead if you don't get down here for the last set! Horus bailed on me!"

He groaned and carefully sat up from the bed. He still had no clue who was calling, but he was about to start yelling and Cynthia would hear him if he didn't leave the room. After stepping out and closing the bedroom door behind him, Nate bellowed, *"WHO. In the flying. Motherfucking fuck. Of fucks. IS THIS?"*

"Nate, please, we have to close at two am if you can't make it! I need someone for the last two hours or we'll lose at least $900.00 from the night. The chill-out set runs until 4 am."

He checked the clock and the calendar on the wall downstairs in the kitchen. It was eleven-forty-five, the Friday before Labor Day weekend. This was pretty much the last party of the summer. *Everyone* was probably at clubs over the weekend. He had to make it worth it if Cynthia was going to be pissed.

"$700.00… plus 10% of the door," he mumbled.

"Nate the last time you were here at Slake, you did the DJ set for $500.00," the caller said.

*Slake! That's the name of the place!* Nate finally put the pieces of the puzzle together. He had only done a few DJ sets in the last four months.

"I'm not leaving this house to take the train to Manhattan for anything less than $700.00… plus 10% of the door."

"$800.00. Up front, in cash, no check, no PayPal, and nothing from the door," the caller countered.

"Okay, I'm hanging up and shutting off my phone…"

He pulled the phone away from his ear as the caller let out a high-pitched scream.

"Okaaaaaaay! Okay, okay, okay!"

"$700.00… 10% of the door… say it." He almost added 'bitch,' but he felt merciful.

"$700.00… and 10% of the door. Be here by 1:45 am." The caller hung up the phone.

Nate nodded and saw a shadow at the top of the stairs. "Holy shit! Baby, you scared the hell outta me!"

Cynthia was glaring down at him wearing a nightie. Her face said it all.

"Baby, I swear… it's just this one time…" he started.

She turned away and walked back to the bedroom and slammed the door.

He hung his head and whispered, "Fuck."

Slake was on 30th Street between Seventh Avenue and Eighth. Nate arrived at the back entrance at one-fifty and knocked. The door opened and the wiry owner of the club along with two security guards led Nate inside. They walked down a long narrow hallway to another door that opened to the back of the DJ booth that was elevated on a stage. Below was a huge dance floor, packed with people.

An Asian guy wearing a flashy hoodie that had spray-painted symbols on it came down from the stage. "You were supposed to be here five minutes ago! I need a 15-minute head start to arrange the end of my set!"

"Blow me, Jeremy Lin. Do what you do and be on your way!" Nate yelled.

"What you say, you fuckin' faggot?!"

The two pushed each other in the small booth until security pulled them apart.

"Hey, hey, hey, break this shit up!" The club owner yelled. "Fucking crazy. Y'all supposed to be professionals, so act like it!"

The Asian DJ climbed back up on the platform and started his final mix. Nate calmed himself down and pulled out his MacBook from the backpack to prepare his setlist.

Eight minutes later, Nate was ready to take over. He looked around the dance floor as he cued the intro of his set, a haunting melodic loop that caught the attention of everyone in the club. He identified himself and played a few hyping sound effects as the loop built up to a climactic crescendo. Nate did a flourish and then dropped a bass-heavy beat, which erupted the dance floor. The party resumed as the torch was passed. His Asian counterpart was less than impressed and exited through the back without saying a word.

An hour in, at three o'clock, things were still jumping.

*Damn, I should have asked for $1,000.00 and 10% of the door. This place is packed!*

He was on autopilot now, with the next 20 minutes pre-programmed. He recorded a few ad-libs and reached for a bottle of water. An odd-looking young man was waving near the booth for attention. It was known for unknown artists to hit up the DJ to play some of their music in hopes of being discovered.

Every person with a SoundCloud account believed they were a musician these days. Nate ignored the guy for as long as he could, but he was persistent. Nate waved him over to the back of the booth and met him at the bottom of the platform.

"Wha'cha want?" Nate asked.

He was white and looked like he was in his early twenties. The attire he was wearing gave off a sparkly vampire vibe, and he had *way* too much mousse in his hair. There was a thumb drive in his hand.

"I got a track here that can really rock the house. Can you play it?"

"I don't play unsolicited music, kid. Get discovered some-where else."

"But it's good, man. I get nothing but positive love on YouTube and Spotify!"

Nate rolled his eyes. "Listen, I play the wrong track, I lose the crowd. They don't like the music, they leave… and I lose money, understand? I have to keep people here, dancing, drink-ing, and spending money!"

"Just give it a listen for yourself!" he pleaded.

Nate saw the hunger in his eyes, he remembered those days establishing himself. He waved his hand. "Alright, let me get a listen."

"I have a copy on my phone." He pulled out a smartphone

and some earbuds then handed them to Nate. He looked at the phone and shook his head. *Android, again? Ugh!* He pressed play on the music app and listened to the track. It *was* a head-banger. The kid looked on and when the song went off, Nate handed back the phone to him.

"I'm no Dr. Dre, but it has potential."

"Thanks. So, can you play it?" he asked.

"Absolutely not… it's not for this scene. Maybe underground clubs or maybe college radio, but not here."

"Aw c'mon man, it's a killer track! Alright, how about this… I'll give you $100.00 to play it tonight, even if it's the last song before we close, please!"

"Sorry man, it ain't happening tonight. I got around 45 minutes to go and my setlist is locked in. All I can tell you is, keep plugging it online, put together an EP, and market the shit out of it. Pretty soon you'll get put on, then look me up if I'm still here."

He looked down and backed away from the booth. Nate climbed back to where the turntables and his MacBook were propped up and shouted some more ad-libs. The crowd responded and he started the final mix of the night.

It was six in the morning Saturday when Nate made it home. He was wired and still feeding off the rush of all the money he made off that set. But, unfortunately, his vibe was killed by the death stare from Cynthia once he opened the door. She was still upset with him.

"The garbage has to go out," was all she said to him.

*Don't yell, whatever you do, don't yell…*

He sighed. "Fine…"

While in the alley throwing out the trash, he noticed Fermin was warming up the lawnmower again. Suddenly, an idea came to him. He rushed back inside the house.

Ten minutes later, he was up in the bedroom and had a pair of speakers attached to his MacBook. His mix playlist from the club was cued up.

"If I can't sleep in… then neither will the whole damn neighborhood… and, HIT IT!" He pressed play, and the speakers came to life with a loud bass drop. He almost wished he got a copy of that kid's song from the club. This would have given him some exposure.

Cynthia flew up the steps and started screaming at the top of her lungs. "NATE! WHAT ARE YOU DOING?!"

"Giving that bastard a taste of his own medicine!" he held his finger up. "Be patient, baby… it won't be long!"

He started hearing people yelling and complaining from neighbors around their block. Then Fermin came out from his backyard and looked up to the second-floor window. He was screaming something, but Nate couldn't hear him.

After another minute, he finally turned off the music.

"…you crazy?" Fermin finished his question. The echo of the sudden silence amplified his voice.

Nate leaned out and looked down at him. "Here's the deal, Fermin! You mow your lawn starting at 8 am and I don't do my Saturday morning mix anymore. Sounds fair?"

The neighbor growled. "Okay Durant, you got a deal." He turned around and marched back to his townhouse.

Cynthia looked at Nate as he celebrated his victory spinning on his heels and doing a Michael Jackson heel kick.

To make it up to Cynthia for taking the DJ gig, Nate promised to watch the most recent two *The Fast and The Furious* movies. Much to his agony. After watching *Fast Five*, they were halfway through watching a downloaded copy of *Fast & Furious 6* when Cynthia started drifting off. He tried to reach for the remote to turn to something else, but she was laying on his arm.

*Damn it! If she falls asleep, I'll have to watch this bullshit movie again!*

"Baby?" he nudged her lightly.

"I'm up, I'm up, I'm still watching…"

She tried to make sense of what she was watching, then asked, "Wait, when did they save Letty? What I miss?"

"Dom did this crazy acrobatic move and caught her in mid-air, then landed on the hood of the car…" he explained.

"Rewind it, lemme see it again…"

"Cyn, you're tired, and it's been a helluva day. Let's go to bed, *together*." He slipped his hand inside her pants for emphasis.

"Honey?" Cynthia asked.

"Yeah?"

"You're dipping in the *red sea* tonight."

He pulled his hand back in a flash. "Okaaaaaaay," he sighed, shaking his hand in the air.

She sat up. "Sorry. You're not mad?"

"Uh, it's cool," he said, with a light chuckle.

She turned off the movie. "I think I will turn in early. Don't stay up too late, okay?"

"I won't… I'll probably come to bed after SNL. It's the rerun with Peyton Manning hosting."

She leaned forward and gave him a peck. "Goodnight."

"Goodnight, baby."

Nate watched her go upstairs, staring at her ass. He was harder than concrete. "If I didn't know better, I'd swear her period comes *twice* a month," he groaned.

He thought about masturbating but looked over to see Brutus watching him from the corner of the room.

"Do you mind?" he asked the dog. He replied by turning his head sideways but still looking at him.

He sighed, got up from the couch, and took a seat at the computer desk. Opening his browser and checking Tumblr. Once his erection subsided, he went on Facebook and noticed Stephanie was online again.

@NatefromNewYork: "Hey…"

@StephanieSymphony: "Hey…"

@NatefromNewYork: "Sorry about before."

@StephanieSymphony: "It's cool. I hope we can still be cool on here. I have to be honest, my page is only for work. I really don't socialize online. You're actually the first person I can talk to. My parents don't speak to me. They haven't since I left Chicago."

*Okay, be careful here, she's doing the victim con again.*

@NatefromNewYork: "Wow, I'm in the same boat. My uncle and cousins aren't online, so I only email them."

@StephanieSymphony: "It also doesn't help that I'm in a long-distance relationship."

His eyebrow went up. *The plot thickens, she just happens to drop that boulder off a cliff like Wile E. Coyote.*

@NatefromNewYork: "Well I'll be damned, Stephanie Anastasia Grace… finally dating someone!"

@StephanieSymphony: "LOL, you funny! I can't believe you remembered my middle name. That is so Friends of you."

@NatefromNewYork: "I need details. Give me some dirt on you and him, c'mon now!"

@StephanieSymphony: "Okay, before I do, I need some dish from you… what's married life like?"

Nate thought about it, rolling the ring on his finger before typing.

@NatefromNewYork: "Marriage is work. It's an adventure. There are highs and lows, good times and bad times. After nearly ten years I can tell you, I am as clueless now as I was that day I said, 'I do.'"

@StephanieSymphony: "Wow, that's deep."

@NatefromNewYork: "I could write a book, which I actually AM doing, among other things."

@StephanieSymphony: "So, I see, photographer, writer, blogger, podcaster, stand-up comedian, AND DJ… geez, who are you? The white version of Donald Glover?"

@NatefromNewYork: "LOL, now there's a comparison I've never heard before! I can call myself Mature Mafioso instead of Childish Gambino."

@StephanieSymphony: "Nah, Nate from New York rolls off the tongue better, it's catchy. Seriously though, what's your book about?"

@NatefromNewYork: "I haven't told anyone the details, not even Cynthia. I'm afraid the idea might get stolen."

@StephanieSymphony: "Cynthia, that's a nice name, is she on Facebook too? You think it would be weird if I sent her a friend request?"

@NatefromNewYork: "She's not on Facebook. She's a teacher, so anything she posts on social media may jeopardize her career."

*Careful, don't share too much, Cyn would freak...*

@NatefromNewYork: "Enough about me and my book, you'll learn about it when it's published. It's your turn. Long-distance relationship, huh? Let me guess. He's a college professor from Oxford across the ocean in England, right? You go out to see him like six times a year?"

@StephanieSymphony: "LMAO! I am literally cracking up over here! No wonder you're good at writing, you have a hell of an imagination."

@NatefromNewYork: "Is that a yes?"

@StephanieSymphony: "No! OMG, I can't believe I'm telling this to someone... okay, he lives in San Francisco."

Nate sucked his teeth and whispered, "Really?"

@NatefromNewYork: "How is that long distance? You're still in the SAME STATE! LOL! I thought it was something crazy, like he was in Texas or something?"

@StephanieSymphony: "Hey, it's a seven-hour drive, ten hours on a bus. That's not easy to deal with three weekends of the month."

*Such a drama queen. Same ol' Stephanie,* Nate thought, rolling his eyes.

@StephanieSymphony: "We've been together for three years. He saw me perform at a nightclub and we just hit it off."

@NatefromNewYork: "Nice, is he going to try to be your manager and make you a star like in The Rose?"

@StephanieSymphony: "Still with the pop culture references. You always found some scenario and compared it to a movie, tv show, or song."

@NatefromNewYork: "You found it clever when I did it, and it was contagious."

@StephanieSymphony: "Yeah, I did it too, back in the day. But then I grew up."

@NatefromNewYork: "Har, har, har… last I checked, I was still older than you. You're not even 40 yet."

@StephanieSymphony: "I turn 40 in April next year, thank you! I've already had my mid-life crisis and come to terms that I'm not having kids. Speaking of, you and… what was her name?"

@NatefromNewYork: "Cynthia… and no we don't have any yet, but there's still time."

@StephanieSymphony: "Really? What, you robbin' the cradle? You got yourself a teeny bopper? She does look like she's in her early-30s. What's the age difference?"

@NatefromNewYork: "Don't change the subject back to me. You met him while singing, together for three years, out in San Fran… why do I feel like something's missing?"

@StephanieSymphony: "Damn, you adding 'Detective' to that list of jobs now?"

@NatefromNewYork: "Okay, fair enough. Keep your secrets, Gandalf."

*C'mon, take the bait, you little mouse…*

The seconds ticked by as Nate thumbed the ring around his finger patiently.

@StephanieSymphony: "ALRIGHT! He's married! There? Happy? Imma fucking sidepiece, and I'm proud of it!"

Nate's eyebrow twitched up at the admission.

@NatefromNewYork: "Wow. Did NOT see that coming."

She didn't reply for a minute, then Nate typed…

@NatefromNewYork: "Feels good to tell someone, doesn't it?"

@StephanieSymphony: "Yeah, actually, it does. I never even told any of the girls at the salon. It's none of their business, really."

@NatefromNewYork: "Ten years of marriage and I haven't shared anything with anyone. Probably because I only have like ONE friend out here in New York. He let me sleep on his couch back in the day while sharing his place with two other roommates. We talk about everything, except what goes on between me and Cyn."

@StephanieSymphony: "Wow. This feels lopsided. I've bared my soul, while you've been pretty limited on what you've said so far."

"Oh bullshit!" he spat.

Behind him, Brutus popped his head up, looking over at him.

"Sorry," Nate said, and the dog lowered his head again. He let the conversation hang for a moment rather than reply quickly.

@StephanieSymphony: "Hello? You there?"

@NatefromNewYork: "Yes, was just thinking. You have a point. What would you like to know?"

@StephanieSymphony: "What's your book about?"

@NatefromNewYork: "The book is off limits."

@StephanieSymphony: "Oh come on! You really think I'll steal your idea? I don't know anything about writing."

@NatefromNewYork: "You can learn. Sorry."

@StephanieSymphony: "Okay, how did you and Cynthia meet? Let ME guess… she came to Chicago for a teacher's conference and y'all met in the lobby of the hotel, then you followed her to New York."

@NatefromNewYork: "Not even close. It all started with 9/11."

@StephanieSymphony: "Whoa, you lost someone?"

@NatefromNewYork: "Thank my lucky stars I didn't, but when it happened, I felt obligated to help somehow. So, I sold everything I owned, let my lease go up, and took the Amtrak here."

@StephanieSymphony: "That is craaaaaazy. What did you do for money?"

@NatefromNewYork: "Well, IPS didn't have anything after Miami, so I filed for unemployment in July. They didn't contest it. We WERE on assignment for two years straight."

@StephanieSymphony: "Holy shit, I didn't think of that!"

@NatefromNewYork: "I was still using my old Chicago address but had my mail forwarded to a PO Box in a UPS store, then asked them to forward the mail to New York. I even went back to check in and show them I was looking for work. Eventually, the state caught on, but it was good while it lasted."

@StephanieSymphony: "Okay, but how does the future Mrs. Durant come into the picture?"

@NatefromNewYork: "Well, after helping out at Ground Zero for a while, damn near dying of a heart attack, they finally sent me home. The three guys I was staying with were trying to develop the next great app and they taught me to code. I learned Java, C++, and Python. I took what I learned and got certified for IT."

@StephanieSymphony: "Hmmm, I always said you missed your calling. You only stayed in document scanning because it was easy."

@NatefromNewYork: "Well, after doing infrastructure work at various places, I volunteered at a few elementary schools."

@StephanieSymphony: "And that's where you met Miss Cynthia… awww, what a touching story. No infidelity, no BDSM, no weekends of torture and degradation."

Nate's head jerked back from the screen after that last message.

@NatefromNewYork: "Excuse me?"

@StephanieSymphony: "Oh, sorry, I didn't mention… Heathcliff and I are Dominant and Submissive."

He rubbed his eyes to make sure he read the screen correctly. *Okay, she's fucking with me! Any second now she's going to type 'Just kidding.'*

@StephanieSymphony: "Hey? You still there?"

@NatefromNewYork: "I… I'm just waiting for you to say that you were joking…"

@StephanieSymphony: "You'll be waiting for a long time then."

@NatefromNewYork: "Holy shit, are you for real?"

An attachment started uploading in the window. Once it was finished, a picture of Stephanie's entire body bound by rope, wearing a leather collar with spikes and a ball gag flashed on the screen.

"Jesus Christ," he whispered.

@StephanieSymphony: "As real as a heart attack."

*The Tumblr picture situation just took a backseat to this.*

@StephanieSymphony: "Don't tell anyone about this. I'm trusting you more than anyone else I know."

Nate's fingers started to shake as he typed.

@NatefromNewYork: "Who the hell am I gonna tell? Shit, Stephanie, I thought the naked picture online thing was risqué. This is a whole other layer on the onion!"

@StephanieSymphony: "Which is why I embraced it so easily. Bottom line, Nate… I'm a grown woman, living on my own, and I'm not in Chicago anymore."

@NatefromNewYork: "No, you are not."

There was a pause between their messages as Nate went into deep thought… then he typed.

@NatefromNewYork: "The Librarios."

@StephanieSymphony: "Huh?"

@NatefromNewYork: "That's the name of my book. It's Latin for 'The Librarians.' It's about the staff of a library in New York that take on strange cases of the occult. They entrap monsters and demons in books categorized by the Dewey Decimal number. Sorta like Pokemon meets Lilo & Stitch."

@StephanieSymphony: "Okaaaaaaaaay."

@NatefromNewYork: "Each of the staff are special. One's a wizard, there's a Japanese ghost, and a Jinn. There's a trio of teenage witches, they're like a coven. There's an immortal, and their newest member is a necromancer who is somehow the last descendant of Christ. It's batshit crazy, but I tie it all together like some sort of comic book super team."

@StephanieSymphony: "Wow… how far into it are you at?"

@NatefromNewYork: "12 chapters, 200 pages, over 115,000 words so far… I'd say around 35% completed so far."

@StephanieSymphony: "What the fuck, who are you, J.R.R. Tolkien?"

@NatefromNewYork: "Hey! I'm sharing a lot here now, too… Miss Fifty Shades of Gray!"

@StephanieSymphony: "Do NOT go there! That book is a gross misappropriation of the lifestyle and I do not support it one bit!"

Things were getting testy between them again. Nate decided to de-escalate their conversation and apologize.

@NatefromNewYork: "Okay, sorry. Now you know about the book. I'd like to think we both learned a lot about each other tonight."

@StephanieSymphony: "Yes, we have. I apologize for knocking your work. I'd like to read some of it one day."

He sucked in a breath at the thought. *Anyone* reading his writing made him nervous.

@NatefromNewYork: "Uhh, we'll see. Just be thankful you actually know about it, let alone reading some of it for now."

@StephanieSymphony: "Okay, say… It's getting late. Wanna call it a night?"

@NatefromNewYork: "Isn't that my line since I'm three hours ahead of you?"

@StephanieSymphony: "It's just that my fingers are getting tired, maybe next time we can just do a video call, or we can exchange numbers and I can just call you?"

Nate tensed up as his eyes darted in all different directions.

@NatefromNewYork: "I'm up for video calls,
but that's about it."

@StephanieSymphony: "Right. Don't want to
overstep boundaries… have a good night,
Nate."

@NatefromNewYork: "You, too."

They both signed off, and he checked the clock on the wall.
It was one forty-five in the morning! They had been chatting
online for over three hours.

*Holy shit!*

Nate turned the desktop off and went around the living room,
turning off the light. He noticed Brutus hadn't moved from the
corner where he was sleeping. Nate finally went upstairs and
took off his clothes. As he approached the bed, he noticed a
small, dried stain on Cynthia's pillow. She had another
nosebleed.

*What the hell?*

He checked to see if she was still bleeding, but apparently, it
dried up. It wasn't even that hot lately. What was the cause of it?
Nate made a note to bring it up to Cynthia the next morning and
climbed into bed. The two images of Stephanie floated in his
head. Polar extremes of the spectrum, completely naked in an
artistic pose… to being bound and gagged. It would be a long
time before he finally drifted off to sleep.

**9**

---

## TEARS AND LOSS

IT WAS THREE O'CLOCK IN THE MORNING AND VANESSA GOSS was doing 90 on the West Side Highway. She was driving her father's 1993 Porsche 911 Carrera. It was worth over $200,000.00 and originally had *six* miles on it. The car only had a CD player, so she was playing a single of "See You Again" by Carrie Underwood on repeat.

She was crying hysterically and trying to sing along with the lyrics. The George Washington Bridge shined in the distance as she weaved through cars, switching lanes, going left and right. Coming up on a long, straight stretch of road, she shifted to third gear and gunned the engine, passing 100 miles per hour.

There was no said destination as she passed exit after exit. Vanessa was driving aimlessly until she either ran out of gas or was stopped. She contemplated driving upstate to Hastings-on-Hudson and then back down to the city in an endless loop, then just leaving the car on the side of the road.

A pair of flashing lights brought her back to reality as a police car was closing in behind her, the siren blaring into the night.

"Shit!" she hissed. "Okay, try to keep up!" she said, inviting a challenge. She floored the gas pedal, and the car pulled away.

The cruiser gave chase and once it got close, a voice came from its loudspeaker, "POLICE! PULL OVER!"

Vanessa finally came to her senses and slowed down. She was emotionally drained as the car came off the road and stopped. The patrol car stopped behind her and a New York State Trooper stepped out and approached her driver-side window.

"License and registration, Miss," he demanded as he shined his flashlight in her face.

Tears were still running down her face as she turned off the CD player, then reached over to the glove compartment.

Upon examining her papers he asked, "Ma'am, have you been drinking tonight?"

She continued to wheeze and mumble incoherently, just looking at the trooper. He noticed the registration was in her father's name and asked another question, "Miss, is there any particular reason you were speeding in what appears to be an irrational state of mind? I require a verbal response!"

Vanessa gathered herself, panting in shallow breaths, "I… I… I've had a *really* bad day, officer. And I… I… just don't know what to do anymore."

The trooper stepped back. "Miss, I'm going to need you to step out of the vehicle. Slowly."

She nodded and wiped her face. "Okay," and unlocked her seatbelt.

Something was wrong, something was very wrong. It was five o'clock Sunday morning and Nate couldn't hear anything. No Brutus running around in the living room, or up and down the steps, and he wasn't at the side of their bed. He remembered Brutus had stayed in the corner as he turned off the lights last night. Nate jumped out of the bed and scanned the dark while slowly walking down the steps.

Cynthia woke up a few minutes after seven. She had slept hard the night before and her whole body felt stiff. Her arm stretched out as she felt around for Nate. When she didn't feel anything, she sat up with a puzzled look. The hallway was still dark when Cynthia stepped out of the bedroom. She heard some faint muttering coming from downstairs.

As she descended the staircase, she wondered why the lights were still off. The sound she heard was Nate whispering to himself in the living room.

"Nate?" she called out.

"Cynthia, don't move. Don't turn on the lights. Don't come any closer, please." Nate ordered. His voice was hoarse and shaky.

She heard him resume his muttering. The living room was dark and after a moment it sounded like he was… crying?

"Honey what's wrong?" she asked.

"He… he's gone, Cyn… he's… *gone*." Nate's voice cracked.

She strained her eyes in the dark, Nate was in the corner of the living room, kneeling over Brutus' lifeless body. It was still too far to hear what he was saying. She took a step closer.

"Baby, I really don't want to raise my voice," he warned. "Please stay where you are and let me do this. I don't want you to see me… this vulnerable."

"I just want to comfort you…" she started.

He simply shook his head.

From that moment, she understood. Nate had Brutus before they met. When they started dating, it took a while to get used to him. Nate loved that dog as much as he loved her. She would never admit it, but he was the closest thing they would have to a son. Without saying another word, she turned and climbed back upstairs to the bedroom.

Nate heard Cynthia climb the steps and gave in to the wave of grief and despair overcoming him. The average lifespan for a bull terrier was 14 years. He purchased Brutus as a puppy, when he was six weeks old, at the end of 1999. There were no signs of his health deteriorating, but the moment Nate realized his pup wasn't running around the house, he knew. The tears fell from his face. In ten years, Nate never cried in front of Cynthia. There would be times while watching a movie he would shed a tear, but nothing like this.

*Not since Miami had he sobbed like this.*

"I'm sorry, son," he whispered, as he pet the back of Brutus' head. "I should have been here, in your final moments, I should have spent more time… I'm so…" he stopped to take a breath as his shoulders collapsed. He looked up to the ceiling and whispered, "Oh God…" then sunk his head into his chest. He wiped away the tears from his face and looked down at his dog one last time. "Goodbye, boy… you're home now. You're good. You're free…"

He took off his tee-shirt and covered the dog, then stood up and turned the lights on. Cynthia was back, standing at the bottom of the stairs. They stared at each other. He had no idea how long she had been there, what she heard, or how she came back down without him hearing her.

"I'm sorry baby," she whispered.

He said nothing. He had no idea what to say or what to feel. The blank emotionless stare suddenly disappeared, replaced by a hard scowl. He started marching forward. Cynthia winced in fright for a second, believing he would lash out at her, but was shocked to see him pass her, heading for the front door.

"Nate!" she called out behind him.

Nate stormed out into the street as an incoming car nearly hit him. He didn't flinch and kept walking as the driver honked his horn until he arrived at Isaiah and Jorge's door. Cynthia looked out from the entrance and saw where he was heading.

"Nate, wait! Don't!" she yelled, but it was too late.

With a perfectly placed heel kick, the door split open off the hinges in three pieces. Nate stepped in and saw Alexis charging towards him. He hissed and pointed sharply at the dog for a heel command, and she stopped immediately inches from him.

A voice came from the kitchen. "What the fuck?!"

He turned to see the couple sitting at their dining table. Jorge was already standing up. Nate took two steps and before Jorge could react, he backslapped him across the face. Jorge yelped in a high-pitched gasp and dropped to the floor. Nate grabbed Isaiah and slammed the side of his face on the table.

"What did you give my dog?!"

"I told you! Just some hormones! What the fuck…?"

"Bullshit! He's dead because of you!"

"What?! I swear I didn't know it could be fatal, he was probably too old, and it accelerated…"

"I don't give a fuck! You killed my dog and the only reason I don't beat the shit out of you is because I have family members that are gay…" he pulled him off the table and then slammed him against a wall. "I should take you out like they did to Marsha Johnson!"

Isaiah gasped in horror at the comparison.

"…and have you floating in the Hudson!"

"How DARE you!" Isaiah yelled.

Nate pulled him inches from his face. "I'm shutting you down for good," he hissed, and pushed him back against the wall, leaving the house.

Cynthia stood outside the busted door frame with a terrified look on her face. "Are you out of your goddamned mind?! They're going to call the police!" she yelled as he emerged and passed her, going back to their house.

Once inside, Nate picked up the phone and dialed the number for the ASPCA. She pulled the phone out of his hand and hung it up.

"What are you doing?" she asked.

"I'm reporting them to the ASPCA and then asking them to send someone to pick up Brutus. I don't know the exact procedure, but I believe they're the ones who'll cremate the body."

"You don't have any proof Isaiah and Jorge are illegally breeding dogs."

*Don't yell, whatever you do, don't yell…*

"Why are YOU defending them?" he asked. "You should be thankful I'm not…" he caught himself. He dare not say it out loud.

"You think this is *my* fault? You're actually blaming…" she started.

"I didn't say…"

"You didn't have to!" Cynthia yelled. "Nate, I loved Brutus! He wasn't just your dog, he was *ours*."

"Cyn, you never liked cleaning up after him, walking him, even buying food for him… he was a *burden* to you."

Cynthia looked hurt. "Nate, I…"

He waved his hands, turned, and headed for the door again. "I can't do this right now. I'm going for a walk."

"What about the police? What do I say if they come looking for you?" she asked.

"Tell them about Brutus and if they want to question me, tell them to come again later. I'll be back soon. I just need to clear my head." He slammed the door behind him.

Vanessa sat in a holding cell Sunday morning. Remarkably, she was the only one being detained at the moment. An officer approached the cell calling her name. "Goss, Vanessa! You made bail." She rolled her eyes and stood up.

Outside near the front desk waiting for her, Barbara was pacing back and forth. The family lawyer, Saul Rosenberg, escorted Vanessa out the hallway from the back of the precinct.

"Dear God! Vanessa!" she exclaimed.

"Mom, I'm fine." Barbara wrapped her arms around her daughter, holding in her tears.

"You have nothing to be concerned about, Mrs. Goss." Saul assured the mother. "Vanessa blew a 0.4 on the breathalyzer that they administered here, rather than the actual stop. That's below the legal limit. She's only being charged with reckless driving, rather than a DUI. We've also taken precautions that the press doesn't hear about this since it was outside the city."

"Where's Dad?" Vanessa asked.

"That's all you have to say?" Barbara asked, "What the hell were you thinking?"

"Don't say another word here, let's talk in the car," Saul instructed her, as he ushered the two women outside.

Nate walked slowly through East River State Park. He loved walking Brutus there, for him to interact with other dogs and their owners. He couldn't imagine a life without his beloved pet.

His eyes began to water as he yearned to talk to someone. He thought about his father or Sean, after pulling out his phone, he noticed Stephanie was online on Facebook.

@NatefromNewYork: "Hey, you're up early."

@StephanieSymphony: "Couldn't sleep, I'll probably take a nap in the afternoon. What's up?"

@NatefromNewYork: "You remember my pup I had just got when we started the first job for Old Republic Life Insurance?"

@StephanieSymphony: "Yeah, you called him Julius or Gailus…"

@NatefromNewYork: "Brutus."

@StephanieSymphony: "Oh, yeah. You showed me pictures every day. You were such a chick, LOL."

@NatefromNewYork: "He died this morning."

@StephanieSymphony: "OH SHIT! I'm so sorry I said that last remark. OMG, I'm sorry!"

@NatefromNewYork: "These fucking faggots across the street, they're breeding dogs for fights, and they kept bothering us to get him to stud. Cynthia took him over there and they injected him with something… two weeks later, he's dead."

@StephanieSymphony: "Wow."

@NatefromNewYork: "Stephanie, I feel like killing these guys. I mean it. I know people through my father's connections that can make it clean."

@StephanieSymphony: "Nate, Nate, Nate, don't be saying shit like that on here, this shit can be tracked! Fucking Facebook nerds monitoring shit like this, and the FBI will be at your house before you can blink!"

@NatefromNewYork: "I just don't know how to feel, I'm out here in the park on the verge of tears, I can't even look Cynthia in the face because part of me blames her... and I don't wanna take it out on her, damnit!"

@StephanieSymphony: "Where are you?"

@NatefromNewYork: "Huh? I'm in a park, it's like nine in the morning. No one's around."

A couple of minutes went by, Nate thought she went offline when the phone rang with an incoming video call. He looked at the phone hesitantly, his appearance wasn't really camera ready. After wiping his nose and eyes, he clicked to answer the call and the screen flashed with Stephanie's face filling the screen.

She looked the same as she did in her pictures and his memories of Miami. Full cherub face, strawberry blonde hair, a shade darker than Cynthia's, with a small nose and exotic green-blue eyes.

He noticed that she was staring at him as much as he was at her.

"Um, hello?" he asked, testing the audio.

"My God, it's like looking at a whole different person..." she said, "Like you were abducted by aliens and replaced by this... clone or something."

"It's me, the same guy from Chicago..." Nate replied.

"Okay, now that I'm used to it… you look like shit."

He frowned. "Gee thanks."

"Listen, I know you're hurt, and angry, but you can't do anything to those guys *or* blame your wife. Brutus lived a nice long life, and he went in his sleep."

Nate gritted his teeth, then sighed. "You're right."

"I want you to turn the volume up, okay? Make sure no one's around you."

He looked around and decided to walk towards the East River. He was near the shore, with the skyline of lower Manhattan in front of him, "Okay." he said, looking down at the phone.

Stephanie propped the phone on a flat surface and took several steps back. She was wearing a pink house dress with floral print. Nate was wondering what she intended to do when suddenly she started to sing a rendition of "Bonny Portmore."

After the song, he was rendered speechless for a minute, then he asked, "Was that… the song from *Highlander*?"

Stephanie came close and picked up the phone again, she rolled her eyes. "It's a traditional Irish folk song, usually sung in remembrance of the departed."

Nate smiled. "Brutus wasn't Irish, but the sentiment is well received. Thank you, Stephanie."

"Go home to your wife, Nate. Talk to you later." She ended the video call.

"Vanessa Evelyn Goss! Get your ass in this room this instant!" Christopher Goss yelled from across the hallway. Vanessa and Barbara weren't in the house for two seconds before the family patriarch summoned his daughter. Without hesitation, Vanessa marched across the living room into the den, where she found her father standing near the fireplace.

She froze when she saw what was in his hand.

"Mom, he's got the M1 Garand..." she called out.

Christopher was holding his brother's M1 Garand .30 caliber rifle, which was the military standard issue for infantry during World War II.

"Don't be calling for your mother now, young lady! She can't save you, now," he said. "Plant your ass in that chair right now!" he ordered.

She slowly approached the loveseat her father pointed to and sat down. Christopher started to pace back and forth before her.

"You've done some crazy things that I have forgiven in the past, Vanessa. All to get attention away from your sister. You burned the curtains when you were eight, stole a bottle of Glengoyne worth nearly $300.00, and shared it with your friends when you were 16, and I don't even want to recall what you did in Tijuana back in 2006!"

She said nothing. She just stared at him, waiting for the hammer to come down.

"I know, you're going through some issues getting back to work, but this... this was the last straw!"

She mouthed the end of the sentence as he said it, having heard the speech a dozen times, but her eyes stayed on the barrel of the gun.

He continued his rant. "That car was a thing of beauty. I would explain to you what a remarkable feat of engineering that it is, but it would be lost on you. It's time you realize the consequences of your actions!"

Christopher pulled the rifle up and aimed with the sight at her. She screamed, expecting to hear a gunshot.

"Chris!" Barbara yelled from outside the room.

"Damnit, relax! It's not loaded!" he barked, "What the fuck kind of person do you think I am?"

Vanessa was trembling in the chair now. "D… Daaadddy!"

"Don't 'Daddy' me! Goddamnit, get up! Stand up outta that chair!" he ordered.

It took a moment to gather her nerves, but she finally stood up.

"You have exactly to the count of ten to leave this house. Don't come back… ever! Your credit cards have been canceled and your accounts frozen. Take whatever the fuck you have in your pockets and live your car-stealing ass off someone else's dime!"

Vanessa's eyes went wide. Her father had been angry before, but never like this. She couldn't believe what she was hearing. She contemplated telling him about the abortion. "Wh… wha… what?! Where am I supposed to go?!" she cried.

Christopher began to load the gun this time. "Don't know, don't care. TEN!"

She frantically looked around, waving her hands. "Wait, wait, wait…"

"NINE!" he continued.

She ran out of the den. "Mom!" She found Barbara still at the entrance, a defeated look on her face.

"EIGHT!"

"Mom, he can't do this! I don't have a place to go. I lost my studio when the station fired me! You two *asked* me to move back in, remember? Talk some sense into him!"

"SEVEN!"

"I'm sorry, he insisted. He really loved that car." She reached behind the door and handed Vanessa a travel bag. "This was all I could put together… I tried to sneak in some money, but my purse was empty. There's some clothes and toiletries."

"SIX!"

"You better go… he said he'd call the cops to remove you and he probably has the phone in his hand already."

She took the bag and kissed her mother. Barbara hugged her back.

"FIVE! I'm picking up the phone!" Christopher bellowed.

Vanessa took the warning seriously and ran out the door.

"FOUR… THREE… TWO…"

Christopher stepped out of the den and walked up next to his wife. They both looked out the window.

She sighed. "Did you have to use the gun?" she asked him.

"It's the only way she'll learn…" he replied. "Did you know that car only had—"

"Six miles, yes, yes," she dismissed. "How many miles does it have now, dare I ask?"

"714. She basically turned a $250,000.00 vehicle into a piece of junk. I'd be lucky to get $10,000.00 for it now."

She shook her head. "Just donate it for the tax credit and be done with it."

He grunted, "Should we call Cynthia and warn her Vanessa's coming?"

"No, because she'll find an excuse not to let her in… why do you think she did it?"

Christopher thought about it. "She wasn't drunk, so it must have been something else that made her go over the edge. The police report said she was crying hysterically. Was she dating someone? Maybe she got dumped?"

"She didn't come with anyone to the picnic. I swear, Chris, she's going to be the death of us." Barbara walked towards the hallway to the bathroom. "I'm going to take a long ass bath. That police station made my skin crawl."

**10**

—————

# AN UNEXPECTED GUEST

Nate walked into the house just in time to see Cynthia set two plates down for breakfast. They exchanged glances, then Nate went upstairs to wash up. At eleven o'clock, there was a knock on the door. Cynthia was on the computer. She tensed up as Nate came upstairs from his man cave in the basement. He waved his hand to reassure her as he answered the door.

There were two police officers standing at the doorway. An African American male and a Hispanic female. The male asked, "Mister Durant?"

"Yes?"

"May we have a word with you, sir?"

Nate stepped outside and closed the door behind him. "May I see some IDs, officers? I have the right to confirm your identities before answering any questions."

The two exchanged looks as the male officer pulled out his badge in a flip wallet with his identification. "You seem well versed in the law, Mister Durant."

He examined the wallet, then waited for the female officer to show him hers, then nodded and folded his arms, waiting for a question.

"We received a call from across the street. Your neighbors claim you broke into their home, assaulted one of them, and threatened the other. They feel they were targeted because of their lifestyle and are possibly victims of a hate crime."

Nate continued staring blankly, waiting for a question.

"You mind telling us your side of the story? Or perhaps we can talk down at the station?"

He chose his words carefully. His father always told him, *"Never give cops more information than you have to."*

"Approximately two weeks ago, after bothering my wife aggressively, one of the two neighbors in question invited her and my dog over to their place, to size up my dog for a possible proposal to stud. The two illegally breed for the purpose of conducting dog fights. That night, when I went to retrieve my dog, I saw one of them administering an unknown injection into my dog, with my own eyes.

This morning, I woke up to find my dog dead. In a moment of grief, I was emotionally charged, and I confronted them. My dog was like my child, officers. I don't know if you can relate or not, but my actions were in the heat of the moment."

"Do you have any proof they're dog fighting?" the female officer asked.

"I've been to their basement. They have cages and equipment to hold more than six animals, and on any given day there are at least that many down there. I still have the body of my dog in our living room, and I plan to have them investigate the cause of death. If it has anything to do with what they did, I WILL be pressing charges."

"Okay, before things get heated any further, I want to inform you that your neighbors *do* feel guilty over the death of your dog and they are willing to NOT file charges against *you,* provided you pay for the door you broke and leave them alone," the male officer explained.

"They're only saying that because they don't want me to call animal services on them. Do you believe they should continue to mistreat animals, sir?" he challenged.

"Mister Durant, we have you using homophobic slurs and referencing a hate crime involving the death of a transgender, which neither of them is. They'll be sending you a bill for their door. I recommend you pay it and drop any accusations you plan to press against them."

Nate remained silent, rolling his chin. He almost asked them what consequences he would face if he went forward with the charges anyway, but he knew a good deal when he saw one.

"Sorry for your loss, Mister Durant, but next time, let cooler heads prevail." They both tipped their hats. "Have a nice day, sir," the male officer said.

They walked back to their patrol car and drove off. Nate stared across the street and saw the shadows of Isiah and Jorge behind a temporary screen door at their house. He stood there, daring one of them to come out. His fists clenched as he gritted his teeth. After several minutes, he turned around and went into the house.

Cynthia was waiting with a concerned look on her face. "Is everything—?"

"It's fine. They're not pressing charges, they just want me to pay for their door. The cops didn't care that I told them they're doing dog fights, so they advised me not to report them. It's over."

She sighed. "Thank God. Um, I looked up online. It said 311 is the number to call for… um, you know."

"You can say it, Cynthia… dead animal removal."

She nodded. "Yeah."

They looked at each other.

"I… I'm…" she started, but he interrupted her.

"It's okay, okay? I'm not angry with you, I don't blame you, I… I just need to process this alone. It's nothing personal, baby.

I'll make the call, wrap him up, and we'll take it from there, okay? We're good… we're fine."

Nate picked up the phone after the speech and was about to dial when someone knocked on the door again.

"Fuck!" he spat. He turned to her. "Get rid of them. Don't let them in, don't talk too long. They ask for me, tell them I'm busy."

She nodded.

"If they have a bill for the door, take it and tell them a payment will be sent in five business days. Don't tell them how I feel, don't say *anything* about me. Just keep it brief and close the door, got it?"

"I got it. You should go downstairs so you don't hear them," she suggested.

"Yeah." He took the phone with him and hugged her. "We're fine, okay?" he repeated.

"Okay," she said.

Nate went downstairs and closed the door behind him. Cynthia gathered herself and answered the door.

Vanessa was disheveled and holding the gym bag so tight her knuckles were white. She tried to use her phone outside her parent's house to call an Uber, only to find out her credit card couldn't charge the fare. With no other options, she had to buy a MetroCard and take the subway to Cynthia's house. It was humiliating.

The door opened and Cynthia was shocked to see her. "Van?! What on Earth—?"

Vanessa broke down. "They kicked me out! They actually kicked me out of the house! He pointed the damn gun, Cyn!!

THE GUN! Mom just stood there and did nothing. I don't know what to do! They canceled all my credit cards, froze all my… my…" She lost her train of thought for a moment, then ranted some more. "I had to take the *subway* here! Jesus Christ, the SUBWAY! Oh God, Cynthia! They kicked me ouuuuuuuut!"

She couldn't hold it together anymore. Vanessa started bawling and wrapped her arms around her sister's shoulders. Cynthia cringed as her younger sister sobbed uncontrollably into her cleavage.

Nate emerged from the basement slowly after hearing the hysterics. "Uh, Cynthia?" he asked.

She waved her arm dismissively and then guided Vanessa inside, closed the door, and maneuvered her past the kitchen to the spare bedroom in the back of the house.

He shook his head and whispered, "I don't even wanna know."

A half-hour later, Cynthia and Vanessa were still in the bedroom, so Nate wrote her a note and placed it on the kitchen counter. He then got a white pillowcase and left the house with Brutus' body. Nate climbed into the Tahoe and placed the pillowcase on the passenger seat.

"No trunk for you, boy… you're riding shotgun one last time." He started the car and pulled off.

The Brooklyn Animal Care Center was in East New York, across town on Linden Boulevard and Shepherd Avenue. He made several calls and found the nearest place that would accept the body right away with a small donation. When he pulled into the parking lot, he cut the engine and sat for a moment. Memories came flooding back to him. Bringing Brutus home in

Chicago, introducing him to Cynthia, and making him the ring bearer at their wedding.

He closed his eyes as the tears fell again, and he bit his lip. "Here we are, boy… last stop." He sighed.

The door opened and he stepped out. He entered the building through the glass door and walked up to the front desk.

"Uh, hi, I'm Nate Durant, I called earlier…"

The woman behind the counter nodded, remembering him from a few hours earlier. "Yes, I have your appointment here. There's a $50.00 fee for this… service. Will that be cash or credit card?"

Nate fished out the money and filled out some paperwork, then a man in scrubs walked up to him at the desk. "Very sorry for your loss, sir. I'll take him now."

"Okay." He looked down and handed the pillowcase to him. The man turned and walked through a pair of double doors. He watched the man walk for as long as he could through the window, then walked back out.

There was a metal green bench outside where Nate sat and pulled out his phone.

Sean answered after a few rings. "Hey man, wassup?"

"You doing anything today?"

"Nah, you wanna go to a movie or something? How about *The Butler*? Or maybe *Kick-Ass 2*?"

"Meet me at Pizza Hut on 63rd Drive and Queens Boulevard."

"Did… did you say Pizza Hut? Shit, did you and Cynthia get a divorce?" Sean asked.

"Worse." He ended the call.

Nate drove to Queens. The pain over losing Brutus was not going away. He hoped this relapse in his eating habits would help him. If not, Isaiah and Jorge were going to have a *very* bad day in their future. Homicidal thoughts aside, he pulled up and parked a block behind 63rd Drive on the corner of the Boulevard and stepped out of the car.

Sean was sitting at a table in Pizza Hut when Nate walked in. He looked up at his face and knew exactly why they were there. Nate always gorged on stuffed-crust pizza when he was depressed, even after the surgery. He looked like hell. Sean was always there to talk and eat, even before Cynthia.

"I already ordered the pie," he said to Nate when he sat down. "What happened?"

"I found Brutus this morning. He passed away."

"Fuuuuuuck," Sean whispered.

"It was those fags across the street."

"The ones doing the dog fights? How?"

"One of them injected him with something. I thought nothing of it at the time, but it's the only explanation."

"He… he was kinda up there in dog years, Nate," Sean said. Nate gave him a hard look.

"Number eight! Kelvin!" The cashier yelled from the counter.

Sean took that moment to get up and get the pizzas. He brought everything back to their table. Nate opened the top of the box and inhaled the scent of an extra-large stuffed-crust pizza with pepperoni, black olives, and green peppers.

"It's been a long time, my old friend…" he picked up a slice and placed it on his plate.

"Ugh," Sean grunted. "All you need is some mushrooms on that, and you'd be a ninja turtle."

Nate held out his hand and Sean pulled out a pair of plastic utensils. "You're the only person I know who eats pizza with a knife and fork," Sean said, handing them to Nate.

"I'm from Chicago. Old habits die hard," he replied with a shrug. He began cutting the piece in half, then made two vertical cuts for six square pieces. With the fork, he picked a square and held it up to his nose.

"You have *any* idea how long it's been, man?"

"Let me guess… March 18th, 2006, right? The day you told Cynthia you were having the surgery." Sean said.

Nate nodded. "She was *soooo* angry that day, one of the rare instances that I yelled at her, that we yelled at each other. She thought it was a mistake, that I could die, that we could lose the weight together…"

"So, you left, came to my place, where we ordered like $40.00 worth of pizza and breadsticks… then ordered a six-hour block of the Playboy channel. Which you still owe me for, by the way."

Nate was finally starting to feel better and he laughed while chewing. "God, I wish they served beer here."

"Got you covered." Sean pulled a flask from his jacket and passed it to him.

"You are the man!" Nate grabbed it and took a swig.

Sean helped himself to a slice, taking off the toppings then folding it in half and taking a bite at the front end. Eating pizza like a true New Yorker. "You know you're not supposed to be eating and drinking at the same time."

"I'm only eating two slices," Nate replied.

"Yeah, okay." Sean rolled his eyes.

"Hey, remember when I found my place and had to wait until the first of the month to move in and my cousins brought Brutus up early? I brought him to your place, and you said…"

"Oh, hell no!" they said in unison, followed by laughter.

"Yeah, that was a looooong weekend. In 48 hours, he managed to knock over my garbage can, gnaw on my ottoman, and destroy my toilet paper dispenser."

"You said I should have named him 'Beethoven,'" Nate said, smiling at the memory. He took another swig from the flask.

"He was a good dog, Nate. He lived a great life," Sean said.

"Yeah," he raised his fork. "To Brutus…"

"To Brutus." Sean held up his slice.

They both howled and barked like dogs. Nate was drawing attention to himself, being a bit louder than Sean. "C'mon, bark louder than that!" he encouraged. "Bark like DMX, nigga!" he started to giggle and then caught himself, sobering up.

"Did I just say the N-word?" Nate asked quickly with a straight face.

"Yes, yes you did," Sean said, deadpanned.

"Did I say it the right way, like Denzel Washington?"

"Yes."

"Are you cool with it?"

"No, because you're embarrassing yourself."

"Oh… tha… that's my bad," he whispered.

Sean looked at him.

"Did I just say 'my bad?'"

"Yes."

"Are you cool with it?"

"No. You're still embarrassing yourself."

Nate's eyes darted left and right a few times, "Sorry."

"That's much better," Sean said, with a nod.

They continued to finish the rest of the pizza in awkward silence, then Sean smiled and said, "You should get another dog and name him 'Popeye.'"

Vanessa was finally asleep in the spare bedroom as Cynthia opened a bottle of Black Cordon Chardonnay. She needed answers from her parents. Cynthia decided to try her mother again, picking up the phone and pressing the redial button.

"Hello?"

"Oh, finally, mom. I've been calling all afternoon, where have you been?" Cynthia asked.

"How are you calling *me* asking where have I been, young lady? I have a life, you know."

"Sorry." *Excuse me!* she thought. "It's just that Vanessa came here all hysterical and making no sense, so I let her sleep it off. What happened?"

"You'll have to get the story from her. Your father and I have been enjoying having the house to ourselves for the first time in several years."

Cynthia's eyes went wide. "What's *that* supposed to mean?" She then figured it out and her mouth dropped. "You mean…? Oh my God, gross! Mom!"

"What? We're two consenting adults alone in this big ass house. You know damn well we're going to do it in every room…"

She winced at the imagery in her head. "Mom, stop! My ears! Can you put Daddy on the phone then so I can ask *him* what happened?"

Barbara let out a sultry sigh. "I'm sorry, he's getting his second wind. You know he's not the war horse he was in the 60s… there was a time he had the stamina of Jack Nicholson in *The Postman Always Rings Twice…*"

"Oh my God, I'll call back later!" She hung up the phone and fought several urges to gag.

Sean opened the door to his apartment and stepped in, carrying Nate's arm around his shoulders. Nate staggered next to him on legs of jelly.

"You sure your car will be safe out there in Queens all night?" Sean asked.

"Tomorrow's Labor Day. Alternate side of the street parking is suspended," Nate replied. Sean let go of his arm and he collapsed on the couch in the living room.

"Holy shit! After twelve years you still got this same couch?"

Sean lived in one of the last few rent-controlled apartment buildings in the lower east side. When Nate first stayed with Sean, the rent for the two-bedroom apartment was $1,200.00, which he split between him and a pair of brothers who slept on bunk beds in the second bedroom.

"You still doing *Three's Company* with the two brothers going to med school?" Nate asked while feeling around the familiar couch.

Sean shook his head. "Nah, I only have *one* roommate now."

As if on cue, the door to one of the bedrooms opened and a short African American woman walked out. She was wearing a cut-off top, with biker sweat shorts that appeared painted on, over her wide waist and huge derriere.

"I know I must be drunk because I just imagined Lil' Kim walking through your living room here."

Sean smiled. "That's Jade. She's Japanese and Black mixed. Slanted eyes, with tits and ass for days."

"Tiger Woods don't got shit against her… goddamn! You and her…?" He made an obscene finger gesture.

"We have an understanding. We have sex with each other, but neither catches any feelings."

"What a time to be alive." Nate giggled incoherently.

"Okay, I'm calling Cynthia to let her know you're crashing here tonight. How's your stomach?"

"I… might destroy your bathroom… please tell me you still don't have that damn yellow toilet seat."

Sean was about to answer, but Jade came out of the kitchen and gave him a sly look as she walked by, returning to her room. She left her door open this time.

"Ah, um…" He picked up his phone and started dialing with some urgency. "Let me make that call already…"

Sean stole a glance at Jade's door, not missing her implied signal.

It was late in the evening and Cynthia was starting to worry about Nate when the phone rang.

She walked over and answered. "Hello?"

"Hey Cyn, it's Sean. Nate's at my place. He parked the car out in Queens. He's a bit twisted about Brutus, got himself drunk off his ass."

"Awww shit, really Sean?"

"Yeah, so he's sleeping it off here. When he wakes up tomorrow, I'll send him home, okay?"

Cynthia was furious. Nate rarely drank to the point of getting sloppy drunk. Without his stomach to slowly absorb alcohol, two drinks of champagne can get him tipsy.

"Let me speak to him! You two better not be at some whorehouse or strip club!"

"Cyn, it's not like that. You want to speak to him? Fine, here he is."

A second went by and then Nate got on the phone. "Honey, I'm in no condition to drive."

"Let me send an Uber there to pick you up."

"Nah, nah, nah, naaaaah… see you in the morning, love you!" He hung up the phone.

"Shit!"

"Cyn…?" a voice called out.

Vanessa came down the hallway barefoot, wearing an over-sized tee-shirt that Nate had from when he was bigger.

"I'm starving. Got anything to eat?" she asked. Cynthia just looked at her.

"It's 7 pm, the kitchen is closed," Cynthia said flatly, while crossing her arms.

The sisters exchanged glances for a minute then Cynthia asked, "So, what did you do this time?"

After looking around, Vanessa countered with a question of her own. "Where's Nate?"

With a long sigh, Cynthia explained everything with Brutus passing and Nate storming out. Two hours later, Vanessa was finishing a pint of Chinese food that was ordered while Cynthia drained a bottle of Shiraz. The television had an episode of *Law and Order: Special Victims Unit* on.

"That car had only six miles, Van. What were you thinking?"

"You know," she began, slamming down the carton on the table. "I'm sick of everyone asking me that!"

Cynthia stared at her sister, while taking another sip of her wine.

Vanessa shook her head, "I… I fucked up, Cyn. I've done some shit in the past, yeah… but now I'm crashing and burn-ing… like Reese Witherspoon during that traffic stop."

She heard a light chuckle from Cynthia and gave her a hard look.

"I'm laughing at the Reese thing, not you!"

"Really? What the fuck? How about some sympathy, please?"

"Oh, come on, don't act like shit's all a bed of roses on *this* side of the grass! In case you haven't noticed, I—"

"I know, I know…" Vanessa interrupted. "But…" She thought about it for a moment. *Should I really tell her?*

Cynthia stood up and walked around the table, she knelt and looked at her face to face, "Whatever it is," she began, "you can overcome it. I know you can."

She did the exact same thing when she was scared to tell their parents she dropped out of college, then after the meltdown on the air. The sisters had always been there for each other. Yes, there were secrets between them and for tonight, the abortion would remain one of them. Vanessa hugged her sister as a tear fell down her cheek, then noticed that Cynthia was snoring, and she frowned.

# 11

## WHY SETTLE FOR PIZZA, WHEN YOU CAN HAVE PIZZA AND FRIES?

NATE WOKE UP THE NEXT MORNING WITH A SERIOUS CASE OF cottonmouth and a hangover. He sat up from the couch and sprang up, looking around. That was a mistake because vertigo kicked in. He was brought out of his dizzy spell by sounds coming from one of the bedrooms.

Sean and Jade were enjoying each other's company as Nate checked a clock on the wall that read eight thirty-seven. Jade was screaming in Japanese between grunts and pants of pleasure from Sean. Nate nodded with approval and whispered, "Damn."

He grabbed his jacket and left a note of congratulations while also apologizing for drinking the last of Sean's orange juice, which he used to wash his mouth. After 20 minutes on the train, he was back in Queens where he left the Tahoe. He climbed inside and thought about calling Cynthia.

*It might be too early, wouldn't wanna wake her up... and what if Vanessa is still there?*

Nate shook his head and started the engine, then pulled out into traffic, heading back to Brooklyn.

The door slowly opened as Nate peeked his head in and tiptoed into the living room. The television was still on, now showing a holiday edition of The Today Show. On the couch, he saw a hand resting on the top of a blanket that was draped over a female figure sleeping on the couch.

"Cynthia?" he asked.

A long, nonverbal grunt was the only reply.

*She must have been too tired after Vanessa left to go upstairs.* He thought.

The blanket started to stir as Nate took a seat next to her and then pressed the top half down gently, "No, no, no… stay here, baby." he started stroking her shoulders, with the blanket still over her head. "I… I wanna apologize for before, Cyn."

There was another grunt of approval.

"Huh?" he asked.

"I… I killed the baby… my baby," she said.

"No, noooo," he soothed. "You didn't know." he moved down from her shoulders to what he believed was her back, petting her like a rabbit.

"I never knew you considered him *your* baby, thought you felt he was a package deal that came with me." He leaned down, hovering right over her head, with his hand moving all the way down for a cup of her ass. "Maybe we can get another *baby* from the shelter, together this time," he whispered.

That was when *Vanessa* shot from underneath the blanket and screamed, "ANOTHER BABY?!"

Nate jumped out of his skin and went flying off the couch. "Fuck!? Van?!"

"What *other* baby!? Who's fucking Van?! What, what,

what?!" Cynthia screamed from the top of the stairs, stomping her way down.

"Did you touch my ass?!" Vanessa yelled.

"Huh! Wha… WHAT?" Nate stammered.

"Answer the question!" Cynthia demanded.

Nate's head kept looking from the stairs to the couch as both sisters converged on him. "I… I… I thought it was *you* on the couch, Cyn!"

Cynthia folded her arms. "Why don't you go upstairs for a shower and change of clothes?"

"You talking to *me* or *him*?!" Vanessa asked while covering herself, still wearing the oversized shirt from last night.

Annoyed at being given an order, Nate went on the defensive and pointed. "You wanna tell me first why the hell *she's* still here?"

"Hey!" Vanessa yelled, feeling insulted.

"Dad threw her out of the house, she's staying here—"

"Whoa, whoa, whooooooooa!" he interrupted. "The hell she is!"

Vanessa sidestepped past the couple and headed down the hallway to the back of the house. "I'll leave you two to talk it out…" when she passed the stairs she called back, "I hope one of y'all start breakfast!"

The couple waited until she was gone, and they heard the door slam shut before they started talking at the same time.

"She is NOT staying here!" Nate insisted.

"*Yes,* she is!"

They stared each other down, then Nate said, "Two days."

"A week," Cynthia countered.

He let out a sigh. "I'm being generous here. Three days."

Cynthia folded her arms once again. "So am I. Five days." Nate shook his head.

"I'm not budging, Nate, she's staying for at least—"

"Okay, hold on," he interrupted. "You've had a rough couple

of days, especially with your job search. I realize you're frustrated."

Cynthia remained silent and just glared, waiting for him to continue. Nate figured the only way out of this argument was to offer something *else* as a distraction.

"I have a few jobs coming up… why don't you tag along for some of them and see how it feels to do freelance work?"

She made a face, wondering what did one thing have to do with the other? But if hanging with him will make Vanessa stay for a few days…

"Okay," Cynthia nodded. "Vanessa stays for three days, and I'll follow you around, watching you do whatever you're doing. We splitting the money?"

"Sure, wouldn't have it any other way."

She smiled and they shook on the agreement. He then pulled her close and gave her a peck on her cheek.

"Thank you for understanding. I'll keep her out of your hair," she said.

"*Yes,* you will."

Cynthia gave him a pinch on his arm. "Go on upstairs and wash up. I'll have breakfast done for *all* of us in forty-five minutes."

Nate turned and started up the stairs while she walked to the kitchen.

The Goss sisters left the house at noon. Cynthia didn't say, but if Nate knew his wife, he figured she would be helping her sister cope with some retail therapy. Something he didn't want to dwell on.

His stomach had been wreaking havoc on him since breakfast. Clearly, a result of his indulgence yesterday. He had irritated his pouch and suffered a serious case of the foamies, followed by more dumping after a previous bout at Sean's place.

His phone rang and he rolled his eyes, not wanting any business calls over the Labor Day weekend. Luckily, the caller ID showed Sean's phone number, so he answered it.

"How's it going, Wesley Pipes? You done laying Miss Lil' Kim out?"

Sean laughed. "We weren't too loud, were we?"

"They could hear you two in Albany! What's up?"

"Just checking in on you. How'd it go this morning? Cynthia waiting with a rolling pin and curlers in her hair?"

"I should be so lucky."

After Nate brought Sean up to date about the chaos that morning, his friend was at a loss for words.

"So, what the hell do I do, man?" Nate asked.

"You, my friend, have a rare opportunity to take advantage of…"

"Meaning?"

"Sisters have no problem *sharing* a guy… if you play your cards right."

"Get the fuck outta here!" Nate screamed. "You obviously don't know *these* two sisters, or me for that matter! It's hard enough to deal with one woman, why would I try to please two!?"

Sean laughed. "Why settle for pizza when you can have pizza *and* fries?"

Nate winced and looked at his phone in disgust. "I'm hanging up now. Not even when I was fat was I *that* damn gluttonous! With that type of thinking, I'm seeing a lot of trips to the Maury show in your future!" He ended the call and tossed his smartphone on the couch.

After surveying the living room in silence, he sighed. The place wasn't the same without Brutus around. He could feel himself getting choked up over a favorite memory and quickly went to the computer to occupy his mind. Since he wasn't doing any photography or reporting gigs, Nate decided to open his latest novel draft and give it a quick read.

*The Librarios* was originally a pitched skit while Nate was interning on Saturday Night Live. After multiple rejections, he played with the idea of making a treatment and proposing a comedy series for television, in the likes of *3rd Rock from The Sun*. He eventually sat on the project for a few years to improve his writing and then decided to turn it into a book.

His manuscript was becoming quite long, and he was stuck at the end of the second act. A notification on Facebook popped up on the screen with an Instant Message.

@StephanieSymphony: "Hey, shoot any oxen lately?"

A smile came over his face as he typed a reply.

@NatefromNewYork: "Yeah, shot over 3,000 pounds of meat but was only able to carry 200 pounds back to camp."

@StephanieSymphony: "Didn't that always suck? How are ya holding up?"

@NatefromNewYork: "Sister-in-Law is crashing with us. I've eaten and thrown up more pizza than all the ninja turtles combined, oh and everyone is having sex except me... living the dream."

@StephanieSymphony: "Well, ain't that the truth? I had a hell of a weekend with Heathcliff the weekend before this one. I'm finally getting the sensation back on my nipples as I type this."

> @NatefromNewYork: "Oh gee, thanks for rubbing it in."

> @StephanieSymphony: "He did more than rub it in 😊"

Nate pouted as he let a minute go by without responding.

> @StephanieSymphony: "Okay, I guess that was over the top, sorry… I forgot how sensitive you were."

He narrowed his eyes and then quickly typed…

> @NatefromNewYork: "Yeah, and sensitive guys aren't your type if memory serves me."

*Take that, you condescending bitch!*

There was no reply, not even after Nate resumed checking his manuscript. The exchange was over as quickly as it began. He seriously contemplated unfriending her for the second time in a month, to make a clean break. It was obvious old feelings were presenting themselves and he didn't need any additional stress.

It was nice catching up and solving the mystery of the picture from Tumblr, but Stephanie was someone he had put out of his mind (and heart) for a reason. He was playing with fire, and it was time to put it out.

"Damn girl! I forgot how tall you were, Gloria!" Vanessa yelled. "It's been a while since sis brought me along to hang with you and Jennifer. You're a mountain!"

Gloria rolled her eyes when hearing Cynthia's immature

sister cackle at the observation. "Gee, I wonder why," she replied dryly.

The four women were spending the holiday off across the river at the Newport Centre Mall. Cynthia went to Forever 21 but soon discovered that Century 21 was much better, honestly believing that the stores were connected somehow.

Her friends and even her sister found the mistake hysterical, attributing it to having a *Dumb Blonde* moment, which upset her slightly. She was tired of being the butt of their jokes, but they were the only friends she had, so she continued to take the abuse.

"Who wants to check out a movie? My treat!" Jennifer suggested.

They were sitting in the food court finishing a light lunch with some drinks, with shopping bags surrounding their legs.

"There's really nothing out I wanna see," Cynthia pouted.

"I'm going to the bathroom, be right back!" Vanessa stood by and excused herself.

When she was out of earshot Gloria hissed, "Let's ditch the little snot at that *One Direction* movie and head back to the city!"

"Oh, stop it. She's just overly emotional, after Daddy kicked her out of the house. I gotta find a way to get them to take her back."

"Better do it fast, Cyn… I wouldn't put it past her to make a move on Nate." Gloria said, followed by Jennifer agreeing. "Yeah, another woman in the house always adds up to trouble."

"Please, Nate and Vanessa are like oil and water."

"Correct me if I'm wrong, but doesn't oil float *on top* of water?" Gloria asked. "You got a Mayflower Oil spill situation, girl!"

Cynthia had finally had enough of their snide remarks. "Shut up! I won't hear any more of this!" she snapped at her laughing friends. "Triflin' bitches, always trying to fuck with my head. I'm sick of this shit!" She stood up and grabbed her bags. Vanessa came back just in time as Cynthia waved her in the opposite direction, storming off and leaving Jennifer and Gloria open-mouthed in shock.

"Damn, what the hell we gonna do, now?" Jennifer asked, "She was our Uber out here."

"What happened while I was gone back there?" Vanessa asked her sister.

They were riding the escalator down to the first floor and toward the exits.

"Nothing, this mall is a great spot, and they have condo apartments nearby." She nodded and asked, "Wanna check 'em out?"

She hoped this change in the subject would distract Vanessa from noticing how pissed she was at her so-called friends.

"What makes you think I can afford to live out here?"

"Mom and dad will pay for it, just to keep you out of their hair. It's time you lived out on your own again, Vanessa."

They walked off the escalator and through the exit.

"And besides," Cynthia added. "I just might want to check this place out for us."

"Right, like you and Nate would ever sell your place and leave Brooklyn!" Vanessa scoffed.

The walk was a quick two blocks east. They walked into the lobby and found the rental office. It took a few minutes to get the attention of the building manager, who looked like a cross between Antonio Sabáto Junior and John Leguizamo.

"May I help you?" he asked, with a condescending tone.

"Yes, um, my sister and I were wondering if you had any vacancies and if we could check one out."

He snorted and smiled. "Normally you would have to *schedule* a tour of our condos…"

Cynthia opened her purse and flashed a hundred-dollar bill in front of the building manager.

"…but I believe we can squeeze you in for a tour in about ten minutes." He took the bill and pocketed it. "Please wait here," he instructed with a pleasant smile.

They walked over to a couch and waited.

"Cyn, I really don't wanna waste this guy's time," Vanessa said, with some apprehension.

"It'll be quick, don't worry."

"What if there's an application fee?"

Cynthia turned to her. "You just wanna stay with me," she said, with a grin.

"No, I don't wanna be in over my head. Let's wait until I have an actual job before committing to a place like—"

"Relax, you'll find something, you always do…"

"Um, we're ready for you now." The building manager called out.

They stood and followed him to the nearby elevators.

Nate was downstairs in his man cave playing Tomb Raider. He was less than impressed with the new reboot of the franchise, having played the original PC version in 1996 during his first data entry temp assignments for Adecco.

It was a few minutes after ten o'clock at night when Vanessa carefully climbed down the steps into the room. "Knock, knock!" she announced herself.

Nate was still focused on playing, he didn't even turn his

head to acknowledge her. "Shouldn't you be sleeping… upstairs?"

"I heard you got a setup down here and I could use a drink."

"Bars at the left wall, help yourself," he said.

"Thanks."

He didn't know it, but she was already drunk, having raided Cynthia's stash of red wines in the kitchen. Nate was a social drinker since the surgery but had an impressive collection of vodkas and whiskey that would make James Bond jealous. After several minutes, and drinks later, Vanessa called out to Nate.

"Hey, Nate?"

"Yeah?"

"You and Cynthia ever wanna have kids?"

Still not turning to talk to her, he replied, "We thought about it those first couple of years, but we were both too big then."

"How about now? Are y'all careful or you leaving it up to fate? I'm sure y'all ain't stop trying, have y'all had any scares yet?"

The subject was getting personal, but he was focusing on the game.

"There was this one time," he started. "She didn't have her period for two months… but we took a couple of pregnancy tests and got checked. It was a false alarm."

He completed the level and paused his game, raising an eyebrow. "This wouldn't be about that remark you said before, would it?"

Nate remembered the 'killing my baby' remark, but didn't say anything, keeping it to himself. He suddenly heard sounds of her sobbing and turned to the bar to see Vanessa holding a bottle of Jack Daniels and hysterically crying… she was also naked as a Rodin statue!

"I… I… I had to do it!" she blurted out. "I couldn't take care of a baby! With no job, no home, no future!"

"Vanessa, what the fuck?! Put some clothes on!" Nate gasped.

She came from around the bar, holding her stomach. "There was a human being inside me, and I killed it!!" She was screaming at the top of her lungs now.

"It… it wasn't a baby yet, it was the size of a dot, calm down! Keep your voice down! Did you tell Cynthia?"

Nate searched his room for a blanket or any type of clothing to cover her up. He couldn't help to notice, Vanessa *wasn't* a natural redhead.

She wrapped her arms around him, burying her face into his chest. "It was STILL A LIFE!!! And I snuffed it out like a candle in the wind! Oh my God! Princess Di!" She held on, babbling incoherently.

*What is going on?* Nate asked himself. The situation couldn't possibly get any worse.

"Nate!!! What's going on down there?" Cynthia yelled from upstairs.

"Oh shit!" he hissed. Apparently, it could get a lot worse.

He started wiggling around, trying to get loose. For a woman, Vanessa had a strong grip, especially when she was losing her mind.

"Let go! Vanessa let me go! C'mon! Calm the fuck down!"

He heard footsteps from the ceiling above and started to panic.

Vanessa lifted her head suddenly. "Kiss me!"

"What?!"

"Kiss me and I'll let you go!"

"You're insane!" He heard the steps moving towards the staircase and then nodded. "Alright, alright! I'll kiss you!"

She closed her eyes and pouted her lips. Nate cocked his head back and slammed his forehead into hers with a shattering headbutt. Her arms went limp, and she collapsed in front of him. He turned in time to see Cynthia step downstairs into the room.

"Nate?!"

He stood in the middle of the room with her naked sister out cold on the floor in front of him.

"Um, yeah… uh, apparently your sister has this thing where she sleepwalks, um, naked. I think she needs to get that checked out."

Cynthia narrowed her eyes and just stared at him.

## 12

## SORRY

THE KNITTING FACTORY WAS A SMALL PERFORMANCE VENUE
that held a stage and restaurant. Once a chain with multiple locations, it first opened in Manhattan, then Idaho, Washington, Los
Angeles, and then Reno. The current New York location was in
Brooklyn on Metropolitan Avenue. It was an intimate setting,
known to host upcoming artists doing music, poetry, comedy,
and other independent performance art.

Nate flashed his credentials and maneuvered through the
crowd as he came in. He looked around and found Pete from
Hot97 waving him over.

"Hey, thanks for getting me in," Nate greeted.

"Almost thought you were gonna chicken out, man."

"Well, actually, I almost did until Pitchfork offered $100.00
for an article covering .38 Special's listening party. It's got to be
750 words, but I think I can swing it. This is my first gig after
lying low for a couple of weeks."

"Hey, yeah, I heard about your dog, man. That's tough, I'd
take off too if my Yogi died." Pete owned a German Shepherd
named Yogi and gave the puppy his own Twitter account.

It was nearly seven o'clock when the rapper's DJ and

producer stepped on the stage and hyped up the crowd with a loud introduction. Nate was new to the current Hip-Hop scene and didn't have enough music knowledge as a full-fledged critic, but he was good at reading an audience and figured he could ask around for any additional information he needed for the article.

The rapper stepped on stage wearing an inaugural Brooklyn Nets basketball jersey and black acid-wash jeans.

"Kid thinks he's Jay-Z!" Nate scoffed to Pete, recognizing the look.

In front of the pair, a man wearing a hooded sweater with the rapper's logo across the chest turned and stared back at them. "Yo, is there a problem?!" he asked.

"Uh, nah, we cool man, we cool," Peter assured him, with a friendly wave.

Nate raised his brow and gave the radio personality a questionable glance.

"Keep your observations to yourself until you're behind that laptop, man. .38's entourage can be in the crowd ready to set it off," Pete warned.

Nate rolled his eyes but didn't reply, trying to make sense of what he was listening to. The music was very generic, using autotune effects and ringtone beats. The rapper's delivery was less than impressive as he went on and on about clothing brands, expensive cars, jewelry, and having sex with women.

*At least he's not talking about drugs or glorifying violence.*

He looked around and noticed the audience was enjoying the music, but not emotionally driven by it. After the first few songs, Pete turned and asked him, "Not feeling it, huh?"

With a shrug, Nate replied, "It's okay. I guess I'm from a different generation."

Pete agreed with a nod. "Yeah, it used to be about rhyme schemes and storytelling, a message… now, all you need is a good beat, a hook, and the ability to talk about nothing."

They took a break and the crowd responded with a light half-hearted applause.

"I'm heading out. I got all I need for my article," Nate said.

"You sure? What about his new stuff?"

"What, there's *more*? Hey, it's Pitchfork, not Rolling Stone! I'll be alright."

As soon as he turned towards the exit, Nate came face to face with .38 Special himself. Up close, the artist looked younger. He couldn't be older than twenty. Next to him was the guy in the sweater who overheard his comments. Nate turned around looking for Pete, who was nowhere to be found. Two more men approached and stood their ground, confining him in place.

"Uh," Nate let out.

"My man tells me you ain't feelin' my tracks."

With a grin, Nate turned and looked around again. "Um, judging by the crowd, I don't think I'm the only one."

The two men behind him exchanged glances, but the rapper didn't seem phased. "They just gotta warm up. Most of that stuff I just did be from my EP. It ain't been circulated around too well."

"Ah."

"Yeah, my mainstream stuff is coming up. Stick around, you'll be feelin' it in no time."

Nate smiled and nodded. "I'll uh, take your word for it."

The rapper stared down at him after that statement, then walked away.

Nate tried to move towards the exit again when one of the three men stepped in front of him, shaking his head. He narrowed his gaze, sizing the man up and down, then turned back towards the stage.

Cynthia was having dinner with her parents at Natalie's, an Italian restaurant on the east side of midtown Manhattan. The elderly couple appeared in high spirits, which was the first time in years. Smiling, holding hands, feeding each other, and various public displays of affection.

They ordered dessert and Cynthia figured it was time to plead her case, while they were in a good mood. "It's great to get together and talk, eat and—"

"We're not letting Vanessa come back. Pass the chocolate cake, please," Christopher quickly interrupted.

"Daddy, please. She promises to never do anything like this again."

"I'm sorry, honey," Barbara chimed in. "Things have been so peaceful now."

"I scored three contracts thanks to that assemblywoman's endorsement from the picnic. My mind's been more focused, and I think I can finally turn things around," Christopher said, leaning in and rubbing his hands.

"But what is Vanessa expected to do for the rest of her life?" Cynthia asked.

Her parents looked at each other, then turned together and said, "Grow up!"

"We can send her money once she finds a job and a place to stay, but we are through dealing with her shit!" Christopher spat.

"But—"

"End of discussion, dearie." her mother concluded.

They rose to leave while their cake was put in a doggie bag by the waiter as Christopher paid the check and left the tip.

Cynthia was still sitting, looking up in awe, her eyes pleading with her parents.

Her plea fell on blind eyes as the couple took off towards the exit.

The vibration from her smartphone from her purse snapped her back to reality. She left her half-eaten meal at the table and left. When she walked outside, Cynthia checked her phone. It was another text from Jennifer, apologizing for the umpteenth time in two weeks since their fallout at the mall.

She thought about deleting the message, but with this setback with her parents and Vanessa waiting for her at home… she needed *someone else* to talk to. Nate would be back from some concert he was attending at ten.

*Fuck it.* She finally decided to forgive them and texted her back.

A half-hour later, Cynthia walked into Jennifer's apartment, located at 155th Street off Broadway. Gloria was sitting on a couch as Jennifer held up two wine glasses, handing one to Cynthia as a peace offering.

Gloria jumped up first. "Girl, I just wanna say I'm sorry. I was out of line… I've been so bitchy because I haven't got any dick lately."

She wanted to stay angry at her, but smiled instead. "Please, you got no problems in that department, but I forgive you."

The wine was subpar, but it got the conversation flowing. They decided to binge-watch a few episodes of the new Netflix comedy *Orange Is the New Black*.

"This show's pretty good!" Gloria said. "I like that girl Taystee… she reminds me of me."

"Yeah, I think I relate to Piper… would you be my Alex, Cyn?"

"Hell no! I ain't going to jail and if I did, I ain't nobody's bitch!"

They all laughed and refreshed their drinks, Gloria then said, "Tell me that crazy sister is out of your house now so we can go back to hanging out."

Cynthia groaned. "Ugh, I just came back from dinner with Mom and Dad. They weren't hearing it, so I'm stuck with her."

There were disappointed sighs all around the room.

"And things are getting… creepier. She's been acting funny around Nate."

Jennifer turned around and gave Gloria a hidden hand signal to change the subject, but she ignored her and asked, "Acting funny how?"

Jennifer rolled her eyes as Cynthia began to recap the incident in the man cave while they drank more wine.

"Sleepwalking my ass! She butt naked in the room and drunk? She was definitely making a move!" Gloria agreed.

"But Nate had all his clothes on, and was playing his video game. I think she snuck up on him!" Jennifer defended. "You shouldn't let your imagination trick you into something that's not happening. Nate's a good guy."

Cynthia finished her glass. "I know, I know. But Vanessa's got to go. It's time to break it to her and get down to what's going on with her and Nate."

Nate always liked writing at night. That special hour before and after midnight. He called it "The inspiration wormhole." When, if your mind was clear and at peace, ideas would come out of your head like a runabout emerging from the Bajoran Wormhole on the television show *Star Trek: Deep Space Nine.*

He was sitting at his desk, putting the finishing touches on his article about the listening party. It wasn't too scathing, but based on what he heard tonight, he was positive the young rapper's career wouldn't be very long.

An email notification popped up on his mail app that caught his attention. With a click of the mouse, a new window opened with a message from the file-hosting cloud service, Dropbox. A media file has been uploaded and shared with him, with private access only from the link enclosed. Nate immediately assumed it was spam or a virus and nearly discarded it, but the file name made him pause. It was one word, "Sorry.avi".

*Was this from Stephanie?*

He checked the sender's email and confirmed it was from Dropbox and not a phishing email then clicked on the link. A new window opened with a media player webpage. A screen capture of Stephanie standing in her living room, similar to those on her YouTube channel appeared. Nate rolled his eyes and clicked play.

The video started with Stephanie speaking to the camera, "Hey, Nate... kinda noticed we haven't been chatting on Facebook lately. I think I was out of line during our last conversation, and I just want to say I'm sorry... I hope we can still be friends online. Hopefully, this song will convince you to reach out and accept my apology."

Nate half-expected her to break into a rendition of Brenda Lee's "I'm Sorry." But instead, she performed "We Are Young." By Fun. He couldn't help but smile because she was very talented. After the song, she took a bow, and he knitted his eyebrows when he noticed there were still six minutes left to the end of the video.

Stephanie looked up at the camera. There was a sinister

smirk on her face, "Still watching?" she asked, letting out a giggle.

"What the…" Nate whispered.

"Ohhh, I hope you still are…" she said, and proceeded to slip off her top, revealing her ample, natural breasts. Nate's jaw nearly dislocated and his eyes grew big as saucers. His entire body froze. He willed himself to turn away or turn off his computer, but his gaze never left the screen. Stephanie stripped off all her clothes and pulled out a long purple dildo, then sat down in a chair and began to masturbate.

He said nothing as he watched, then played the video again from the end of the song a second time, then a third time. Ten minutes later, a Facebook Message notification popped up on his screen.

@StephanieSymphony: "Hey, is your tongue on the floor, yet?"

He gathered his composure and started typing.

@NatefromNewYork: "First off, not only is my tongue on the floor, my jaw is too! Second, I AM a married man, woman!"

@StephanieSymphony: "Oh c'mon, you said you take pictures for adult websites. I'm sure you've seen that kind of stuff before!"

*Cotton Candi got nothing on her!* he thought.

@StephanieSymphony: "And you saw that picture on Tumblr, so don't act like you haven't seen me in all my glory!"

*Glory indeed.*

@StephanieSymphony: "Look, we're both
consenting adults, and we go way back… two
fat nerds at the top of our pop culture game.
Quoting movies, playing video games, and
being smart-asses. I miss those days and I
want to keep in touch, maybe even hang out
one day if you ever come out here…"

Nate was surprised by this outpouring of emotion. "Is she serious?" he asked himself.

@StephanieSymphony: "So… we cool?"

He let a minute go by before replying.

@NatefromNewYork: "Yeah, we cool… but
never do this again. I'm serious!"

@StephanieSymphony: "You have my word…
so what's your latest assignment? Catch
me up."

@NatefromNewYork: "I've been on break
actually, mourning Brutus. Tonight I did a
listening party article for this upcoming rapper,
.38 Special."

@StephanieSymphony: "Hmm, never heard of
him."

@NatefromNewYork: "And you probably never
will."

They went back and forth until four o'clock in the morning, then said their goodbyes. Nate saved Stephanie's video on his cloud server in a password-locked folder, then erased the email and emptied the trash. After logging off, he stood up and noticed he was rock hard with a serious erection.

Cynthia had enough. She woke up Friday morning at four and started cooking an extravagant breakfast with baked vegetables, a protein shake, and several other healthy dishes. Two hours later, Vanessa and Nate made their way to the table with puzzled looks.

"Baby, what's all this? What's going on?" Nate asked first.

"Yeah, wha—" Vanessa began.

"Sit down, both of you… now!" Cynthia barked. "We're having breakfast and getting to the bottom of this."

Nate looked behind him, wondering who she was talking to. "Um, can I wash up first?"

"Nope, the two of you have been acting funny and it's time to cut the bullshit."

Vanessa darted her eyes back and forth. "Cynthia," she began again.

"Mom and Dad aren't letting you back home, Van… so if you want me to help you find a place to live today, you will *sit your ass* down."

Nate squinted, but he was familiar with this tone from ten years of marital experience, so he sat down at the table, followed by Vanessa.

Cynthia put their plates of food in front of them and then took a seat at the head of the table. She sipped on her shake and said, "Start talking."

Nate and Vanessa exchanged glances.

"Am I speaking in Portuguese?" she asked, spreading her hands apart.

Nate sighed and was about to say something when Vanessa cut him off. "I had an abortion," she stated flatly. "That's why I took Daddy's car. I couldn't bring myself to become a mother. I didn't want to have it adopted. I had no choice but to kill the life inside me."

She began to cry after the speech. Nate turned to Cynthia, who began crying as well. "Oh, Van… I'm so sorry." She stood up and hugged her sister. They took a moment to wipe their faces, then Cynthia looked at Nate coldly.

"What?!" he gasped.

"Was it yours?" she hissed.

*Don't yell, whatever you do, don't yell…*

Vanessa pulled away from her sister in shock, while Nate closed his eyes to contain his rage. "What?" he did a double take. "Cyn… I… Jesus, Cynthia, she's nearly fifteen years my junior, how crazy would that be? Are you actually serious?"

"Cyn," Vanessa whispered, Cynthia put her finger up, demanding silence.

He fought all his anger to stay calm, while flabbergasted. "For you to even *think*… to ask me, outright… after ten…" he turned away for a moment, then turned back. "No, Cynthia, it wasn't mine, I have never had sex with your sister. She's an emotional mess, who got drunk while naked, and told me she killed her baby."

He left out the blackmail for a kiss because it wouldn't help how hurt he was feeling.

Cynthia heard through his tone how outraged he was and immediately felt guilty, then Vanessa said, "Child, I would *never* sleep with Nate," and scoffed. "What kind of woman do you think I am?"

Cynthia looked at Vanessa and then turned back to Nate with an apologetic look, she then looked down as Nate let out a breath.

"Well, I'm glad we got *that* settled. Vanessa, can you give us a moment, please?" Nate asked sharply.

Vanessa looked at her sister, then stood up and headed to the guest bedroom. Once they were alone, Nate folded his arms. Now it was time for him to get some answers.

"Nate I'm sor—"

"Are you using cocaine?" he interrupted deadpanned.

She gasped at the question. "What?!"

"The nosebleeds, spending all this money, and now these goddamn paranoid delusions…" he ticked off with his fingers.

"How dare you?! I have a right to be paranoid about the way you've been acting…"

He stood up. "I have never given you *any* indication I was doing anything other than what you have been seeing me do."

"Oh yeah?! Then who the fuck is Stephanie?"

Nate didn't even flinch. He had been careful, but Cynthia must have been snooping, "An amateur singer I was asked to interview for a music blog. I watched a few of her YouTube clips for research."

Inside his head, he was screaming.

"After all this time, everything I do… and you still haven't answered my question," he said, while pointing at her.

"I'll piss in a cup right now! No, Nate, I am not using cocaine! Or any other drugs, for that matter!"

"Then neither of us has anything to hide, but I really think it'll help the situation if Vanessa's not here by the time I come back home." He stormed downstairs to his man cave.

Cynthia slammed her fist down on the table. *Cocaine! Of all…* she shook her head and started to clean the table.

"Four-letter word for 'Cry like a baby'?" someone asked.

"Any letters?" Nate asked.

He was back at Bryant Park behind the library, trying to cool off from the confrontation this morning. There was nothing on his schedule, but it was early. Hopefully, someone would throw an assignment his way.

"No, no letters."

"Try wail or bawl," Nate suggested.

"Or blub," someone else suggested.

"Is that a word in the singular?" he asked. "I've heard of blubber or blubbering…"

"Blub fits."

"Well, how do you know it's blub, and not bawl? You said you had no letters," Nate challenged.

"The last letter down clue was a seven-letter word for auguries, that would be bodings, wouldn't it?"

Nate thought for a minute. "Yeah, I guess…"

"What the hell are auguries?" another writer asked.

"It's like foreshadowing. A method of showing something that's going to happen in the future, like a sign… or an omen," someone else answered.

"Oh, like that poem by what's his name, 'Auguries of Innocence?' Who was that who wrote it?"

"I thought a chick wrote that. It was a book of poems. Patti Smith was her name!"

Nate tuned out the inane debate and stared at his MacBook home screen. He was trying to figure out how Cynthia found out about Stephanie. Could there be some kind of spyware on his phone? The computer at home? Or the MacBook? No, Cynthia wouldn't do that. She would have no clue how.

*Unless those two friends of hers helped.*

He had been so careful. Once again, he thought about cutting communications with Stephanie, but then again, Cynthia already knew about her and what he told her. Lying to Cynthia was something he only did in an extreme situation. In their ten years of marriage, he had probably lied to her five times, but never about a woman. He honestly didn't see the harm in talking to an old friend from Chicago, even a female friend.

*She's more than an old friend, at least to you... even if Stephanie herself doesn't see it that way.*

He was annoyed with the private thoughts he was having as he scrambled for a sensible course of action. A phone call snapped him back from his thoughts. He pulled out his phone and answered, "Hello? Nate from New York Photography?"

"Hey Nate, it's Pete from Hot97. I think you need to check out social media. You're trending."

"What?!" Nate gasped, and opened his web browser to Twitter.

"I warned you. These rappers don't take kindly to bad reviews…"

He clicked out a few posts and noticed several popular trending hashtags related to him and .38 Special were becoming popular. WorldStar had an article stating the rapper had called him out in a series of videos on Instagram and Facebook. After searching a few web pages, Nate learned that Pitchfork outsourced his review to several magazines.

"You gotta be kidding me!" he yelled, attracting everyone around him.

After blushing from embarrassment, Nate stood up to find an isolated spot in the park. Once he was away from everyone, he turned on the sound for one of the videos on Instagram.

"…if I see you in the street, I'm stomping you out! I don't give a fuck about who your daddy, granddaddy, or any of them Chicago mafiosos your family know are! I'll be checking for you, BITCH!"

"Oh, my God!" Nate gasped.

Never in his life did he believe one of his reviews would bring this much trouble.

*I hope Dad doesn't find out about this.*

He needed to do some damage control of this situation and

the only way to do that was to talk to .38 Special directly. After checking the musician's Twitter feed, Nate learned he was making another appearance at a local sneaker store. He normally would take the bus or subway, but this was serious, so he used his app and called an Uber.

# 13

## YOU TALK IN YOUR SLEEP

"Cocaine! Can you believe that shit? He had the nerve to wanna drug test me! I'm telling you, Van, if you *were* fucking him, I'd be talking to a divorce attorney right now."

The sisters were walking down Astor Place heading west from Broadway towards Lafayette Street. Vanessa listened to her older sister rant while walking quietly, wondering where they were going.

Reading her mind, Cynthia answered the question. "Look, until we get through this… I don't want to call it a *rough patch*, but this thing we're currently at, I need you to stay at this loft Gloria uses for her hookups. She never lets men in her relationships know her regular address unless she's been with them for at least a year."

"For how *long*?!" Vanessa gasped.

"For as long as it takes for you to find another job and your own pla—"

"You're kicking me out, too?" she screamed and stopped walking.

Cynthia turned to her. "Don't make a scene. I can pay the

rent and utilities for six months. You'll have to get food and household products on your own."

"With WHAT MONEY, Cyn?!"

"Hey, work at Starbucks for all I care. You'll figure it out, but you're not staying at my house! It's not you I don't trust, it's *him*!"

"He just told you he ain't doing anything, and you know about my abortion now. I don't have any more secrets."

"But *he* does. He's been talking in his sleep, saying the same name over and over… someone named 'Stephanie.'"

"Who the hell is Stephanie?" Vanessa asked.

Cynthia grunted. "I don't know, but I'm damn sure going to find out." She stepped forward and grabbed her hand. "Until I do, you're staying here!"

They stopped in front of 416 Lafayette Street.

"Whoa, is that Blue Man Group doing shows down there?" Vanessa asked, pointing south.

"C'mon!" Cynthia yelled, pulling her inside.

"A third-floor walk-up?! Are you insane?!"

Cynthia sighed. "Look, I would have put you up in those condos, but you're afraid of heights."

"That place was over 30 stories and all the ones they had available were starting on the 25th floor!" Vanessa interrupted. "None of them faced the river, either! What's the point of being up that high and having a shitty view?!"

"Be that as it may, this place is better suited for you. At least I won't have to deal with tolls to check up on you."

Cynthia unlocked the door, and they stepped inside. She did a flourish and explained, "There's a TV with a basic Optimum Cable package, a computer with internet service so you can do job searches. If a guy named Leroy stops by, just say Gloria's out of town and she'll call when she comes back."

Cynthia turned to see if Vanessa was listening and noticed she had a frantic look on her face.

"Cyn, if I stay here for more than two days, I will steal that fucking Porsche again and drive myself off a cliff!"

*Christ, she is so melodramatic!* "Girl, sit down." She gestured to a couch in the middle of the room.

When Vanessa obliged, Cynthia sat next to her and wrapped her arms around her distressed shoulders. It was time to talk.

"So… who was the father?"

Vanessa sighed. "Is there anything to drink in here? I need to be soused if I'm going to tell this story…"

Two hours and a bottle of white wine later, they were giddy and laughing together.

"Arena football?! Are you shitting me? You couldn't even get a *real* football player?" Cynthia asked.

"Shut up! Arena is just as good as the NFL!"

"What kind of name is *The Philadelphia Soul*? I have never heard of them! You always were attracted to jocks, though. Remember that baseball player? Wasn't he in the minor league, too?"

"Ohhhh yeah. Jamie." Vanessa purred at the memory. "Hung and dumb," she added, with a wide smile.

"Just like you like 'em! You feeling better now?"

"Yeah…" Vanessa sighed. "But seriously, check in on me here after a few days… and tell Daddy to change the code to his garage. I'm going for the Jag next."

Cynthia stood up, hugged, and kissed her sister. "Next time, pick me up too, will ya? How did it feel out there? On the freeway, without a care in the world?"

"Like flying, Cyn… it felt like flying in the wind."

Her eyes were half-closed, it was four o'clock. She leaned back on the couch and drifted off to sleep. Cynthia took the opportunity to sneak out, locking the door behind her.

Cynthia stepped back outside after ordering an Uber to pick her up. She stopped cold in her tracks when she saw someone standing in the middle of the sidewalk.

"Motherfucker," she hissed.

"*Well*, fancy meeting *you* here," Sylverton Withrow III greeted her, with a grin.

"If I didn't know better, I'd say you were stalking me."

"Quite the contrary. I was just picking up some tickets at Will Call. I do, however, believe in serendipity. Because, it just so happens, I heard about a private school that could use a substitute teacher."

Pedestrians passed them by as she stared icicles at him.

"I'll pass… thanks."

Sylverton took out a piece of paper and a pen to write the information down. He extended his hand out to her. "Here. I just want to help."

"I'd sooner suck your dick than receive any help from you!" Cynthia spat.

"I doubt that. You never liked doing it when we were married. Not that you were any *good* at it in the first pla—"

Her slap across his face was so fast and hard, Sylverton saw white as his face snapped sharply to the left. He was able to stay on his feet, but by the time his vision refocused, Cynthia was nowhere to be seen.

"Bitch," he whispered with a grin, feeling his red cheek.

An hour had gone by, when Vanessa was stirred awake from her nap by the ringing of her cell phone. Luckily, Cynthia reactivated it after her parents terminated the service.

"Hello?"

"Hey, Vanessa, it's Josh. Got some good news. The producers loved your tape and they're willing to give you a permanent weekend spot. You'll be groomed for a while, shadowing the weather *and* traffic people, then they'll bring you in for holiday weekends starting around Thanksgiving."

She sprang up. Reporting traffic was beneath her, but she didn't care. "Josh that's amazing! Oh my God, thank you!" She wiped an imaginary tear of joy trying to compose herself. "How much are they starting me with?"

There was a moment of dead air over the line, she almost thought they got disconnected. "Um, hello?"

"They can only do 15," Josh said, deadpanned.

She rolled her eyes and sighed. "Well, it's a step down from what I'm used to, but I guess I can do $15,000.00 a month."

"$15,000.00… a *year*."

Vanessa dropped her phone. It clattered on the hardwood floor as her eyes rolled to the back of her head. She struggled to stand, swaying on the balls of her feet. It looked like she suffered a stroke, as she collapsed on the couch. She took a moment to breathe and then she reached down and brought the phone back to her ear.

Josh was in mid-sentence trying to explain. "…I tried to talk them into giving you more, but bringing you in…"

"Are they open to at least a bonus?" Vanessa asked. "I'll even sign a morality clause if they give me a little bit more. Throw me a bone, Josh."

"I'll see what I can do, *if* you keep out of trouble… try not to steal any more cars from here on out."

She gasped. "How did you—"

The phone clicked off before he could give her an answer.

"Well," she said to herself, while looking around. "I have officially hit rock bottom. At least there's nowhere to go but up."

"Man, just when I think your life can't get more complicated," Sean said, with a laugh.

He was spotting Nate as he benched 175 pounds in the weight room of their local gym. Over the past hour, Nate and Sean had been talking about .38 Special and the rapper's threats on social media.

"This isn't funny, man. My father called me. I don't even know how he found out, but I had to talk him out of sending up some of his old friends to track this kid down, if you know what I mean."

"Yeah, he really called you out, putting your personal business out there… give me five more!"

Nate grunted with the last presses and then placed the weight back on the rest. He sat up, did a few stretches, and then followed Sean to the treadmills as they continued their conversation.

"I just missed him at that sneaker store. He was only there for two hours. Luckily, he's doing another show at some club in The Bronx. I'm going there tomorrow night to try to talk some sense into this guy."

The two men were an updated version of Rocky and Apollo, challenging each other in friendly competition. They were equally matched, with neither one letting the other waver.

They started a slow, ascending walk on a set of StairMasters.

"At least Vanessa's out of the house. It'll help smooth things out with Cynthia," Nate said, with a deep breath.

"I'm surprised she didn't cop to doing cocaine, man," Sean

replied. "No offense, but from what you told me she was showing all the signs of rusty pipes."

They increased their pace to a light trot.

"I think the best way to get on her good side again, is a vacation outside the city for our anniversary, after we do these gigs together." Nate checked his pulse by putting two fingers on his neck. "It'll take her mind off this fucking job search slump that has her really feeling down."

"Any ideas?" Sean asked.

"I'm drawing a blank. We haven't been anywhere in like six years."

"How about somewhere down south? Myrtle Beach? Miami? Atlanta?" Sean suggested.

An idea popped into Nate's head suddenly. "Hmmm… I *did* tell Cynthia I'm doing a story about Stephanie. Maybe we can take a trip out to San Diego…"

Sean stopped in his tracks. "Now, you're thinking… kill two birds with one stone *and* get some much-needed 'closure.'"

He emphasized the last word with a pair of air quotes and a smirk.

Nate rolled his eyes. "Please."

His friend let out a chuckle and resumed his trot.

"I still can't figure out how she found out about Stephanie…" Nate mused to himself, scratching his head.

They were alone in the steam room, each with a towel around their waist.

"I think I know…" Sean started.

"Huh?"

"I meant to tell you… um, when uh, me and Jade were…" he did an obscene finger gesture.

Nate nodded. "Right…"

"She was on top of me, doing reverse cowgirl, and…"

Nate stared at him and narrowed his eyebrows.

"Heh, sorry, um, yeah… in the middle of all that, she thought she heard me say another girl's name and started cursing in Japanese. I swore up and down that it wasn't me, turns out… it was *you*!"

"Me?!" Nate squeaked.

"You talk in your sleep… loud."

"Bullshit!" he scoffed.

Sean shook his head. "I'm not joking, man. You need to record yourself or something."

Nate leaned against the wall, completely shocked. "Great."

After getting dressed, the men stepped out of the building and stopped in front of the entrance. They did a fist bump and went their separate ways. Nate climbed into his Tahoe and checked his smartphone. He had several missed Facebook messages from Stephanie. He quickly erased the notifications and put his phone back in his pocket, then started the car. His idea was forming into a plan, but he needed to be careful. One false move and it could go sideways quickly.

Cynthia came home, still pissed after her encounter with Sylverton. Socking him did put a smile on her face, though. With her sister out of their hair, she now had time to do some research on this 'Stephanie' person that Nate seemed *too* interested in. Nate had been careful to wipe his browsing history on their computer nearly every night, BUT, not on his iPhone, which she had been accessing remotely.

With all the websites Nate accessed on his phone, Cynthia was able to find the Facebook profile of 'StephanieSymphony,' but she had her privacy settings on, and without a login, Cynthia was only able to see typical game notifications of what she played.

*Candy Crush Saga. Real fucking mature, bitch!*

She thought about making a fake profile and trying to befriend her, but nixed the idea, afraid of becoming obsessed with this person.

*Would that actually be bad?*

Upon doing a general search on Google, Cynthia discovered a connection to the Facebook username and a hair salon called Hair Escape… located in San Diego, California.

*Was that where she lived? Nate never talked about knowing anyone from out on the West Coast. All he knows are people from Chicago and here.*

She went back to YouTube and pulled up her channel with clips of her performances. Since hearing Nate say her name a few weeks ago in his sleep, she immediately thought he was having an affair with the woman. After all her searching, she still wasn't sure. Could it be harmless? Was she really only a musician he was doing an article on?

Cynthia stood up and opened a bottle of Riesling. She had a lot to think about.

Nate had another adult photoshoot with Destro as he directed another scene, but unfortunately, Cynthia couldn't be with him. This time he was in a fancy apartment located on the upper west side of Manhattan. He flashed his credentials and signed in a guestbook at the lobby, then took an express elevator to the penthouse. After stepping off, he looked around. Destro was waiting for him at the end of the hallway.

"I know, right?" he asked with a smile. "This place is off the charts. Is your dick hard, yet?"

*There he goes again,* Nate thought. "It's cool," he replied, with a shrug.

"Heheh, pretend to be unimpressed if you want. You'll thank me once you meet our new performer from across the pond."

"Across the what?" Nate asked.

They entered the apartment and went to the bedroom. Once again, Cotton Candi was there, getting ready. She gave Nate a playful wave and adjusted her top. He gave her a faint wave back and focused on getting into professional mode.

"Okay, we'll be shooting in five, so places! Where's our British import?" Destro asked.

Nate registered a confused face until one of the other doors opened and another full-figured woman stepped out.

Professionalism flew out the window once he laid eyes on her.

Destro saw the look on his face and introduced the newcomer. "Gentlemen, Miss Shanice Richards!" then leaned over and whispered to Nate, "Ahem… say, 'Thank you, Destro.'"

"Thank you, Destro," he quickly mumbled.

Miss Richards was extravagant. Granted, all the women Nate had seen were beautiful in their own right, but Shanice reminded him of every woman that was out of his league when he was his former, heavier self. Tan skin, long hair, and a little taller than Cotton Candi. She stood at five-foot-seven, with an impressive 38-JJ bust. At a little over 240 pounds, she wasn't as heavy as her co-star, but still had the typical 'double coke bottle figure' that was to die for. Not only was she beautiful, but when she spoke, Nate swore he heard a chorus of angels singing. Her posh British accent nearly made his knees buckle.

"Nice to meet you," she said, with a smile.

He didn't want to be caught staring, so he composed himself quickly and spoke in a deeper-than-usual voice. "It's an honor, Madam… to be involved in this production."

Cotton Candi wasn't about to let him slide. "Are you speaking in a deeper voice?"

He coughed and stammered for a second. "N-no, no! Of course not, I always talk like this. Um, I'll be over here preparing the shot." He moved to a corner and pretended to fumble with his camera.

Destro and Cotton Candi exchanged glances, then resumed working. The scene was for the upcoming Halloween holiday in two months. Shanice was wearing cat ears, with whiskers drawn on her face, and a tail attached to her panties. Cotton Candi had her hair up in pigtails, while wearing a white lace bra with a plaid skirt, for the typical naughty schoolgirl look.

The lesbian shoot went for nearly 45 minutes when Destro called cut, then congratulated the two ladies.

"Excellent as always… that's a wrap!"

Several interns handed out robes to each of the performers and started cleaning up. Cotton Candi stole a glance at Nate, then walked to another room. Shanice held her robe on her arm and approached Nate. She was still nude, so he concentrated on her whiskers to prevent himself from staring.

"Um, nice scene," Nate said, still using his deep voice.

"Why thank you! Such a gentleman."

He tried his hardest not to, but melted like the cheesiness of his wide smile.

"Are you doing anything after? I could use a guide to show me around the city and see… *the sights.*"

Nate was flabbergasted by the invitation. He opened his

mouth to reply but Destro quickly shouted, "He's married, Shanice! Be nice and stop toying with the photographer!"

He turned to Destro with an annoyed look.

Shanice pouted. "Oh poo. All the nice ones are, I guess." She put on her robe and started wiping her face paint off.

Nate watched her walk by and Destro came forward.

"What the hell, man?" he hissed at the director.

"Look, kid. You never date the performers. It gets ugly. I've been married seven times and four were in the business. It's just not a good look. You love your wife, don't you?"

Nate took a beat to answer. "Well, yeah, but—"

"Then just think about her while fucking your wife. She won't know, and she'll even thank you for the extra effort you put in." He slapped his shoulder and walked away. "On to the next one! Keep your phone on!"

He shook his head and realized Destro was probably right.

Cynthia was on the couch, finishing off a salad while watching the evening news. She was wearing sweatpants and one of her old, oversized shirts. There was an empty wine bottle in front of her on the coffee table. She heard Nate pull up to the driveway and turned to see him enter through the front door and close it behind him.

Instead of his usual haggard look, he had a sly grin on his face.

"Hey?" she greeted skeptically.

Nate came over in front of her and started kissing her neck. His hand slid down and squeezed her ass.

"Ooooh, someone's frisky!" Cynthia purred.

"Hmmm, more than that," he replied, and suddenly hooked her legs, lifting her in the air.

"Ooomph!" She giggled, and they started to kiss passionately.

He carried her up the steps to the bedroom and they were naked in seconds. Nate tossed Cynthia on the bed as she opened her legs. His erection was bright red and engorged. She rarely saw this side of him. This was beyond spontaneous. It was full on blood lust.

Nate wished that it was actually Cynthia he was seeing before him, but it wasn't. In his mind, it was Shanice Richards on the bed in front of him. Lying on her back with her huge, thick legs spread wide and a full, luscious belly, ready to envelop him. He imagined her calling to him in her British accent.

"Show me what you Yanks got!"

He leaped onto the bed and shoved himself deep inside her, then proceeded to give her the pounding of a lifetime as if The Star-Spangled Banner was playing in the background.

"Holy shit, baby!" Cynthia gasped. This was the most intense Nate had ever been, and she was loving every minute of it!

*He damn sure ain't cheating! Fuck it, let him cum in me, I don't care!* She thought. "That's right, motherfucker!" she encouraged. "Drain your fucking balls in me!"

"Yeah!" he growled. "Turn over!" He propped her up and they switched positions.

Nate imagined Shanice's gigantic ass in front of him, as he brought his head down and took a bite of her left cheek like it was an apple.

"Oooooh!" Cynthia gasped.

"Pull my hair, Daddy! I like it rough!" Shanice whispered to him, and he obliged.

"Hey!" Cynthia objected. Now he was getting *too* intense.

Nate pulled a handful and pounded himself deep inside her ass. Cynthia was feeling violated now.

"Time out! Stop! Stop it!" she protested, as he continued. "Goddamnit, Nate! STOP! Get the fuck off of me!"

She kicked him off the bed and pulled the sheet to cover herself as he landed on his ass with a confused look on his face.

"What!?" Nate barked.

"What the fuck was all that extra shit!? You never pulled my hair before!" she screamed. "And when I stay stop, you fucking *stop*! What is wrong with you?"

He looked down and felt ashamed, "I… I… I'm sorry. I just got caught up in the moment."

"There's 'caught up' and then there's *rape*. You better learn the fucking difference if you ever want to touch me again! I didn't consent to anal, either! You check with me before crossing that line!"

"Sorry! It… just slipped."

She stared back at him, and he took the hint. He grabbed his drawers off the floor and backed out of the bedroom, heading downstairs.

When she was sure he was out of earshot, she finally let her body tremble and fought the urge to cry.

# 14

## THE LEGEND OF NATE BOURNE

Nate slept until 8 am the next morning in the guest bedroom. He felt so guilty that he didn't want to leave the room until Cynthia had left the house. When the sounds and scent of breakfast crept in from the kitchen, he finally decided to wash up and come out of hiding.

He was shocked to see Cynthia cooking scrambled eggs and actual bacon for breakfast.

*Okay, there's no way that's for us, this must be a trick!*

He opened his mouth to speak, but she held up her finger and then pointed to the chair. Nate closed his mouth and took a seat at the kitchen table. Cynthia finally finished and brought two BLT's to the table on separate plates, hamburger buns and all. With a side of hash browns for him and scrambled eggs for her.

It was at that moment Nate realized what was happening. The breakfast was exactly what Cynthia served the morning after their very first fight. He just looked at the plates as she took a seat across from him.

Neither one of them started eating. They just looked at each other for two of the longest, quietest minutes.

Cynthia finally spoke first. "So… what happened?"

Nate thought about his reply *carefully*. "First of all…"

"No, no, no," she interrupted. "No, *first of all*, just tell me…" she gestured with her right hand.

He sighed. "I got a little too excited at this photoshoot they were doing, and I brought that excitement home." Nate took a breath and then continued. "I'm really sorry. It… it kinda felt like… like I was a porn star, myself."

He looked hurt, like a teenager who had gotten caught masturbating by his mother. Now that she knew where he was coming from, she couldn't stay mad. It actually was kind of funny. Cynthia dared not crack a smile, though.

She stood up, walked over to his side of the table, sat on his lap, and playfully tugged on his ear. "My personal *Dirk Diggler*, huh?"

He grinned and chuckled slightly. "Yeah,"

Now that the ice was broken, it was time for step two, groveling and offering her the world.

"Please let me make this up to you. Whatever you want. Name the place. We'll go wherever you want for our anniversary."

She pretended to think about it for a moment. "Okaaaaaaay… how about… hmmm, San Diego?"

Nate was taken aback. "Um, as luck would have it… Rolling Stone offered me an upgrade on the blogger's story looking into that singer I was researching. Ah, she um, lives out in San Diego…"

"Oh really? Well, two birds one stone, eh? A little bit of business *and* pleasure… you can write off the expenses."

He studied the look on her face. *There's no way she's this clueless. She wants to confront Stephanie. She knows something's going on.*

"You know what? Let's do it. The beach would be a nice change of scenery."

Nate tilted his head. "Yeah?"

"Sure. I'll even get some new swimwear. Something skimpy and scandalous that leaves nothing to the imagination."

He knew she was serious and testing for his reaction, knowing well she'll do whatever she wants despite his objections.

"Okay, now that we've settled that…"

She stood up and picked up his plate, then walked across to collect hers.

"Hey!" Nate protested.

"I made my point, and you learned your lesson. You better not *ever* do anything like what happened last night again!"

"Okay, I won't but…" He reached out.

She looked back at him. "Huh? Oh. You didn't think we were going to *eat* this, did you?"

Cynthia dumped the food in the trash as Nate gave a disappointed look and sighed.

"Where did you even hide all that fatty food?" he asked.

"I have my secret hiding places."

Nate just shook his head and shrugged with his hands. "Alright. I'll set up the flight," then stood up and gave her a peck on her cheek. "Thank you, baby. This interview can boost me into getting something permanent with a magazine. I got a podcast to record at noon. We'll get together with some of my upcoming gigs soon!" He backed his way to the door and headed upstairs.

Now she was certain something was going on between the two of them. For him to use their anniversary as an excuse to meet her… that was all she needed.

*I can't believe he thinks I'm that stupid! I'll show him!*

She started cleaning the table when the phone rang.

"I got it, honey!" Cynthia yelled to Nate upstairs and answered the phone.

"Yeah?"

"Hey sis, surprised I'm still here?" Vanessa asked.

"Actually, I am. Wassup?"

"Well, it's not much, but I got an offer. I'm starting at the bottom, but hopefully I'll be back in no time!"

"Heeeeey! That is awesome! We should celebrate!" Cynthia said.

"Well, that's where *you* come in… how's about you buy a few bottles and bring your friends to throw a little party?"

"Little Sis, you read my mind. See you in a few hours."

She hung up the phone.

Club Cyclone was on Boston Road near 222nd Street. After his podcast guest spot, Nate stepped out of the Uber that took him up to The Bronx. He was dressed in his best social clothes and walking alongside the long line that was forming to get in. The bouncer recognized Nate immediately as he approached.

"Yo! You're that online reporter! Holy shit! You come here to throw down with .38? You gonna need backup, my man!"

"Nah. Nah, I'm here to talk peace with him. Is he inside? Can you let me in?" Nate asked.

He waved them through. "It's your funeral. Just make sure to stand alone somewhere so no innocent people get caught in the line of fire. Good luck!"

Inside, the venue was packed. Nate felt overdressed compared to most of the fashion choices of everyone else.

*I guess it's more of a Hip-Hop scene instead of an actual nightclub scene.*

Being a DJ himself, he was used to the loud music and little personal space. Maneuvering through the crowd, he first stopped at the bar. When Nate didn't see the rapper there, he figured he had a secluded VIP booth somewhere. There was a bottle of

Christal sent off. He made a beeline to follow the server and found a corner that was cut off from the main floor with a velvet rope.

"Bingo," Nate said to himself out loud.

He pulled his collar and approached the corner. As he moved closer, Nate recognized the two security goons from the listening party. He stopped in front of them and waved.

"Wassup!" he yelled.

The two men exchanged glances and grinned.

"Alright, let's try this again… hey, is .38 Special back there? Tell him it's me and I just wanna squash this. I'm sure he's reasonable and this is all just a misunderstanding."

One of the men rolled his eyes and turned to look behind him. He made a hand gesture to someone else, who then made another hand gesture to someone else and got the rapper's attention. .38 yelled back and then turned towards Nate, who gave a faint wave back.

He jumped up and came across the area to the velvet divider.

"You gotta lot of nerve coming up in here, motherfucker!"

Before Nate could reply, he felt a flurry full of money thrown in his face.

Then something strange happened. .38 quickly waved him to come closer. Nate barely saw the motion but moved a step closer.

"Yell in my face and make it look convincing," the rapper whispered.

"Huh?"

"You gonna apologize for that bullshit review, you know what I'm saying!?"

He pulled a magazine from his jacket and waved it in Nate's face. Once again, he mumbled something under his breath. "I'm going to push you, so act surprised and flail your arms around. This some good PR shit. I'll spot you 50k if you sell this right, you feel me?"

Nate barely had time to react before he was pushed back a few inches. He exaggerated his reaction and raised his arms over his head, finally understanding what was happening. What better way to sell your music than some drama with an online critic? He decided to play along for the hell of it and suddenly grabbed the magazine out of .38's hand.

"Yo, who you think you're talking to, punk?" Nate yelled, then gave a quick wink with a nod.

The two security guys pretended to brace each of them as they continued to fake their argument and escalate it further.

A few onlookers around them started pulling out their smartphones.

.38 looked around and whispered, "Okay, wait for the cue…"

Nate didn't know what to expect. Was this guy really going to hit him? Hopefully, he would telegraph it so he would have time to react.

They kept pushing against the two security guys, looking like they were about to come to blows. The anticipation got too much for Nate and he just decided to react. The rapper threw his punch a second too early, missing Nate completely, as he swung the rolled-up magazine like a baseball bat and hit him square in his eye.

.38 let out a high-pitched shriek and immediately collapsed on the floor. Nate froze in complete shock at what had transpired. Flashes went off in the club, and before the security guys could react, he ran for the fire exit. The door opened and an alarm went off, which sent the nightclub into complete chaos.

"Ohshitohshitooooshiiiit!" Nate repeated, as he ran up the street.

He had no clue if anyone was after him and he dared not look back to find out. There were no subway stations nearby, so he climbed onto the Bx30 bus heading to Co-Op City, paid his fare, then went to a seat in the back.

Twenty minutes later, he got off and took an Uber back

home. It was 1 am and his hands were still shaking. The last time Nate punched someone, he was in high school. He never got into any fights, arguments, or disagreements to the point of violence. Luckily, Cynthia was asleep when he got home, so he went upstairs and immediately climbed into bed. He stared up at the ceiling, unable to fall asleep for nearly a half-hour before he finally drifted off.

The next morning, Nate's cell phone woke him up. He had forgotten to put it on vibrate before falling asleep. Cynthia was nowhere to be seen, probably downstairs, so he answered the incoming call, praying it wasn't a job.

"H'ullo?" he mumbled.

"Dude, you made the front page of the Daily News! You're a celebrity!" Sean cheered.

Nate sat up on the bed. "What?"

"They said you bitch-smacked .38 Special in a club! Even reading it with my own eyes I still find it hard to believe! What happened? You got drunk with some liquid courage and turned into Jason Bourne or something?"

Nate put the call on speaker and checked several gossip websites, finding articles about the confrontation.

"Awww fuck!"

The posts had several different videos to back up the story. It was all over Instagram, Twitter, and Facebook.

"Damn, I gotta get control of this, um, meet me at that restaurant near The High Line."

"Cookshop?"

"Yeah, around noon."

"I'll be there."

Nate ended the call and got up. Hopefully, Cynthia hadn't gotten the newspaper yet. He walked to the bathroom to wash up.

Cynthia was waiting for him when Nate came downstairs. She was holding the newspaper in front of her, with an annoyed look on her face.

*So much for that,* he thought. "You gotta believe me, baby. I had no idea this would blow up like this!"

"What is this? What the hell happened?" she asked.

"I… I gave this rapper a mediocre review and he took it personally. I tried to de-escalate the situation, but apparently, he decided to use it to create some publicity," Nate explained.

"What does that mean? *'Create some publicity?'*"

"Um, how can I say this in terms you'll understand?"

She looked blankly at him and he rolled his eyes.

"Basically, he's making up this *'beef'* to give him some 'street cred.' More people will buy his CDs if he's seen as a badass, picking on a white critic who probably knows nothing about the music. Beef is their word for…"

"I know what beef means. I grew up listening to Biggie and Tupac," she said dryly.

"Well… yeah. So it's all exaggerated. If I stay away from him, it'll die down. Unless he tries to find me to retaliate…"

Cynthia raised an eyebrow.

Nate waved his hands. "*But* it won't come to that, I'll make sure of it!"

Cynthia threw the newspaper on the coffee table and walked past him to the kitchen. Nate let out a sigh of relief, then jumped when their home phone rang.

*Who the hell is THIS?* he asked himself.

He beat Cynthia to the cordless receiver and pressed the 'Talk' button to answer. "Hello?"

"My son! You rocked that nigger's ass!" Jeremy Durant cheered.

Nate cringed. "Oh my God, Dad! Don't say that word, at least not with the 'er' at the end!"

His father laughed. "When my friend Pauly showed me the video on his Facebook page, I was so proud! I'm getting free beers down at the pub just for telling people you're my son. You think you can have pictures printed and autograph them? I could make a killing here."

Nate shook his head. "Dad, it wasn't real. It was a publicity stunt to sell his music. I just messed up and accidentally hit him for real."

He couldn't believe the words as they came out of his mouth. Who would have thought going to a listening party would lead to all this drama?

"What are you talking about?" his father asked.

"You know how WWE wrestling is fake? It's like that. It was scripted. We… planned to look like we were arguing. Look, I'll explain later, Dad. I gotta go. Call you later, okay?"

Nate hung up the cordless phone before his father could say something else, then placed it back on the charger.

"I hope no one else tries to call me. If they do, just let the machine answer it."

Cynthia started mixing a protein shake in a blender. "Works for me. You have any gigs I can tag along with you today?"

"I'm meeting up Sean for lunch, but I *do* have a DJ set tomorrow evening. It's from 10 pm to 2 am, so you'll need to sleep in, okay?"

"Jesus! I don't think I've ever *been* anywhere in the city that late at night!" she gasped.

"10 pm or 2 am?" he asked, with a grin.

"2 am! I'm not a *total* square, I'm just not a night owl."

"It'll be fun, and best of all, it's a gay club. I won't have to worry about anyone hitting on you."

"Oh, how convenient," Cynthia replied sarcastically. She poured a cupful of her shake as Nate prepared some black bean toast. After breakfast, Nate watched some television while Cynthia did some job-hunting on the computer. They were still walking on eggshells since the other night, but hopefully working together the following evening will smooth things out.

Sean was running behind but still managed to beat Nate to the High Line. He was checking out a few ladies when Nate finally showed up.

"Hey," Nate greeted.

"Hey," Sean replied.

They started walking and Nate noticed Sean was acting sheepish, trying to hide his appearance. He was wearing a baseball cap and sunglasses with a hooded sweater.

"Are you for real, right now? Take off those sunglasses! You're ashamed to be seen with me?"

Sean removed the glasses and lifted his cap but pulled the hood over his head. "Not ashamed! Just laying low," he said, looking both ways.

They came down the steps onto the sidewalk and started walking when a truck buckled from hitting a pothole and Sean dove behind a car. Nate just stopped and stared at him.

Sean got back up and smiled with a light chuckle. "Um, I uh, fell, man. Must have tripped over something."

"Must have." Nate rolled his eyes and resumed walking.

They made it to Cookshop and got a table. A waitress

brought two glasses of water and they each ordered their usual order of a bacon, lettuce, and tomato sandwich. When they were left alone, Nate recalled the incident at the nightclub and explained the rapper's false bravado.

"Wow, so he's all talk, huh? Figured as much."

"Yeah, so while he tries to repair his image, I come off looking like some vigilante. Everyone's calling me 'Nate Bourne,' 'Nategyver,' or my favorite, 'Kung Fu Nicky.'"

Sean snickered at that last one and Nate gave him a look.

He cleared his throat and said, "Um, sorry. Change of subject, how are things with you and Cynthia?"

"We're okay, but she's playing 'chicken' with me about this trip for our anniversary."

"You really going through with it?" Sean asked.

"I'm not backing down. The two of us are going to prove nothing's going on between me and Stephanie to Cynthia."

"Nate, she obviously didn't pull 'San Diego' out of her ass. She knows you've been talking to her! You're asking for trouble having your wife meet an ex."

"She's not an ex, she was just a friend!" Nate quickly corrected.

"That you had feelings for. It's the same thing in their mind."

He waved his hand. "Look, we leave in two weeks, it's a done deal, okay? Part of me needs this, this closure. Once Cyn sees there's nothing between us, she'll be satisfied and eat crow. Then I can spend the rest of our lives rubbing it in her face how faithful I am to her."

"Eat what?"

"Huh?"

"You said Cynthia will be satisfied and eating *what*?"

"Crow, eating crow… admitting you made a mistake? Being embarrassed? You never heard that before?" Nate asked.

Sean just shook his head. "You white people and your weird ass phrases."

Nate rolled his eyes. "We didn't come up with it."

The waitress came with their orders and placed them on the table.

"Now this is more like it! Prompt service!" Sean exclaimed.

Nate nodded in agreement. "Yes!" and grabbed his sandwich for a huge bite.

After chewing it down he said, "Can you believe she actually threw away *two* perfectly good BLTs like these this morning!?" gesturing with his hand to the sandwich.

"Bullshit! Really?"

"Put them right in the garbage can, just to prove a point!"

"Damn! While children are starving in Ethiopia." Sean shook his head and continued eating.

After the meal, Nate and Sean went their separate ways. Nate was walking back up Tenth Avenue and decided to give Stephanie a video call through Facebook Messenger.

"Hey, Nate. How's it going?" she answered.

He stopped walking for a moment.

"Um, there's been a development."

"What the hell does *that* mean?" Stephanie asked with an alarmed tone.

"Cynthia somehow learned that you and I have been talking…" he saw the concern grow on her face. "But don't panic, I uh, told her you were… an amateur singer I was doing a story on for a magazine."

"What?! Are you crazy? She's not going to believe—"

"I know, I know…" Nate interrupted. "I'll think of something, but she still hasn't tried to contact you, so for now, all I can assume is that she *did* believe me. But when we get there…"

"Wait a minute, y'all are coming *here*?!"

"Well, yeah. For Rolling Stone, you'd think it would have to be a face-to-face interview…"

Nate resumed walking as Stephanie started to freak out.

"Oh my God, Nate! Was coming out here your dumbass idea or *hers*?"

"Um…" he swallowed hard. "Hers."

"And you really don't believe she knows something?" Stephanie asked.

"Relax, we'll be there in two weeks, it's also our wedding anniversary," Nate explained.

"Oh, that's reassuring!"

"We'll pretend to have an interview, go out for drinks, you two meet each other and talk… she'll be convinced that nothing's going on between you and me, then we'll go back to New York and live happily ever after." He did a dismissive gesture with his right hand. "Nothing to worry about."

Stephanie simply shook her head. "I forgot how delusional you can be sometimes. You're the type to wait 90 days before having sex with someone, then ask them to move in with you after another three months."

Nate pouted. "Okay, on *that* note, I'm ending this call… goodbye!"

He pressed the hang-up button and put his phone away. He caught his reflection looking back at him from one of the store windows.

"It's gonna work," he told himself.

Whether he actually believed that was yet to be seen.

# 15

## OUT WEST

It was the last weekend of September. Nate and Cynthia took the train to Queens. They approached the Pink Ribbon Club at nine o'clock. Nate had his backpack with the MacBook inside. There was a bouncer guarding the back entrance and the owner of the club was a few steps behind him.

"You the next DJ?" the bouncer asked, while twirling a toothpick in his mouth.

"Yeah."

The bouncer looked past him to Cynthia and asked, "Who's this? You mentoring now?"

"Uh, yeah… this is my intern. Just showing her the ropes… don't worry, she's a lesbian… right?"

"Uh… yeah, I love that pussy." Cynthia said, with little enthusiasm.

He snorted and joked, "Whatever. Guess it's 'take your daughter to work' night."

Nate narrowed his gaze and stared at the bouncer for a moment, then whispered to Cynthia, "Wait here."

He walked past him and whispered something to the club

owner. The man then walked over to the bouncer and counted five ten-dollar bills into his hand.

"Here you go. You're fired."

"What?! Why?"

"First rule in any club. Don't insult the DJ. Without him, there's no music, and without music, there's no party. Now, get the fuck outta here!"

Nate folded his arms in front of his chest with a smirk.

"C'mon! What if I apologize?"

"Forget it. Take your money and go. In five minutes, I'm making a call and whoever shows up next will put you through the windshield of whatever car's parked outside!"

Nate gave a friendly wave from inside.

The bouncer flipped the toothpick in his mouth again, contemplating whether it was worth it to start something. Then grunted and walked past Cynthia, heading towards the street.

"Wow!" Cynthia said, and walked over to Nate.

"That's power, baby…" he replied with a grin.

Most nightclubs either have levels of floors with different music or one big dancefloor with a bar and surrounding tables. The Ribbon was different, with a large stage for live entertainment on one side and a smaller hall for dancing on the opposite side. Each weekend was dedicated to a different genre of music. Tonight, it was Goth Night.

Nate and Cynthia made their way to the front and approached a long table, with a sound system full of components, connected to the surrounding speakers in the hall. Nate pulled out his MacBook and started connecting plugs, preparing to take control of the music.

Cynthia gave a puzzled look. "I don't get it, where are the turntables? The… whatchamacallit? Mixer? The microphone?"

Nate chuckled. "This is the mixer, and instead of turntables we have these CDJs" he gestured to the table. "This is how we work, now."

The familiar signature cue played over the speakers and Nate began the set with an earth-shattering bass drop. The shock of the loud chord made Cynthia jump out of her skin.

"JESUS!" she screamed.

Nate laughed maniacally and set up the first arrangement of music.

"Sorry, I should have warned you!" he yelled, then handed her a pair of noise-canceling earbuds. "Here, put these in! They're not earplugs, but they'll drown out the sound so you can still hear!"

After sticking them in each ear, she noticed the reduction of sound. "HEY NOT BAD!" she yelled.

They looked at each other, giving a thumbs-up and bopping their heads.

The music drew in a noticeable crowd within the first hour. They made a great team. Cynthia played hype-girl for Nate, jumping and cheering him along with full energy. Halfway through his set, he waved her over.

"Let's record a few ad-libs to play on top of the beats…" Nate said, handing Cynthia a microphone headset.

"What do I say?" Cynthia asked.

"Anything, just off the top of your head… like this…"

He turned on a separate microphone and motioned to the crowd. "RAGE THE SYSTEM!"

They screamed the same message back to him.

"See? It gets them hyped! This type of music is called Dubstep," Nate explained.

"It sounds like two Transformers fucking."

He stopped moving and gave her a look. She just shrugged.

They started rocking again and Nate said, "I'm going to build the kick, and then point to you… say something crazy and then I'll drop the bass. Everyone will go nuts, okay? So, when you get on, just scream something, anything, into the mic."

"Alright." She nodded.

After a two-minute build up, he turned and pointed to her.

"This cow needs an enema!" Cynthia yelled.

Nate dropped the bass and shook the room as the crowd went berserk. It was insane. The two of them started jumping around. It was such a rush.

When two o'clock finally came, Cynthia's ears were ringing. After the set, they went to an after-hours lounge to come down from the high they were still feeling. She hated drinking beer, so she settled for Gin and Tonic while Nate nursed a Heineken.

"I don't know how you can do this three times a week!" she said, a little louder than normal, still on her party volume.

"You get used to it… are you still wearing those earbuds? You're still talking kinda loud."

She adjusted and concentrated on talking at a regular volume. "No, I took them out. Sorry." Cynthia couldn't help but smile at the moment. It felt good working with her husband, and the money was nice, too. He let her have his cut of the gig tonight. It was play money to her, but it was nice after a long dry spell of job leads going nowhere.

"Hey, babe?" Nate began, after a swig of his beer.

"Yeah?"

"Where the hell did you get 'This cow needs an enema!' from?"

She laughed. "Jack Nicholson said that as the Joker in the first Batman movie."

Nate shook his head. "That wasn't what he said, Cyn."

"No?"

He waved his hand. "Forget it, it worked." He chuckled. "We

make a good team. Maybe we can get some helmets to wear and be America's answer to Daft Punk."

"Who are they?"

Nate rolled his eyes. "I'll tell you later."

They drank quietly for a few minutes then, Cynthia said, "Nate?"

"Hmmm?"

"This is cool for a hobby every now and then, but you don't wanna be doing this when you're sixty, do you?"

He sobered up at the question and put the bottle down on their table. "Meaning?"

"Look, I'm the last person that should be telling anyone how to live, but… I know you have more potential than this. And yes, you're not the 400-pound computer nerd anymore. I get it… but maybe you can be the handsome, 175-pound IT guy that all the women in the office wanna bang."

Nate tilted his head. "Would you actually prefer that? Me batting women away with a stick as they undress me with their eyes? You don't even *trust* me now?"

She quietly cursed at the valid point. He had her in a corner. "Look, it's great that you're doing all these gigs, but sooner or later you're going to have to find something stable. And before you start on me about not working myself… *don't*. I will find something, okay? We both can't be unstable, since you won't accept my parents' help. I see the attraction, for sure. This shit is fun, I get it, but the appeal won't last forever."

Nate just watched her during the speech. Cynthia wondered if her words struck a chord in him. He finished his beer and stood up. "We should go."

She sighed and stood up. They walked towards the exit and took the train back to Brooklyn.

Nate and Cynthia emerged from the train station and Nate pulled out his phone to check his Twitter feed. There were several popular hashtags trending, and he stopped in his tracks when he noticed one.

"Holy shit!" Nate gasped.

A few steps ahead of him, Cynthia stopped and looked back. "What?!"

"Look what's number three trending on Twitter…"

Cynthia walked back and squinted. "What is it?"

As he held up his phone, she read the list of trending hashtags on the side of the timeline and noticed that the third one down was '#cowneedsanenema' with over a thousand posts and counting.

She snorted in amazement. "Well, ain't that something!"

The plane approached from the east as the sun was rising and landed on the runway without incident. It taxied to the nearest gate, opened the doors, and the passengers began filing out. Cynthia walked down the long connecting hallway and headed towards the luggage carousel. Nate followed closely behind with his carry-on bag.

As Cynthia waited for the suitcases to appear on the conveyor belt, Nate decided to find a seat and read a magazine. More people waited near the belt and were starting to get impatient. After twenty minutes, the belt started to move, and the flight's luggage started to appear. Cynthia and the crowd around the carousel began scanning the belt for their labeled bags or suitcases, then filing out to the nearest exit. It felt like a feeding frenzy.

Nate shook his head. *We're only here for four days, why couldn't she just bring a carry-on, like I did?*

He pulled out his phone and noticed Stephanie was online in Facebook Messenger.

@NatefromNewYork: "Hey, we just landed, jetlagged and getting used to the time change. This sucks. How can you possibly live like this? Three hours behind on everything!"

@StephanieSymphony: "You get used to it, you big baby. I can't believe you're actually in town!"

@NatefromNewYork: "Yep, some boring story on yet another musician. I needed to get out of town and lay low for a while after some nonsense happened with my previous review."

@StephanieSymphony: "Yeah, like bitch-slapping some rapper like you're Steven Seagal in his prime?"

Nate gasped and typed,

@NatefromNewYork: "OMG, you heard about that?! Even out here? And also… Steven Seagal? When was the last time you saw an action movie? 1996?"

@StephanieSymphony: "Do I have to remind you I work in a hair salon? We were talking about that shit for days."

Nate was about to type his reply when Cynthia suddenly appeared next to him and asked, "Who ya talkin' to?"

He jumped and nearly dropped his iPhone. "Huh? Oh, nobody, just check some news blogs." Nate smiled and let out a chuckle.

"It kinda looked like you were Instant Messaging someone. You had a goofy look on your face."

Nate handed her the phone. "See for yourself," he said, nonchalantly.

Cynthia looked down at the phone, then up and stared at his face for the longest sixty seconds. She then shrugged it off. "It's okay, I believe you." *Not.*

Nate squinted and stood as Cynthia held up the luggage bag she had been waiting for. "I got my bag, let's go."

"Alright, hotel's across town. Wanna rent a car or just take the bus?"

Cynthia crunched up her nose. "They have buses out here?"

"Of course, they do!" Nate scoffed. "I took the liberty of learning the city's public transportation system."

"Is it as good as New York's?" she asked.

"Is *any* city better than ours? They run every 25 to 40 minutes, depending on the route."

"Okaaaay, where's the nearest rental company? I'll pay." She stopped in her tracks and started looking around.

Nate let out a sigh. "I figured."

The couple found the nearest Avis and rented a 2010 blue Toyota RAV4, much to Nate's disgust. Cynthia drove it out of the parking lot and used the GPS to find directions to their hotel.

"You're such a car snob," she told him, while watching the road.

"I just prefer to drive American. My father would disown me if he saw me behind the wheel of a foreign car."

"This is *just* like a Chevy Tahoe. In fact, they're damn near identical! And don't you dare say I don't know cars because I'm a woman. I'll fishtail this sucker and have you out the window before you can say 'Michelle Rodriguez.'"

Nate stifled a laugh, believing the threat, and was quiet the rest of the drive.

They arrived at the Marriott hotel in the heart of Gaslamp Quarter. Cynthia stepped out and tossed the keys to the valet, but he dropped them. Nate kept a straight face, but he was cracking up inside at her attempt to be cool. After walking in, Nate gave the concierge their name, and they received their electronic keycards.

Inside the elevator to the 18th floor, Cynthia asked, "Do we have a view?"

"Yeah, we can see the beach."

"Hmmm."

*What the fuck is she thinking about?* Nate thought.

They stepped off the elevator at their floor, and walked down a long hallway. The rooms were spaced out as Cynthia counted only three doors on each side at their section of the building. Nate pulled out his room keycard and stopped in front of room 1804 at the end of the hall.

"A corner suite?" she asked, a smile growing on her face.

"It's been a while, but I still remember all your *preferences* when it comes to travel accommodations," Nate replied.

She leaned in and gave him a peck on the cheek. "You spoil me so well…"

The door unlocked and Nate pushed in, holding out his arm to let Cynthia walk in first.

Just when she thought Nate had done everything right, her

personality soured at the sight of the room. Everything was terrible. The color of paint on the walls, the furniture. Had it been *that* long since she took a vacation that hotels lost their sense of style? The only bright side was that there was a balcony, and since they were eighteen floors up, they had a great view of the city.

Their suite *was* huge, though. With high ceilings, they pretty much had this side of the floor to themselves, but the walls were nearly soundproof to minimize the VIP parties that the hotel might host.

Cynthia was less than impressed. She walked across the room and opened the door to the balcony. The view was nice. At least they were able to see the beach and ocean off the horizon.

*He could have picked a better place.* But she decided not to hold it against him. There were more important things to attend to. "Okay, I'm going to take a shower and change into something for a nice stroll on the beach. Are we meeting your *musician* interviewee tonight?"

Nate couldn't help but notice the emphasis when mentioning his assignment.

*She knows that assignment is bullshit, I know it.* "I have to call and set up a meeting spot. They told me she'll contact me tomorrow."

That gave him time to think of some way to have Stephanie meet Cynthia and him at a neutral place nearby.

She nodded. "Okay." Then she walked from the balcony to the bathroom, closing the door behind her.

Nate checked his phone for a second and began to unpack.

After a light lunch from room service, Cynthia convinced Nate to take a stroll. He was still jet lagged and wanted to sleep it off, but relented. They took the elevator downstairs and walked out of the hotel.

Nate was wearing sweatpants with a blue sleeveless tee-shirt. Cynthia was turning heads, in a tight shirt with cut-off denim shorts. Despite it being cool for October in New York, San Diego was still hot, with temperatures in the mid-nineties.

There was quite a distance between the couple as they walked down Market Street. He wondered why she was walking so far ahead and where she was going while looking around. They passed several boutiques with Cynthia showing no interest in shopping for clothes.

*What the hell?* he thought as he finally caught up with her.

Cynthia looked back at him and held her chin. "You know, you could use a haircut."

"Huh?"

She then snapped her head and said, "Yeah, and I could use a change-up from this pixie cut, maybe get some extensions or a different color. Let's check out this salon over here…" and started walking up to a nearby establishment called Hair Escape.

It looked familiar to Nate, and he stammered, "Sa… Sa… Salon?" while walking nervously.

She walked over and opened the door, walking in, Nate slowly approached the entrance, mumbling to himself, "Wait. No way, did she…"

He stopped and froze at the sight of Stephanie Grace turning and looking back at him.

# 16

## A DEER IN THE HEADLIGHTS

Despite face-timing each other these past few months, and watching her YouTube videos, even watching that private video multiple times… Stephanie still took Nate's breath away in person. She was wearing jeans and an oversized black blouse, with a blue smock wrapped around her waist.

There were three main chairs, two with someone sitting while a stylist stood behind them. Stephanie turned to them at the entrance from behind the empty middle chair. Nate was still frozen stiff by the sudden meeting. He was certain Cynthia did some research and discovered where Stephanie worked, then came here in the guise of a random excursion.

He started to panic, and he thought quickly of what to say or do. Cynthia was still surveying the premise with her back to him, so he decided to bite the bullet.

"Stephanie?!" he pretended to act surprised. "Oh my God, it *is* you! Heeeeeey, How ya' doing? I didn't know you worked here!"

He conveyed a look with his eyes that Stephanie caught, just as Cynthia turned her head to him.

Stephanie was unsure what was happening, but played along.

"Is that Nate? Nate Durant from Chicago?! What are you doing here?"

Cynthia turned back and looked at Stephanie with a questionable glance.

"I was just in town, doing a story and *my wife* here just happened to walk into *your salon*, here!"

She took a few steps towards the couple. "Wow, *what* a coincidence!"

Nate and Stephanie exchanged big, fake smiles as he gestured to Cynthia. "Um, this is my wife, Cynthia."

Cynthia put her hand out for a handshake, but Stephanie extended her arms and said, "I'm a hugger!" then embraced the unsuspecting woman while mouthing over her shoulder to Nate, *"What the fuck?"*

He quickly mouthed back, *"Just go with it!"*

She released the embrace and put on the fake smile again. "So, can I take it you're interested in… something?"

Cynthia shifted her glance between the two of them and then said, "Um, yes, I actually wanna new color for my hair. Switch up to something… *darker*. What do you think?"

Stephanie looked at her hair. "Hmmm, I might have JUST the color for you."

"Um, I'll just take a haircut. You have a barber here?" Nate asked.

"I do, actually," Stephanie replied, with a nod.

In an isolated corner, an African American man stood up from the barber chair he was sitting on and waved him over.

Nate gave Cynthia a goofy look to her deadpan face as they proceeded to separate chairs.

The salon was pretty big, so Nate was just out of earshot of the ladies as they started conversing. The barber wrapped his neck with two strips of disposable paper and then fastened a cape cover on him.

"What'll it be?" he asked.

"Um, just a shape up."

"You got it."

As he began, Nate looked at the two women talking across the room with a worried glance.

After a few snips with his scissors, the man leaned in to Nate. "We already know your story," he whispered. "Bringing your wife to an old female friend's establishment? You walking on some hot coals, my man."

"I know, I know!" Nate hissed. "But it's not like that. We were just friends!"

He scoffed. "Yeah, she ain't gonna care."

Cynthia took a seat as Stephanie sized her up then started mixing her hair coloring.

"So," Cynthia began. "You're a friend of Nate's?"

Stephanie decided to keep their conversation vague, unsure of what Nate had told her. "We worked together a long time ago, but, um, he reached out to me recently after discovering my videos on YouTube. He mentioned something about an article. I thought he was bullshitting," she laughed. "I mean, why would Rolling Stone want to do a story about a hairstylist who occasionally sings, right? That must be crazy."

"Uh-huh, yes. Crazy."

With minimal small talk, Stephanie gave Cynthia a dark shade of red to her short pixie cut and changed it with a nice part on the right side of her head. She went from looking like Beyoncé to looking like Kelly Rowland.

Nate approached the chair, nodding with approval. "Wow. Red looks good on you! I didn't believe it was possible to improve on perfection," he added, with a chuckle.

Cynthia still sensed the awkwardness in the room, but she had to admit, it was a noticeable change for the better. "It looks great! Thank you very much. What do I owe you?"

"Fifty. I applied my discount," Stephanie replied.

"Aww, you didn't have to do that."

"No, I insist." She waved with her hand.

"Well, here's eighty. Thank you very much." Cynthia handed her four twenty-dollar bills.

The two women exchanged awkward looks at each other in a long moment of silence.

Nate coughed, breaking the tension. "Um, we should go, babe. It's been a couple of hours, and I'm kinda hungry."

Cynthia snapped to attention. "Okay, um, we should all get together in the evening while we're here." She turned and asked Stephanie, "Would you like to have dinner tomorrow night? Our treat, of course."

"Oh, um, Saturdays are our busiest days. I have appointments until 7 pm. I'll also be um… entertaining company coming to town tomorrow."

"Cyn, I think she means she rather no—" Nate began.

"That's great, then we can do a double date!" Cynthia exclaimed. "Me and Nate are late sleepers, and we absolutely love the nightlife! I think the four of us can meet for some late-night shenanigans, what do you say? I insist."

Stephanie looked past her to Nate, who rolled his eyes.

"Sure, what the hell? You only live once, right?" She put on her fakest smile.

Cynthia looked back at Nate and then nodded in front of Stephanie. "Excellent. I'll send a car to pick you up here, let's say… 8:30 pm?"

Stephanie tilted her head. "Um, make it 8:45 pm, just in case." She snuck a glance at Nate and then hard blinked. "Wow, it's like *that*? What exactly do you do for a living, Nate?"

Nate was about to answer but Stephanie cut him off. "We'll talk more tomorrow night. Looking forward to it!"

Cynthia turned around, hooked her arm into Nate's, and led him out of the salon.

They were halfway back to the hotel when Nate finally said something about Cynthia's vice grip on his arm. "Um, are you taking my blood pressure or something?"

She hissed through her teeth, "I am squeezing you like this to prevent myself from screaming at you in front of all these people out here."

With that, he braced himself for the worst, once they got back to their hotel room.

Once they arrived and took the elevator to their room, as they walked down the hallway Nate pleaded, "Can we at least get something to eat first?"

She simply shook her head, and they entered the suite.

Cynthia finally let go of Nate's arm and he flexed it a little bit to return the blood circulation. *Okay, here we go.* "Look," Nate began. "Before you freak out…"

"Do I have 'stupid' on my forehead?" Cynthia asked in a sharp tone. "You don't have no article in no damn magazine to write! Admit it!"

"Okay, okay… yes, I lied. I just wanted to come out here to get away from that bullshit in the city annnnnnd catch up with an old friend…" he gestured with his hands. "We're having fun, aren't we?"

"Did you fuck her?" she asked.

"Huh?"

"Motherfucker, you heard me," Cynthia replied sharply.

Nate twisted his face at her tone. *"No!"*

"Do you *want* to fuck her?" she asked quickly.

"Of course not!" As if that were an option. "Can you please relax and stop cursing like you're from 125th Street?"

"I'm fucking serious. If given the chance, would you?" She pointed her finger at him. "If I gave you permission… like that stupid-ass Owen Wilson movie, *'Hall Pass.'* You get only ONE opportunity to have sex with her, no guilt, no consequences, and no revenge fuck for me. You wouldn't take it?"

"NO!" Nate gasped. "That ship has sailed, okay? It hit an iceberg, sank, and not even The Discovery Channel can find it. No fucking way."

"You're gonna have to convince me because I *don't fucking* believe you!"

"Okay, if we're going to have this discussion, I have to eat something first." He stormed past her towards the door. "I'm getting something from the lobby. You want anything?"

"I'll order room service! I think we both need some time to ourselves. We'll talk about this later, but if I get any signals from either one of you, tomorrow I will *check* her so fast, your head will spin."

Nate sighed, then opened the door and left.

Cynthia went to the bedroom, took a pillow, and held against it her face as she let out the loudest scream.

Nate walked down the hallway to the elevator and took it to the lobby. There was a bar on the right side of the front desk. He didn't need a drink but hopefully, they offered some decent food with their spirits.

Inside, there were tables for couples and a few booths for

groups, so he just took a seat at the bar. The bartender was a woman wearing a uniform, but her shirt was open a few buttons, revealing some noticeable cleavage.

*Fuck, is this San Diego or Los Angeles?* He thought.

She approached and he pretended to look above her as if he was in McDonald's checking their Dollar Menu.

"What can I get ya?" she asked.

"Um, you have anything to eat here?"

She turned around and looked where he was looking, then turned back around. "You blind or something?"

Nate sighed and then lowered his gaze. "No, I was trying not to look at your tits, M…"

She pointed suddenly and warned, "The next word out of your mouth better not be, 'Madam' or 'Miss!'"

"…myyyyy dear bartender." Nate finished, politely. "I'll have a beer and some nachos if you have them."

"We don't," she replied sharply. "But we have peanuts."

She slid over a bowl of roasted peanuts and handed him a bottle of Michelob.

He pulled out a twenty-dollar bill and placed it on the bar. "Keep the change and I'll keep the bowl."

She picked up the bill and stuffed it in her shirt.

As she walked away, he whispered to her back, "I hope you don't get a rash…"

A notification hit his phone and he pulled it out. It was from Stephanie on Facebook Messenger.

@StephanieSymphony: "Nate what the hell? Why didn't you tell me you and your wife were coming to my salon?!?!?"

@NatefromNewYork: "Obviously I didn't know. I was just as surprised as you were when we walked in."

@StephanieSymphony: "Yeah, I noticed. You looked like a deer in headlights. So, I take it you haven't told her the real reason we started talking again and why?"

@NatefromNewYork: "No, that would have been a very awkward conversation, 'Hey baby, I found this naked picture online of an old female friend from back in the day, so I was wondering if I could look her up and see if she was okay with it being on the internet.' How do you think that would have went?"

Nate sighed and took another handful of peanuts.

@StephanieSymphony: "No need to get snippy, Nate. Let's just go over the game plan for tomorrow. I was looking forward to some mind-blowing sex this weekend with Heathcliff."

*Ah yes, there's a nice image to put in my head.* He fought his reflex to gag and typed,

@NatefromNewYork: "Well, there's nothing to go over, now. I came clean and told her there's no magazine article. She's pretty much livid, but what's done is done. Now, we'll just have a late-night dinner, talk some mindless conversation for an hour, then go our separate ways. Once we convince Cynthia nothing happened between us, and apparently, nothing ever will, we can go back to New York. You can go back to living your life, and this nightmare will be over."

@StephanieSymphony: "Gee, you make it sound so easy..."

Nate chuckled and shook his head, then grabbed another handful of peanuts.

> @NatefromNewYork: "We're celebrating ten years. I think I know my wife by now."

> @StephanieSymphony: "Nate, last weekend I had twenty laundry clips attached to each of my tits. Trust me, after meeting her once, I already know your wife has layers you haven't even scratched the surface yet."

She went offline as Nate held his phone quietly. Stephanie made her point, but he was turned on by what she just shared with him. He probably couldn't walk straight if he wanted to.

She knew she would regret it in the morning, but Cynthia, being the emotional eater she was, went crazy and ordered nearly every dessert on the hotel's menu. A slice of cheesecake, with an ice cream sundae, two fudge brownies, and finally, a cinnamon roll the size of a basketball.

And goddamn, it felt so good to eat it all.

She sat in silence on the floor, while cutting small pieces of the roll with a plastic knife and fork, when the room's telephone rang.

*It wouldn't be Nate. He would have called my cell. Did I leave this number to the girls?* She asked herself.

Reaching over her head, Cynthia found the hotel suite's phone and answered, "What?"

"There she is…" Vanessa said triumphantly. "I called three other hotels that were up to your taste in San Diego. This was my last pick."

"You know me sooooo well!" Cynthia replied.

"Uh-huh. Let me guess, there wasn't any article for Nate to write, right? It was all bullshit."

"Give the girl a cigar!"

"So now you're up to your elbows in food, while Nate is sulking off somewhere, because you finally caught his ass cheating with someone he wanted to meet over there, right?" Vanessa concluded.

"THAT'S still a fuckin mystery! I was right about her being some singer he was following on YouTube and Facebook, who was also running some salon out here, but Nate keeps saying they're just old friends. I'll find out more tomorrow."

"How?" Vanessa asked.

"Double date!" Cynthia said, after eating a bite of her cinnamon roll. "She apparently has a boyfriend who's in town, so we're getting together in the evening. It's time to settle this shit!"

"Okay, just make sure he's actually cheating, Cyn. If this is some innocent thing and they really are just friends… I'm just saying, he's not worth losing over you making an ass of yourself."

"The fuck's that mean, Van?"

"It means, if you drop him over some stupid shit, he'll be the next girl's great catch. Then you'll be oh-for-two. Be careful."

Vanessa hung up the phone and her last words stayed with Cynthia.

After finishing with Stephanie on Facebook Messenger, Nate got tired of peanuts and found a pizza place down the street from the hotel. His cell phone rang just as he was sitting down with a couple of cauliflower slices.

With a sigh, he pulled it out and answered, "This better be important!" to whoever was calling.

"Hello to you, too," Sean replied.

"Oh, it's you."

"Not going well, I take it."

"I'd rather have Frank Thomas take a swing at my balls than live through the last six hours again."

Sean laughed over the line. "You are too funny! Well, now that the jig is up, when are you coming home?"

"Monday. I think things have died down with that rapper. I just have to survive the next forty-eight hours and I'm home free," Nate replied, and took a bite of pizza.

"Meaning?"

He took a sip of his water. "We're going to some restaurant. Stephanie's boyfriend came down here from San Francisco, and Cynthia talked her into them spending the evening with us."

Sean laughed again. "You're gonna size him up, aren't ya?"

"Wouldn't be a good friend if I didn't voice any concerns upon meeting the guy, would I?"

"Man, what I would give to actually be there to see this!"

"I'll fill you in on all the juicy details when I get back."

"Looking forward to it. Stay frosty… hell, stay *alive*!"

Sean was still laughing to himself when Nate hung up the phone and resumed eating.

Cynthia took a long bath (which was dangerous after eating so much.) and stepped out of the bathroom with a towel wrapped around her. After flipping through the channels aimlessly for ten minutes, she relented and picked up the hotel's phone, and dialed Jennifer's number.

"Hello?" Jennifer answered, obviously annoyed.

"Well damn, did I interrupt something?"

"Did you remember the time difference? It's almost 11 o'clock over here."

"Oh fuck. I forgot, sorry."

Jennifer sighed. "You're fine. I'm more pissed that Ryan Gosling isn't plowing my ass at this indecent hour. What's up?"

"You got three-way-calling? I wanna hear Gloria's take, as well as yours, on what I'm about to tell you."

"Oooh, shit! Let me get some wine while we at it!"

Ten minutes later, Jennifer, Cynthia, and Gloria were talking over each other about their theories of what was going on with Nate and Stephanie.

"Girl, he's fuckin' her."

"No doubt in my mind." Jennifer agreed with Gloria.

"If he didn't already, he wants to, and probably be thinking about it when you two be going at it."

"I don't know, Gloria," Cynthia began. "I would have known about it if he were cheating, but I think *something* happened between them in the past."

"Has he mentioned any exes from his past before?" Jennifer asked.

"Yeah, he told me about relationships he had in New York before meeting me, but nothing about anyone in Chicago."

"Hmmph, he probably didn't think that would count!" Gloria and Jennifer shared a chuckle.

"Good one, Gloria!" Cynthia said.

"But seriously, make sure you *know* what they're doing, and if he's doing wrong, fuck his shit up," Jennifer began. "I've been rooting for y'all, but shit, men cheating is just their nature, like breathing. You have to do *a lot* to keep one!"

"Mmm-hmmm!" Gloria chimed in.

They were all quiet for a moment, then Gloria said, "Look, I know you got doubts, but if you find out the truth and things go south, I have a cousin out there in Sherman Heights near you. He can get you *anything,* if you know what I mean."

"Uh, hey!" Jennifer interjected. "I don't need to be hearing this. I'm hanging up right now for some plausible deniability."

"Wait, if you hang up and you set up the call between the two of us…" Cynthia began, then she heard the click. "Gloria, you still there?"

"Yeah, I'm here."

"Oh, whew, I thought I'd lose you both," Cynthia said, and started laughing.

Gloria laughed along with her, and they continued their conversation.

**17**

---

# CALM BEFORE THE STORM

SATURDAY MORNING STARTED WITH A DOWNPOUR OF RAIN, BUT luckily it passed by four o'clock. The sun was in and out through the clouds when Nate and Cynthia woke up. They took separate showers and ate a light lunch. While Cynthia placed the order for an UberBlack to pick up Stephanie at the salon, Nate searched for a restaurant nearby.

"What about The Prohibition Lounge? They have live entertainment and are open until 2 am," Nate asked. He showed her his phone, which had candid pictures of the restaurant and its patrons.

"How many stars? What are their reviews on Yelp?" Cynthia asked.

Nate rolled his eyes and Cynthia noticed. "Fine, I'm sure that place will be decent." She pointed at him. "*Make* a reservation and get the best table in the house."

"Yes, dear."

Stephanie slept in and left the salon to be opened by one of her other stylists. She actually lied to Cynthia and Nate about her appointments. There was a chance of a walk-in, but in reality, she had only three appointments, starting at one o'clock, and her last one was at six. Heathcliff called her last night and she let him know what this evening's plans were. He was thrown by the announcement but was excited about meeting new people.

Cynthia seemed okay, but Stephanie still had doubts about tonight. She was hurt by Nate keeping certain details about them a secret but understood his reasoning… to a point. Hopefully, the conversation would stay friendly, and the couple would return back east, never to be seen again.

During her second appointment of the day, a text came in on her phone. It was from Cynthia. She informed her that they would be going to some place on Fifth Avenue, off Market Street. An Uber would pick her up and take her back this evening. She never used the rideshare app before, since it only started in San Diego last year. This was putting her outside her comfort zone, but she managed to take it in stride. She had the perfect outfit in mind to wear for the evening and was anticipating having a wonderful time.

Nate had on his best suit as he stepped out of the bathroom and checked himself out in the mirror above the dresser on the wall.

"Hmmm, not old enough for *Casino Royale,* but smooth enough for *Quantum of Solace*," he whispered.

Cynthia was still in the walk-in closet, wearing her bra and panties, searching through the few outfits she brought.

"We have to be there at nine!" Nate yelled.

"We can be fashionably late! That's what reservations are for!" she barked back.

Nate sighed. *Hopefully Stephanie will get there first. They'll seat her and her boy toy, then we'll show up.*

True to his prediction, Stephanie and her boyfriend Heathcliff were picked up and arrived at The Prohibition Lounge ten minutes before the hour. The car that took them there was clean and roomy. They were impressed by the ride, and the restaurant, once they were inside.

Cynthia finally picked a blue dress, and the couple left their hotel suite five minutes after ten. It was a fifteen-minute drive from the hotel, but they arrived, and a valet accepted their keys as Nate escorted Cynthia inside the restaurant.

Stephanie was wearing a shimmering black dress that hugged her body while making her look slimmer. She sat next to a tall African American man who wasn't exactly fat, but wasn't skinny, either. He had a muscular build, as if he played semi-pro football. Wearing a gray suit that looked like it was tailor made for him by someone in Italy. Stephanie saw Nate and Cynthia from across the room and waved them over. As the couple approached the table, Stephanie and her companion stood as she introduced him.

"Nate and Cynthia Durant, meet Heathcliff Robson."

Heathcliff extended his hand out to Nate, who despised him immediately, so he squeezed his hand extra hard to test his strength.

"Nice to meet you," Nate said, with his fakest smile.

Heathcliff cocked his head and smiled himself. "Likewise."

Nate looked at Heathcliff with a fierce stare, who matched it with one of his own, as they continued to shake hands for an extended period of time. They finally broke the handshake, still staring at each other as the couples took their seats. They were sitting close to the stage, where entertainment was provided by various acts.

A waiter arrived and greeted each of them with a nod. "Good evening, my name is Gerrard, I'll be serving you tonight. The kitchen is still open, but only for another hour. After that, it's just appetizers and spirits. No beer or soft drinks, but we will have water. The evening's special is tortellini with clam sauce. Here are your menus. Do you need a minute, and would you like any refreshments to start you off?"

"I'll take a mimosa while looking over the menu," Cynthia said.

"Um, just water for me, please," Stephanie requested.

"Nothing for me, thanks," Nate replied.

"I'm good as well," Heathcliff agreed.

The waiter wrote all their drinks on a notepad and took off.

"Um, excuse me, I need to powder my nose."

Stephanie stood up and walked to the restroom as Heathcliff pulled out his smartphone to check an email. Nate leaned to Cynthia and whispered, "I'm not gonna say something suicidal like *'Pace your drinking,'* but I will *suggest* that you behave yourself and not hit the sauce too hard. Please."

"You're right," she began. "That *would* be suicide to say such things, and I plan to behave." She then turned her face into a crazed and wild-eyed glance for a moment. "Okay?" then went back to her normal face.

The waiter returned with two drinks. A minute later, Stephanie returned to the table and Heathcliff put away his phone. Cynthia took a long sip and Nate told himself it was going to be a long night.

After the full-course meal and dessert, the two couples and the rest of the restaurant enjoyed the live entertainment, with minimal conversation, until midnight. Once the last performer finished, the restaurant started to empty, but the four of them stayed and finally started to reminisce.

"So how long have you been seeing each other?" Cynthia asked.

She had at least three martinis and was feeling very tipsy. *At least she was more pleasant to be with,* Nate thought.

Stephanie was a bit soused herself, despite only having a glass of champagne with her meal. She was leaning on Heathcliff and volunteering more information than asked while petting his arm like one would stroke a cat.

"Six wonderful years… um, I'm sure Nate has told you about… our arrangement."

Cynthia smiled and waved her hand. "No need to feel embarrassed, I'm sure."

"Uh, my estranged wife and I are only staying together until our daughter graduates from high school. We both have plans to move on to our *separate* ways after that," Heathcliff interrupted.

Nate chuckled. "Gotcha."

Stephanie suddenly blurted out, "Me and Heathcliff engage… in extracurricular sexual activities… roleplay, BDSM, spankings… I even peg him on special occasions," she whispered, with a playful wink.

Heathcliff blushed sheepishly, as Nate and Stephanie shared a chuckle, but Cynthia didn't appear to get the joke, looking confused. "Uh, peg him?" she asked.

Nate leaned in and whispered in her ear. Her eyes got extremely wide and her jaw dropped.

"Can *we* try that?" she asked, turning to him.

"No!" he replied, a little too quickly.

They continued their conversation until the host walked up on stage with an announcement. "Evening, ladies and gentlemen. We are very thankful you chose to spend your weekend at our establishment. It's time for our amateur hour! Where we invite anyone out there from the audience to come to the stage and perform. Are there any entertainers out there who can sing or tell a few jokes?"

Stephanie sobered up and felt a wave of apprehension that Heathcliff noticed, but Nate took this moment to put the four of them on the spot. "We have a singer, right here!" he yelled.

Cynthia gave her husband a look, as Stephanie and Heathcliff also turned to Nate.

"What are you doing?!" Stephanie hissed, wide-eyed.

"C'mon, it'll be fun. I saw your YouTube videos!" Nate encouraged her, with a grin.

"That was in the privacy of my living room!"

Heathcliff stepped in. "You don't have to do it if you don't want to…"

She snapped her head. That was all she needed, being defiant to his attempt to control her. She stood up instantly and started walking towards the stage. Nate led what was left of the audience as they all began to clap and cheer her on.

Once on stage, Stephanie felt more relaxed and whispered to the host the song she wanted to sing. He nodded and introduced her, then backed away as the spotlight centered on her. Stephanie proceeded to sing a perfect rendition of Duffy's *Syrup and Honey* that brought a stirring round of applause.

After taking a modest bow, Stephanie walked back to their table and sat down. She looked at Heathcliff and whispered,

"*Never* tell me I don't have to do anything I don't want to do. That's not *your* decision to make."

He gave her a look then broke into a huge smile. "You are such a brat."

She joined him in the laughter, then noticed the blank looks from Nate and Cynthia.

"Sorry." Stephanie's cheeks turned a shade of pink in embarrassment. "We're not used to being out in public and sometimes—"

"Think nothing of it. I completely understand," Cynthia interrupted, with a dismissive wave.

"That song definitely helped liven things up again," Nate noticed, as the after-hours crowd started filling the restaurant again, with more singers performing one at a time.

None were as good as Stephanie, though.

"So, tell me more about yourself, Steph… may I call you 'Steph?' I feel like I know you like a sister now," Cynthia asked, with a wide smile.

Stephanie found the question unnerving as the smile. "Um, any friend of Nate is already family to me as well, but 'Stephanie' will do just fine. Steph always sounds short for Stephen, instead of Stephanie."

Cynthia chuckled. "Sure, no problem… I'm just playing. The vodka's starting to make me giddy."

Stephanie relaxed as the tense moment passed. "So, I actually grew up in Chicago myself. Me and Nate go way back actually," she began. "We've known each other since starting at IPS in 1998."

Cynthia turned to Nate with a fake shocked expression on her face. "Realllllly?"

Nate adjusted his collar and started coughing suddenly. He reached out for his glass of water. But Cynthia quickly reached out and moved it out of his reach.

Heathcliff and Stephanie exchanged looks, then he asked Nate, "You okay over there, man?"

Nate finally grabbed his glass and took a long swallow and cleared his throat. "Ahem, just fine. Think I accidentally swallowed my spit or something."

Cynthia took a napkin and playfully wiped his mouth as if he were a child who made a mess. "He's such a klutz, but I love 'im." She then gave him a small peck on his cheek and whispered, "Grew *up* in Chicago, huh?"

Stephanie smiled and gave Heathcliff a nudge. "Awww, you see? That's true love, right there! You two are too much! You're very lucky Nate! You too, Cynthia."

Heathcliff rolled his eyes and drummed his fingertips for a moment.

Nate was still embarrassed but continued the conversation. "Thanks. Um, enough about the old days in Chicago… let's change the subject. Tell us how you ended up here in Long Beach. I'm pretty sure you still don't know how to swim!"

"Ha! I learned, actually, Mr. Funny-man! But, you know, I hated Chicago with a passion, so when I came back from Miami after that last assignment, I packed up and left town once my lease was up. I moved in with my aunt around 2004."

"You've been out here for nine years? Wow!" Nate said, impressed.

"Yep, my aunt worked me like a Mexican housekeeper while she taught me how to do hair. I was a shampoo girl at first, but I kept my ears open and watched her like a hawk. Learned everything I know now."

She then sighed a breath. "Then in 2009, when she was on her way to open the salon one morning, a bank robber fleeing the police ran a red light and T-boned her at the crosswalk."

"Damn!" Nate exclaimed.

"She was in a coma for three weeks before her body just gave out. Nate, I tell you, I almost went back to Chicago after that, but I kept her salon open, and even after two other stylists left, I worked my way back, and it worked. I finally got back in the black last year. I have loyal clientele, and word of mouth has been good."

"You run the place all by yourself?" Cynthia asked.

"Yep. Hired new hairdressers and even added a barber." She snickered. "Lucky for you, Nate. We all squawk at each other like hens, but the respect is there."

"Well, I'm glad it all worked out. You always *were* an opportunist, Stephanie."

She narrowed her eyes at the comment and there was an awkward moment of silence.

Heathcliff noticed the tension and asked, "So, how long are *you two* in town? I, unfortunately, have to start back for San Francisco tomorrow afternoon to get there by the evening."

"We leave first thing Monday morning, but you're right." Cynthia stood up, sensing the night was over. "We don't wanna take up all your time down here. I'm sure you two have some alone time to get to. I just wanted to get together for a little bit, since Nate here hasn't seen you in *so* many years."

Stephanie chuckled nervously, "Right. Um, let's settle up. You're not paying for everything we had tonight, no matter how much you insist."

Cynthia put her hands in a yielding motion. "Alright. Let the gentlemen sort it out. I have to use the bathroom anyways." She headed to the restrooms on the left side of the restaurant.

Nate pulled out his wallet as Heathcliff checked the bill. "I get the feeling there's more than meets the eye, here," Heathcliff said, as he looked back and forth between Stephanie and Nate.

"It's a long story. Thank you for being civil for *most* of the evening," Stephanie replied. "I'll fill you in when we get home, after some reprimands."

Heathcliff arched his eyebrow, as Nate switched glances between the couple, but said nothing.

Heathcliff closed the bill then fished out a fresh hundred-dollar bill from the lining pocket of his suit jacket.

"This should cover our half and the tip."

Nate took the bill and rubbed it in his fingers to see if it felt real. "Nice clean bill, here. It's a shame we didn't talk about what *you* do for a living, there… 'Cliff?'"

"Yes, I suppose it is… maybe next time." Stephanie turned away from them to put on her coat, as a wide smile came across Heathcliff's face and he suddenly grabbed Nate's other hand for a death grip of a handshake. "*IF* there's a next time," he hissed.

Nate did his best not to buckle, but the pressure nearly brought him to his knees. Cynthia walked back to the table as Heathcliff finally let go and grabbed his coat from the back of his chair.

"We straight here?" Cynthia asked.

"Yep," Nate squeaked in a high-pitched voice. "Been a pleasure to see you, Stephanie. You too, Heathcliff."

The couple left, as Nate put in a few twenties from his wallet with the bill, and left it on the table, then moved his fingers to get the circulation flowing in his hand again. It was the second time someone had put him in a paralyzing hold in twenty-four hours and he was getting quite annoyed with it.

"You okay to drive?" Nate asked Cynthia, once they stepped outside. "If not, I can—"

"Nope, I'm alright," she answered, and took the keys from the valet when he pulled up and stepped out of the car.

He recognized the tone of her voice. It was going to be a long drive back to the hotel.

As they started back, Nate got right to the point. "What's

wrong?"

Cynthia stopped at a red light, then turned to him. "Why didn't you tell me she was from Chicago?"

"It slipped my mind. That was over ten years ago."

"And the fact that she worked with you at… what was it? IPS?"

The light turned green, and she resumed driving. Nate kept quiet and Cynthia asked, "Whattsamatter? Now, you wanna be quiet? Yeah, *that's* what's wrong."

Nate finally had enough. He was in a corner… and it was time to put all the cards on the table.

"Alright, fine!" He said with a forced breath. "She broke my heart, okay? Smashed it into a million pieces! We were co-workers for nearly four years doing document scanning gigs and I liked her. We were good friends, hung out, went to a couple of movies, but she didn't want to take the next step, okay? You see she's into all that crazy, aggressive, alpha male schtick… and I tried to act like that, as a front. She saw right through me and at the end of our last scanning assignment, I told her how I really felt."

Nate took a breath and bit down on his lip in frustration, then continued.

"And she left. Walked out on me. I never saw her again… until three months ago, back in August."

He pulled out his phone, unlocked it, and brought up the picture from Tumblr, then held it up. "I found this picture online and I looked her up, thinking it was some sort of revenge porn. We started talking again. And that's the God's honest truth."

He finished his speech and looked for an emotional response from Cynthia. She stopped at another red light, reached over, and took the phone out of his hand. She studied the picture for a moment, then looked up at him.

"This the only picture?" she asked.

He simply nodded, unsure what she was thinking.

Cynthia nodded slowly and pressed to delete the photo. Then checked the phone's trash and deleted the picture *permanently*. When the light turned green, she handed him back the phone and resumed driving. She didn't say a word the rest of the drive, even as Nate pressed and persisted until they pulled up to the hotel.

They went back inside and took the elevator up, neither one saying anything. Nate was nervous. When Cynthia was quiet it could be a good thing… or a bad thing. It was almost four in the morning, and he was certain they would just go straight to bed. Tomorrow, he would feel her fury after a lengthy period of rest.

But then something weird happened…

As soon as the door slammed behind them, she turned around and began kissing him passionately. Nate was shocked beyond comprehension, but he wasn't about to stop and ask questions. They started ripping each other's clothes off and she pulled him into the bedroom. They necked like teenagers in heat, then proceeded to fuck like both of them were going to separate prisons the next morning.

The raw and animalistic act went on for hours, then they finally succumbed to their limits and fell asleep in each other's arms.

Sunday morning at seven o'clock, Cynthia opened one eye, then slowly slipped out of the bed, grabbed her phone, and tiptoed to the bathroom. She looked back at Nate. He was out like a light. Fireworks wouldn't wake him up. She had to admit, she could barely stand on her rubbery legs herself. Last night they took it to a level that was rarely seen in years. *But she had something else in mind…*

Nate needed closure from this woman, and she was just the

person to give it to him, with some help. She sent a text to Gloria, asking for the number of that cousin in Sherman Heights. Her mind was forming a plan that would have only two possible outcomes, neither of them any good.

The sun was beginning to shine directly in Nate's face as he finally opened his eyes. He was sore as he slowly sat up in bed. After feeling around behind him, he noticed Cynthia was gone.

"Babe?" he called out, thinking she was in the bathroom.

He stood up and felt it immediately in his knees and lower back. "Holy shit," Nate whispered. "I'm not the young man I once was, whew!"

As he started walking to the bathroom, a note on the minibar caught his eye. He went over and picked it up.

*"Wanted to walk around the beach before leaving."*

"Hmmm, I wonder if I can catch up to her," he mused.

Nate went to the bathroom to wash up and put on a fresh change of clothes.

The gas station was in the middle of a nondescript street, with a few people going in and out of the convenience store nearby.

Cynthia pulled up in the RAV4 and stopped at the furthest pump, pretending to get gas.

A Hispanic teenager wearing red shorts and a white tee-shirt approached, as she walked back from the gas tank, waiting at the driver's side door.

"You Gloria's friend?" he asked.

"Yeah… you got that for me?" she asked, pulling out a folded wad of hundred-dollar bills.

He looked around and slipped her a brown paper bag.

"Hope you know how to use it."

Cynthia didn't answer him. She just put on her sunglasses and whispered, "Walk away."

Which he did and disappeared as quickly as he came.

She stepped inside, started the car, and dialed the number to Stephanie's salon.

"Um, hello?"

"Stephanie! Good morning, it's just me, Cynthia. I was just checking to see if you made it home last night and that you're okay."

"Um, yeah. Thanks again for last night. It was great seeing Nate again, *and* you as well." She paused for a moment, then said, "You got a good man there, Cynthia. I hope you know that. Um, treat him as such."

Cynthia didn't know what to say. "Wow. That's nice of you to say. Um, can I ask you for one last favor, Stephanie?"

"Um, sure…"

"I hate to do this, but if you have some time this evening, could you swing by our hotel? Nate told me the truth about everything, including the picture he found on the internet of you, and I just wanna hash things out between the two of y'all while being in the same room… one last time."

There was an awkward silence over the phone, but Stephanie sighed and said, "That's a relief. I really hated lying to you."

"I understand."

"Um, okay, sure. Where are you staying?"

"We're at the Marriott in the Gaslamp Quarter. Suite 1804. I appreciate it. I think Nate deserves some closure."

"You know what? You're absolutely right. I'll be there around… 6 pm?"

"That works! See you then." Cynthia hung up the phone.

The beach was calm, with a few regulars out this early in the morning. Nate wandered up and down the shore, looking for Cynthia. When there wasn't any sign of her, he decided to just walk aimlessly for a couple of hours. If anything happened, he had his cell phone. He probably just missed her, and she went back to the hotel.

It *was* weird she didn't call to check in, though.

A couple of women walked by him. One of them had a lingering eye, checking him out. He flashed a smile and kept walking.

*It's a good thing I don't live out here…*

He stopped walking, found a wall to lean on, and looked around for a moment. He thought about what Cynthia said after their DJ set last week. Perhaps it was time to slow things down and concentrate on their relationship. Nate started thumbing his ring while thinking about Cynthia.

Obviously, the passion is still there when both of them were in sync. If things were less stressful, they would be happier. But there was no way he would be a trophy husband, making social appearances and living off her parent's money. There just wasn't any reason to work ten different jobs anymore.

Nate made the decision to drastically change his workload and focus more on his marriage. He knew it was the right thing to do, and he was going to tell Cynthia his decision the minute he saw her. The tide was washing waves on the beach, so Nate decided to take off his socks and shoes like a bohemian beachcomber and walk slowly back to the hotel.

**18**

___

# WE'RE GOING TO MAKE THIS WORK

NATE WASN'T BACK YET, AND IT WAS A FEW MINUTES AFTER SIX o'clock, but Cynthia wasn't bothered. She knew he would be back at any moment… unless something happened to him. She put the negative thoughts out of her mind as the doorbell rang. Wearing a casual outfit, Cynthia answered the door.

Stephanie stood in the hallway, with a look of apprehension on her face. "Uh, hey."

Cynthia smiled. "Hey Steph, come on in. Nate went out for a walk, but he should be back any minute now."

Stephanie chuckled and entered the room. "Now, Cynthia… I remember telling you about calling me 'Steph.'"

*Bitch, I'll call you whatever the fuck I want.* "Oh, I'm sorry, it slipped my mind," Cynthia replied, with a fake smile, and closed the door behind her.

Stephanie looked around. "Wow, this room is amazing… how can you afford this on a teacher's salary?"

"Nate told you I used to be a teacher?" Cynthia asked.

"Uh, yeah… Used to? What happened?"

The sound of the door opening made both women look in that direction as Nate entered. The door slammed behind him,

253

and he tilted his head. "Stephanie?" he began. "Wh… what are you doing here?"

Stephanie opened her mouth to speak, but Cynthia cut her off. "I invited her here. I felt there was some… unfinished business between the two of you."

"Oh?" Nate's eyes danced, jumping from each side of the room as he remembered what Sean told him about being with two women. He walked slowly to the middle of the room.

"That's right," Cynthia replied, then reached into her purse and pulled out a 9mm pistol.

"Cyn, what the fuck are you doing?!" Nate yelled, at the sight of the gun.

"Wha… wha… what is this? You're robbing me?" Stephanie gasped.

Cynthia snorted. "Ha! With those fake-ass secondhand Jimmy Choo shoes and that cheap knock-off Fiocchi purse? Please! I got more money than you'll ever see, singing in bars and doing hair!"

"Hey! These are *real* Jimmy Choo's, bitch!" Stephanie barked, insulted by the comment.

Nate tried to use that moment to move close to Cynthia, and possibly grab the gun. *Could it actually be loaded?* He asked himself.

She sidestepped to keep the gun on both of them. "Don't you come any closer, Nate, I see you! I know you're thinking you can take this piece from me! Put your hands up, now!"

Nate and Stephanie raised their hands.

Cynthia waved the gun back and forth between the two of them. "You and her obviously have some unfinished business, so we're gonna have some closure right now!"

"What are you talking about?"

"You two are going into that bedroom…" Cynthia instructed. "And *fuck* for as long as you can!"

They both screamed, "WHAT?!"

"You heard me! Now get in there!" She waved the gun to the bedroom. "GO!"

"Baby, please, let's just talk about this… put the gun down." Nate inched forward again, getting closer.

Cynthia held the gun with both hands at Nate. "Don't take another step towards me, Nate! Or I will pull this trigger and blow your head off, then hers, and finally my own because I'm not going to jail!"

"Cynthia this is crazy!" Nate yelled.

"You haven't SEEN crazy yet! You wanna see crazy, Nate?!"

"I seriously do NOT want to see crazy," Stephanie whispered.

"You shut up!"

Nate suddenly reached out to Cynthia, she quickly pointed the gun over his head and fired a shot.

"Holy shit!" he gasped, and took two steps back, as the sound echoed in the room.

"Didn't think there were any bullets, did ya? Now that you know I'm serious," she motioned with the gun to the bedroom, "get in there AND FUCK!"

Stephanie and Nate rushed into the bedroom and closed the door.

"Nate, nothing against you and your girl there… I have to admit… this shit is *really* turning me on!" Stephanie admitted with a breath. "Heathcliff and I only *talked* about sexual gunplay, but she took it to the next level. I'm scared and horny at the same time!"

Nate turned and gave her a look. "Really, Stephanie? *Really?*"

She just shrugged. "Well, we might as well get this over with," Stephanie said, as she began to undress.

Nate turned away, looking back at the door. "What are you doing?"

"Making good of a crazy situation…" she grinned. "We'll have to keep this from Heathcliff of course but… c'mon, don't act like you don't want this!"

Nate waved his arm. "Stop it, I'm not having sex with you! Put your shirt back on!" He then turned to face her again, pointing a finger. "And also, don't act like this thing between us was one-sided, *you* had feelings too!"

"Feelings as friends, that's it! I never once gave you the idea that things could work between us!"

"Bullshit! Friends don't go on dates, they *do not* have phone sex, and they don't make out!"

"Hey, we made out *one* time and I was drunk, that doesn't count. As for talking dirty and getting our rocks off over the phone… well…" She tapered off.

"It was more than what you want to admit… and you know it!"

Back outside, on the other side of the bedroom door, Cynthia lowered the gun and tilted her head.

*Were they… arguing?*

"I'm sorry, I never saw you as anything other than… than…" Stephanie began.

"Go on, *say it!*"

"Than a nerdy big brother. There, I said it, happy? All the comic books, video games, the same taste in music and books. Nothing about you… about *us*, felt sexy." She took a seat on the edge of the bed, still wearing jeans and her bra, with her head down. "You wanted something that just wasn't there, Nate."

He was furious now. "No, *NO*! When I became more aggressive with you, even though you saw through it, there was some part of you, some small part, who was interested in where we could have taken it. You were just scared!"

She shook her head. "You really don't *believe* that, do you? Geez, you're more gullible than I give you credit for."

Nate took a breath and sighed. "I wish I could be that guy for you. That sadomasochist you want to dominate you, to break you into submission, to bring you to my beck and call... but I couldn't... it wasn't me... it's not who I am," he confided.

Stephanie nodded, still looking down. "I know. I've always known. I had you pegged the moment we met. You liked me, and you were pretending to be something you weren't, just for my attention. That's why nothing happened that night. As much as you wanted it to. I couldn't be with someone... fake."

That last word brought Nate back to that night. He buried the memories so deep that he thought he was cured of the pain it represented. The pain of falling off a bike and breaking his leg into a million pieces. He sat on the floor, just to look up to her again, his goddess, worshiping her as she rejects him again... like she did before.

"I'm sorry, Nate. I'm fucked up in the head, my wires are crossed! The only way I can associate true, unconditional love is through violent, life-endangering, torturous, and agonizing-to-the-verge-of-tears pain. Only *he* can do that to me... put the fear of God in me and drenches my panties at the same time." She took a breath, then looked directly at Nate.

"I live to push him to his limits and test how far I can go with him. He's so unpredictable, you have no idea. That little tiff we had in the restaurant? With the song? If he was in company he could trust, he would have choked me right there and I would have *loved it*. I know one day he'll actually kill me, and if that happens, I will leave this earth… fulfilled."

Nate thought back to his hand and that handshake between him and Heathcliff. He gave Stephanie a look of concern as she continued.

"I've always been a spoiled brat. Raised by two parents who gave me everything I ever wanted and let me get fat. We were middle-class suburbanites, living in a house with the white picket fence and getting along with all our neighbors. Do you have any idea how fucking *boring* that shit is?"

She was crying now, the tears slowly coming down the side of her face. "When I was 18, I paid a motorcycle gang $600.00 to run a train on me and take my virginity. I… I couldn't get it any other way. I never even kissed a guy until I was 23." She sniffled and wiped her face. "You deserve someone better. You were one of the good guys. You deserve a woman who would make you happy. Not someone you would worry about all the time if she was cheating on you, making you all insecure. No one deserves that, Nate… especially not you."

Nate stood up. "But that's exactly who I have now. She wasn't always like this. In fact, she only became this insecure after we lost weight! When I was 400 pounds, and she was nearly 350, we were *both* a whole lot happier! Because we *knew* no one else wanted us, that all we had was each other and we were both fine with that!"

He turned to look at the door and clenched his right hand with determination. "Deep down, despite our appearances, despite how everyone else sees us… we can't tear away from our former selves."

Nate turned and looked behind him. He knew what he had to do, and nobody was going to stop him.

The door flew open, and Nate emerged from the bedroom. Cynthia noticed he was moving quickly and since he was still dressed, she surmised nothing had happened between him and Stephanie.

"Nate! I'm not playing! I—" she began, bringing the gun up.

"I'm not playing either, Cyn!" he said, and reached for the gun after taking three long steps across the room.

She closed her eyes and pulled the trigger. The gunshot echoed in her ear. Cynthia had no clue what had just happened, as Nate froze. His hand was covering the muzzle of the gun. The bullet whizzed by the left side of his ear by *one inch*. It took all his remaining strength, but he pulled the weapon out of her hand and called out to Stephanie.

"Stephanie? You can come out now," Nate said, calmly.

She slowly stepped out of the bedroom with her shirt back on. He motioned with his head to the door, and she proceeded to leave without another word.

Nate was running on pure adrenaline, afraid to look down at his left hand. He closed his eyes and chose his words carefully.

*Now… it was time… to yell…*

Stephanie stood there before him, her whole body shaking, barely able to comprehend what had just happened.

"Ten years… ten years of nagging," he began. "Ten years of hearing 'The garbage has to go out,' ten years of dealing with *your fucking* family… ten years of dealing with your *thieving* uncle and his cons, your crazy ass sister… ten years of marriage, of me never cheating, never even *thinking* about it…" he finally opened his eyes. "And you have the nerve to *pull a gun on me?!*"

Nate stepped forward and backed Cynthia against the wall, his right hand was still clenched in a fist, and punched the wall an inch from her face. "If I were my father, you'd have so much foundation on your face to cover up the bruises you would *SHINE*!"

He repeatedly punched the wall in frustration, nearly breaking his knuckles.

"I spend all day in the company of naked women, taking pictures, getting hit on by them left and right, your fucking *sister* even asked me for a kiss, and of *all* the people to get jealous of, you go crazy over some man-eating bitch I haven't seen in over ten fucking years?! REALLY, Cynthia?!"

She was breaking down, now. "I… I can't do this… I can't do this… I… I want a divorce. I know you don't love me anymore. You just love working. You love your jobs. You can't even give me the time of day anymore! Even after ten years, you haven't realized that you don't even *have* to work! You're just ashamed of the possibility of being a trophy husband, that my parents can take care of us if we just let them! There's nothing wrong with a family sharing success!"

"Are you kidding?!" Nate screamed. "I work because you think you're still living with your parents! Your entire lifestyle throughout our entire marriage is just you on autopilot from your first one! When we met, you were a proud and independent schoolteacher, doing what you loved, in order to help children… children you at one time wanted to have before the health scare! But then you got lost… lost in a forest of self-doubt, of wallowing and pity, and now… you're something else."

He took a breath and sighed. There was a tingling feeling coming from his left hand, which he was still afraid to look at.

"If you've given up, if you really can't do this anymore, then fine. But I'm not giving up that damn easily… I love you, and *only* you, Cyn! If getting shot in the hand and *still* being semi-calm is not a sign of that… then I don't know what is! So, we're going to get past this. We're going home and we're going to talk, then talk some more." He sighed. "Then after that, we're going to counseling, and together, we're going to make this work, okay? OKAY?"

She simply nodded.

Nate looked down finally. His left hand was bleeding, with a hole in the middle, but he still somehow managed to keep a grip on the gun. At the sight of the injury, he finally started to get woozy.

"Good, now please pick up the phone and call 911. I think I'm going into shock." He took a few steps back and collapsed onto the couch.

When Nate came to, Cynthia had just hung up the phone after talking to room service. The neighbors had heard what they believed were gunshots and were concerned. She had also called the police and reported an incident with her husband, but they were both fine. They were sending a couple of officers to take a report. Cynthia was frantic, but Nate had a plan.

With the police on their way, he came up with a story to tell them. After the publicized incident with him and .38 Special, he became paranoid and brought a gun for his protection. But Cynthia discovered it in his bag, and he startled her when she pulled it out. The piece dropped to the ground and went off, shooting him in the hand.

He had a CCW made up using his father's connections and even though the gun wasn't registered to him, the police didn't press charges. Chalking up the incident as an accidental discharge. The press even ran with the story and .38 Special used the moment to save face, posting more videos on social media, making fun of Nate. He was a joke now in the Hip-Hop world, but he didn't care.

It was Monday. Nate and Cynthia checked out of the hotel and paid for the hole in the wall in the suite. They were on the flight back to New York, and the captain announced that it would be around fifteen minutes to takeoff. His left hand was bandaged, and neither one of them had said anything since talking to the police.

She finally decided to break the uneasy silence and asked, "That was a hell of an idea you came up with, the whole shooting yourself thing. Where did you get it from?"

"Huh? Oh, *Gimme a Break!* the old TV show from back in the day. It just popped in my head."

She nodded and they got comfortable in their seats. Her thoughts started to wander, and she mumbled something.

"What was that?" Nate asked.

"Oh, I was just thinking of this term I heard. 'Red Eye.' A lot of people call these flights that and I was wondering why."

"Oh, um, flights that go coast to coast, flying over the time zones feel longer than they actually are. Adjusting to that type of time change, a lot of people get jet lagged and their eyes get red like they've been up for 18 hours straight. Hence the term, 'Red Eye.'"

Cynthia nodded again. "You're so smart."

He chuckled. "Thank you."

She looked at his bandaged hand and he lowered it between his legs, hiding it shamefully. They had an awkward moment as she looked away. A tear rolled down her cheek as she began to feel guilty. His bandaged hand came back up and took hers. She looked back at him, looking at her.

"It's going to take some time, Cyn… but we'll get past this, okay?"

She wiped her cheek and nodded.

He let a few minutes go by as the plane taxied towards the runway, then chuckled to himself.

"You know I'm going to probably milk this for at least three months, right?" he asked, jokingly.

"You'll be all 'Hon, the garbage has to go out…' and I'll be like, you shot me in the hand… 'You didn't wash this plate…' well, you shot me in the hand. 'You have to do the laundry…' baby, you did shoot me in the hand…"

"I get it, I get it," Cynthia grunted. "I feel bad enough already."

"I didn't cum baby… well you shot me in the hand, woman. It's a miracle my dick works!" he laughed.

"Oh my God, I hope this plane crashes!"

Gloria was running late for work Wednesday morning, so she checked her phone for a ride downtown to the office. Uber's rates were astronomical, so she switched to Lyft and the app set her up with a car that was five minutes away. She was finally on the sidewalk in front of her building as a blue Ford Taurus pulled up and she climbed in.

The driver turned around and asked her name. "You Gloria?"

She nodded and he took off from the curb.

Two minutes went by, and the car stopped at a red light. Her phone rang in her purse, so she fished it out. Gloria didn't notice the driver put on a gas mask suddenly and locked the windows.

"Hello?" she answered.

"Yeah, this is Mike, your Lyft Driver. I'm in front of the building, but I don't see you."

Gloria looked up and panic took hold of her as she started to feel dizzy. The phone slipped out of her hand and fell on her lap before she passed out, unaware of what was happening.

Two mysterious figures slowly formed as Gloria shook her head and tried to focus. She noticed her wrists were tied to the chair she was sitting on, as the rest of her surroundings became clear. They were in a room on a high floor of a building. She saw the Hudson River and the New Jersey skyline in a window across the room.

"What the fuck is this?!" she demanded.

As her vision finally returned completely, Gloria recognized one of her captors as he stood up from the couch across the room and approached her.

"Hello… Gloria, is it? We haven't been formally introduced, my name's Nate Durant. I'd shake your hand, but I have a slight injury I'm recovering from that I have *you* to thank for, actually."

"Oh, where are my manners? This is Andrew Circoni, one of the best knife throwers in all seven continents. I don't mean those performers you see in the circus, who throws at a wheel from only three feet. Andy here is the real McCoy. Show her, Andy…"

The man pulled a knife out while still sitting on the couch and threw it at her. It missed her face by inches and went into the wall behind her. She gasped and started trembling.

"And that was from 15 feet. Pretty impressive, huh?"

She didn't reply, so he continued.

"Well, now that we're acquainted, I wanted to talk to you about giving my wife Cynthia the idea that I could be cheating on her, or that she should find *your* family member… who is also being dealt with by the way… and acquire a gun!"

A second knife flew by her face, missing it on the opposite side and embedding into the wall.

This time she screamed and started pleading. "You better let me go! I'm a legal assistant to the attorney general! Your ass will end up in Rikers!"

Nate was less than impressed. "Yeah, right… listen here, Ally McBeal. You and my wife are about to become strangers, okay? You're going to unfriend her on all social media, lose her phone number, and *never* see her again, no matter what. That goes for her friend Jennifer as well. You are going solo, from The Supremes to Diana Ross. Got it?"

"She'll never go for that. She'll know *you* did something! I don't care if you didn't cheat on her, you do this, you'll lose her. We've been friends for longer than she's known you!"

"That may be true," Nate admitted. "But eventually she'll forget. Now I'm actually being nice, and as you can tell, this can go another way… with one flick of a wrist."

Another knife hit the wall, coming closer to her face. The knife thrower was examining his fingernails, completely unbothered by their conversation… but ready to act if Nate gave him the signal.

Nate held up her phone. "I took the liberty of replacing your smartphone and duplicating your contacts. Who the hell still uses Sprint anyways? Their service sucks!" He tossed it on a nearby table.

Gloria shook her head. "Hey! That's not mine! It's a government issue, the serial and IMEI numbers have to match what's on file!"

"All taken care of. Just don't try to get it replaced, because

I'll know. I'll be keeping tabs on you to make sure you stay away from Cynthia. I'll track you wherever you go for the next six months until I'm sure you're out of the picture!"

"You're not gonna get away with this! The minute you let me go, you're toast!"

He was quiet for a moment, staring at her, then chuckled. "Yeah, I figured you'd want to do things the hard way, so I have a Plan B. Hey Andy? Do one more blindfolded, then you can leave."

Gloria tensed up, but then Nate waved him off and smiled. "Just kidding. You can go." He then snapped his fingers. Andrew left and from the same door came six huge African American men. They were shirtless and wearing various shorts or sweatpants.

"Okay, so, I won't bother to introduce these guys. They're actually well-known in the adult film industry. Something tells me you probably recognize one or two of them. They're going to pose for some naughty pictures with you…"

Gloria's eyes went wide as he continued.

"…then post those pictures all over the internet and send them to your co-workers. All of them will get exclusive access to *Gloria's Big BLACKED Adventure*. Title pending, of course."

She was still skeptical of his threat. "Bullshit!" she spat.

Nate actually laughed this time. "I am *so* not the one for the bullshit. You have ten seconds to make up your mind… one… five… nine!"

"Alright, alright, alright!" she screamed. "She's ghost, okay? Ancient history… I'll never talk to her again. Fuck!"

Nate grinned and walked up to her. "Glad we have an understanding… now, when you wake up at your apartment…" he suddenly stabbed her with a needle. "You're going to need a shower."

"Wha…?" She gasped then slowly slumped back into the chair.

"You're going to be very, very, sore." Nate completed the thought.

The rest of them encircled her as Nate untied her and instructed the men. "Take some provocative pictures and make a few videos. She'll be picked up and taken back to her place. Be nice…" he said, with a wink, then walked out of the room. They all exchanged smiles and started to remove their clothes.

Thursday morning Jeremy Durant was watching The Today show when his doorbell rang. He got up from the couch and walked to the door. Jeremy pulled it open and was surprised to see his son standing in front of him.

"Nathaniel! When did you fly in? What are—?"

Nate gave his father a hearty embrace, stopping him in mid-sentence.

"I know now, Dad." Nate said. "I get it, I finally get what you were saying… I understand."

"Understand what?" he asked, stepping aside as his son walked in.

"I get what you went through with mom, to have someone you love do something so crazy, your life is in danger."

"Oh." Jeremy simply nodded, closing the door and not asking for details.

"And for a minute dad, for one *long* moment in time, I almost did it. I could actually see myself hitting her. Over and over again… but I didn't. The only thing in my head during that moment was you. I didn't want to follow in your footsteps. I was almost there, but I fought it with every fiber of my being."

"That's good, son!" Jeremy praised. "It's not worth it, no matter how much you may want to, no matter how much it'll feel good in that moment." He sighed. "It's not the answer. If you pick up anything from me, let it be that."

Nate nodded. "So many times I've tried to be something I'm not… someone once didn't think I could be what *she* wanted in a dominating man. To break her spirit and own her submissively. To dominate her, ravage her… and I tried…" he shook his head. "She saw right through me. I just don't know dad… what type of person do I have to be in order to be happy?"

Jeremy looked at his son with a curious glance, wondering who was he talking about.

Nate saw the look. He would probably tell him the whole story another time. "Um, Cynthia and I are trying to work this out, but it just won't be the same… I'm always going to see her… *differently* now," he said, thinking back to when she was holding that gun, and eventually pulling the trigger.

He raised his hand. Now healed, but scarred.

"And *this* will be a constant reminder as well, of course."

"Jesus Christ!" Jeremy gasped. "What happened to your hand?"

Nate knew he was about to tell his father one hell of a story.

# EPILOGUE

Six months later.

It was a nice spring evening, a few minutes after six. Nate was once again at Bryant Park, helping his fellow writers collaborate in a brainstorming session. He was due at his new job, located at 45th Street and 6th Avenue, in a couple of hours. This new group of writers were a bit moodier than the daytime crowd he was used to, but he was a welcomed addition to the wild conversations they usually had.

Nate was sporting a clean, heavily maintained beard and goatee now. He let his facial hair grow, now that he was scaling back on his workload. He finally accepted that he needed more free time in his life, and focus on simpler things.

"...so, who you think gonna replace Letterman on The Late Show next year?" someone asked.

"I think Conan might be picked."

"Nah, I think Craig Ferguson's gonna slide down from his Late Late Show position. He's got first dibs."

A trio of women chimed in on the conversation. "I think they're gonna go radical and have a woman take a crack at being a late-night talk show host."

That made the rest of the group turn towards them. "Who?" one of them asked.

"Chelsea Handler."

The men all broke out in a round of hysterical laughter.

"Hey, her show on the E! channel is a hit, and her contract is up this year. She could take Letterman's place easily!"

One of them scoffed. "You women don't know anything about comedy!"

The debate went back and forth as Nate kept his observations to himself as an incoming message came on his Facebook Messenger.

@StephanieSymphony: "Hey there, stranger."

@NatefromNewYork: "Hey, how's it going?"

@StephanieSymphony: "Any new pictures of me out there? LOL."

@NatefromNewYork: "Well, now that you mention it, I've come across some new pictures in my travels among Porn Tumblr."

He uploaded a picture that flashed on their dialogue screen.

@StephanieSymphony: "That's another old one, geez, where do they dig up these pictures? I was in my late twenties when this was taken. My ass doesn't even look like that anymore."

@NatefromNewYork: "I also found this one. 'sexybbwsluts.tumblr.com Date Stamp: April 17th, 2014'. Check that one out."

@StephanieSymphony: "Hmm... that one's kinda new. I may have to have a chat with him about sharing."

@NatefromNewYork: "Ooooh, trouble in paradise? Happy belated birthday, by the way!"

@StephanieSymphony: "Nothing worth mentioning. We're still in the honeymoon stage."

@NatefromNewYork: "I don't know if y'all qualify since you still don't have official titles, yet. You still have to go down to city hall. Just because he finalized his divorce and moved in with you, y'all just shacking up."

@StephanieSymphony: "Yeah, I guess… or maybe we'll just live together for ten years and make it common law. Like Goldie Hawn and Kurt Russell. But, enough about me, how are you and Cynthia doing? And when are you gonna let me read your book?"

@NatefromNewYork: "We're fine. Did the therapy thing, talked to several counselors and a psychologist. They gave her a script for a couple of medications, Cymbalta and Brintellix. She eventually got an administrative assistant job for an advertising firm. I jokingly call her 'Peggy,' but she doesn't get it. She thinks I'm referencing Married with Children instead of Mad Men, LOL…"

@StephanieSymphony: "LOL! I love that show!"

@NatefromNewYork: "Meanwhile, I've scaled back a bit. Ditched writing articles, doing podcasts, and yes, even my photography. Concentrating instead on screenwriting and still the occasional stand-up comedy bit. I also found a contract IT job that pays well. It's even third shift so I'm working those 'gargoyles' hours."

@StephanieSymphony: "Nice."

@NatefromNewYork: "Yeah, ten years is a long time to throw away a relationship. God forbid Cynthia tried a stunt like this at the beginning of our marriage…"

@StephanieSymphony: "Why? Would it matter? You wouldn't have gone through with it."

There was a pause between their conversation.

@StephanieSymphony: "Right?"

Nate started typing again.

@NatefromNewYork: "I… I don't know."

@StephanieSymphony: "What makes you say that?"

@NatefromNewYork: "Because… I'm a married man… who loves his wife… but I'm in love with TWO women."

Nate rested his hands on the keyboard and looked at the screen, reading what he just admitted. He wondered what Stephanie was thinking as she read the same thing 2,700 miles away. Seconds ticked away like hours.

@StephanieSymphony: "We should never meet again,"

she typed with certainty.

@NatefromNewYork: "I agree."

@StephanieSymphony: "Good. In the meantime, are you ever gonna let me read your book?"

@NatefromNewYork: "Maybe. But I have a good idea for a short story you can read around six months from now."

THE END

# ABOUT THE AUTHOR

Syntell Smith was born and raised in Washington Heights, Upper Manhattan in New York City. He began writing while blogging his hectic everyday life experiences in 2004. After gaining an audience with a following of dedicated readers, he studied scripts and plays and got into screenwriting. Syntell has written three books in his award winning *Call Numbers* series. He loves comic books, video games, and watching reruns of Law and Order. Syntell is active on Twitter, Facebook, & Tumblr and currently lives in Michigan.

# ALSO BY SYNTELL SMITH

**The Call Numbers Series**

Call Numbers: The Not So Quiet Life Of Librarians

Book Endings: Loss, Pain, and Revelations

Hold Circulation: Trial and Redemption

www.ingramcontent.com/pod-product-compliance
Lightning Source LLC
Chambersburg PA
CBHW072028220726
48293CB00016B/566